THE RECKONING

AUTHOR'S NOTE

THE RECKONING is fiction, using personal experiences and memories from my childhood, as well as actual details involving the U.S. invasion of Iraq in 2003. The characters are also fictional, with the exception of Saddam Hussein's younger son, Qusai, who plays a small role in one of the later chapters. He headed Iraq's feared secret police, the Mukhabarat, and so, while this is fiction, it is not unlikely that he would have taken personal interest in an American prisoner.

The talented Iraqi artist, Vian Sora, graciously allowed me use of her painting "Nostalgia" for the cover. She lives and works in Dubai now, due to the situation in Iraq, but her work can be viewed online at www.viansora.com. Another Iraqi, Mohammed Al-Sadr, whose mother tragically died in prison, provided invaluable resource information.

I want to acknowledge my family for clarifying certain memories and being willing, along with several good friends, to read early drafts and provide important feedback. My friend and fellow writer, Brenda Sartoris, used her literary skills for an important final edit. In particular, however, I want to credit the Interrobangs, my writers group back in Hemet, California, who helped guide me through this endeavor from its infancy. I hope Ann Dunham, Christine Gordon, Carolyn Straub, Judie Mare, Rey Madueno, Shirley Messmer and the rest will forgive the change of title.

Most of all, I want to thank my husband, Michael, who has been completely supportive of my writing. He, along with my children, Allison and Jason, sacrificed much to see this completed, and I will always be grateful.

To my father,
Whose vocation allowed us to travel and live far and wide
And whose avocation as a writer has inspired me to create
stories of my own.

ONSET

(Santa Monica, California—1969)

It hovered like a fly trapped inside her skull, crowding out the squeaking of sneakers, the banging of the basketball. Drained, the fourteen-year-old sank down on the bleachers and the low-pitched buzz between her ears evened to a soft hum. She swallowed twice. Perhaps this episode would end now. Gently. She prayed there would be no hallucinations.

Eyes fixed on the gym floor, the girl reached back to pull off the band holding her sun-bleached hair in a ponytail. As the elastic slid from her damp strands, the floor seemed to fall away. She gasped and drew back. Then, slowly, she craned her neck forward.

She looked down into the pool at Baghdad's exclusive Alwiya Club. But instead of the expected blue water, the girl viewed miles and miles of mud-brick sarifa villages. Like the ones in back of their house when they lived in Iraq some years ago. Not the first house, but the big new house they had moved into in Park Saadoun in1962. Shortly before her seventh birthday.

She gazed at the vast brown wasteland. The stench of water buffalo excrement rose up her nostrils, mixing with odors from open sewers and ditches where naked children played. She gagged, and the gagging brought another image—a crater-like scar on a man's face, where a boil had burst and healed. Two inches in diameter, the mark reminded her of the cheek of the old Iraqi who had shined their shoes each Thursday. As she stared, transfixed by the dimpled, whorled scar tissue, she felt the press of a hand on her shoulder. Then nothing.

The neurologist told her later that she had suffered a full-blown seizure, shaking and convulsing for several minutes. She remembered only the scar and the hand.

RETURNING

(Northern Iraq—August 24, 2002)

At Jalal's signal, Theresa dismounted and crept forward. Small pebbles and rocks littered the grassy knoll. She swept them to the side with her good hand to clear a space, and eased her long-boned figure flat against the ground next to the Kurdish guide. Theresa still hurt from the bruises of last night's fall and every movement pulled at her aching, middle-aged body. Grunting, she took the binoculars he offered.

"*Shu hatha*, Jalal? Did you see something?"

He pointed left to an area in the valley below. "Ansari, Miss Fuller. There."

Squeezing the binoculars tight against her forehead, she adjusted the lenses and scanned until she found them. Four armed figures weaving in and out between the boulders a few miles below. Her jaw clenched and she sucked in a breath. Had last night's mercy shot alerted the fighters of Ansar al-Islam to their presence? When her horse had stumbled on the dark mountain trail, she fell too, landing against sharp, angled rocks and cutting her left hand, but her cuts were nothing compared to her mare's leg. A complete break. They had tried to muffle the gunfire. Apparently, they failed. The Ansari were definitely heading in their direction.

Theresa lowered the glasses. "I see four. *Araba'a, na'am?*"

The sixty-year-old Kurd shook his head. "*La. Saba'a.*" He pointed down further to the right of the creeping figures.

Seven? She brought the binoculars up again, found the original four, and panned right until she sighted the other three. All carried Kalashnikovs. Theresa groaned. She and Peter had taken extra precautions, heading two days out of their way through the high hills of the Zagreb mountain range in Northern Iraq, all to avoid this precise situation.

"What's up?"

Peter had shimmied up beside her. Jalal's oldest son, Barham, also stole forward for a look, leaving his younger brother, Massoud, back with the horses.

She handed her cameraman the binoculars. "Ansar fighters. Down there."

Peter peered through the lenses a moment before passing them over to Barham. "You think they know we're here?"

"They know someone's up here. They're not herding goats."

Jalal tapped her arm and started scooting away from the edge. "Come. *Yalla*."

All four snaked backward several feet until they were out of sight from below. Once clear, they stood and ran toward Massoud, waiting with the horses behind a large outcropping. While the elder Kurd explained the delay to his younger son in their native tongue, Theresa tried to answer Peter's questions.

"How can they be Ansar? I thought we were skirting around them." His ready, dimpled smile had vanished and he ran his fingers like a comb through his blond locks.

"We must have come closer to their area than we realized when we fumbled in the dark last night. One thing is clear. We can't afford to stay here. Our visas are only good for Kurdish-controlled territory."

"Maybe they're not Ansar."

Theresa didn't respond immediately but removed her *khafiya*, the black and white traditional scarf headdress, and shook out her shoulder-length hair. She had dyed it a deep brown for this excursion and still wasn't used to the change. Arab men had a particular taste for blondes, and she wanted as little attention as possible.

"If Jalal says they're Ansari, that's good enough for me. I'm not willing to take risks with fundamentalists. These guys hate Westerners. Particularly women."

She used the cloth to dab at beads of sweat around her hairline brought out by the hot August sun. Holding the scarf between her knees, she drew an elastic band from the pocket of her pants and pulled her hair back into a ponytail. With her left hand bandaged as it was, it took a little longer than usual. Finally, she wrapped the khafiya around her head again, hiding everything but her eyes.

If they were caught, she knew the Ansari would show a woman little respect. Small breasted and tall, Theresa hoped to pass for a man as long as possible.

At Jalal's signal, the five climbed onto their horses. With one less horse, she rode in front of Peter on his mount. They spurred the old mare forward to consult with their Kurdish guides.

"Jalal, this is too dangerous. I'm not sure the story we're after is worth this kind of risk. We should turn back." Theresa gave Barham time to translate her concern into Kurdish.

Jalal's thirty-year-old son had studied English for two years at the University of Sulaimani in Kurdish-controlled Iraq and served often as a guide for foreign journalists. While he stumbled over some current American idioms, Barham learned quickly and his command of their language equaled Theresa's grasp of Arabic.

Father and son spoke and gestured back and forth for several minutes before Barham turned back to Theresa and Peter.

"My father says we cannot go all the way back now. Not the way we came. Our supplies are few and we need to reach a village to buy more. We are not far from Halabja now."

"We're also not far from Ansar," Theresa argued.

"True, but my father knows of a cave we can hide in for the night. They will not find us. In the morning, when we are sure they are gone, we can make our way down to the lake and on to Halabja and Bamuk."

"That sounds reasonable," Peter said.

Barham pressed his family's case. "Please. It is an important story. America needs to know."

She considered how much this meant to Jalal and his sons, in terms of sacrifice and money. And Barham was right. If Bush were going to invade this country, either later this year or in 2003, then Americans needed to understand its people. That meant the Kurds, among others. The story needed to be told. Looking back at Peter, she shrugged off her sense of foreboding, and nodded.

The group began climbing a new mountain trail. Several times she turned to look over her shoulder, uneasy at the near brush with this particular group of Islamists. Rumors held that Ansar was aligned with Saddam Hussein, as well as Al-Qaeda. She shivered as she thought about how close they might be to Iraqi troops.

As dusk came on, casting the hills in shadows, Theresa relaxed and removed her khafiya. She was exhausted from their five-day trip through the high backcountry of southeastern Turkey and Kurdish-controlled Iraq, and longed for a shower and a soft hotel bed, with or without fleas. Instead, it would be even more cold nights on the hard ground. Aches and pains had spent every night with her on this venture, refusing to leave in the morning. Her head drooped down and her eyes closed for a moment.

"Tired?" Peter's breath warmed her right ear. "Go ahead and lean back. Pretend I'm a recliner."

"What do you mean pretend?" She smiled, but sat up straighter. "I'm okay."

"Are you calling me lazy? Who helped break camp this morning?"

"Hey, you claim to be the cowboy. I was just letting you show your stuff. Have you sold that ranch in Alberta yet? Who takes care of that place for you, anyway?" Theresa knew if she could keep him bantering they'd both stay alert and keep their minds on business.

"I can't give up the land. My younger brother's in charge while I'm gone. It's been in the family for decades and one day I hope to pass it on to my son."

"Then what on earth are you doing here? Go home, find a wife, and get married before your brother steals it out from under you."

"What, and leave you to have all the fun? No way. You're not getting rid of me that easily."

"I'll bet your horses miss you," Theresa teased.

"More than you likely would. Anyway, I sold all the horses but one. I ride my range in a Jeep. A true Canadian cowboy, eh?"

Theresa chuckled and glanced down at his hands gripping the reins. She noticed he still wore the gold ring she had given him a year ago for his birthday. A

Beirut jeweler had custom engraved a maple leaf into its surface as requested. It glinted now in the rising moonlight, and she looked away.

She liked Peter. He had been a good colleague and friend—one of the few friends she allowed in her solitary life. As a freelance journalist, she had crossed dozens of borders, dealt with hundreds of officials, and met thousands of individuals. But she still preferred the solitude that cocoons the frequent traveler.

Her lifestyle allowed her to keep certain things to herself. Things she didn't even tell Peter. For the most part, she even kept her family at bay. She always moved on, leaving the old, seeking the new. These past five years, Peter had simply moved with her. Theresa knew he wanted more than friendship. She had responded to his initial physical advances because he was attractive and she thought she felt strong enough to end her isolation. But when he began to talk about family, about children, something inside her froze. The ring had been meant as a symbol of their friendship, and a way to keep him close without promising anything. Instead, it seemed to have only strengthened his hope.

She knew any future with her held no hope, at least for now. She sought for something more than a man. Something bigger pushed her from country to country, causing her to constantly search for a story—the kind that would make a difference.

Theresa had contacts in most major capitals, but her area of expertise had always been the Middle East. A working knowledge of Arabic, the local customs, and Islam—both Sunni and Shia—opened doors for her closed to most other American journalists. A phone call from a source and Theresa, unencumbered by a husband or children, could be packed in thirty minutes, on a flight two hours later, and on the ground rounding up interviews the next day.

It was her familiarity with Muslims, as well as fieldwork with Human Rights Watch, that had led to her first prime assignment from CNN in Bosnia...and Peter Cranston. The network hooked her up with the Canadian cameraman after his former partner, Lou Davies, had been killed covering the Serbian cleansing squads. Together, Theresa and Peter tracked down story after story of rape and so-called "ethnic cleansing."

Within two years, she had developed a reputation for doggedness, clarity, and excellent sources. She no longer had to pitch ideas to the executives in New York. She simply tracked a story down and scripted it. Following her outline, Peter shot fifteen to thirty minutes of film. Editing came easily because the message had been clear from the outset. Her writing and on-air talent, combined with Peter's gift for the visual, had even earned the team a Peabody.

But by the late-90s, foreign news had become less and less important. Network budgets were being scaled back. Americans had grown tired of the on-again, off-again Arab-Israeli crisis and so had Theresa. With foreign news bureaus closing or consolidating, particularly in the Middle East, she and Peter began chasing stories beyond the mainstream. She hated to admit it, but her stories were getting harder to sell.

Then came 9/11. After that day, the world's eyes quickly refocused on the Middle East. And she and Peter were busy again.

In January of this year, when Theresa had wanted to document the plight of the Kurds in Southern Turkey, Peter talked her out of it. He reasoned that they might need Turkish officials on their side to cross into Iraq and cover what most journalists acknowledged was inevitable—a showdown between Saddam and Bush, Jr.

He had been right, though they hadn't come to document any build-up to war. After bribing a Turkish border guard five days ago, they crossed at Habur between Silopi in Southern Turkey and Zakho in Northern Iraq. Following a day's rest in Sulaimaniya, where they met up with Jalal and his sons, they set off to chase yet another story. A better one, she hoped.

Hers was essentially a search for justice, so her stories always dealt with victims. It was easy because the earth grew victims daily, like blades of grass. She could find them in every corner of the world. Although she had avoided it as long as possible, Iraq was no exception. She somehow sensed she would find her fill here. Perhaps this was the place her wandering might cease.

"What are you thinking about?" Peter's question startled her and she jerked. "Sorry, didn't mean to scare you."

"No, I'm fine. I was just thinking about the story."

"Naturally. I thought you were going to get some shut-eye."

"You haven't really asked about it. I mean, the details about Jalal's family."

"I expect it's some variation on all the others. Someone has been hurt or wronged. Probably Jalal in this case. You know, the powerful feeding off the weak. You can tell me when we get to the village."

His apathy surprised Theresa. "Have you really become so jaded? You know no two stories are exactly alike. What's happened to your compassion?"

He chuckled. "Sorry, I think it went to bed two hours ago. I'm exhausted. But what's keeping you awake? Are you really interested in the people involved or what their story might lead to?"

Theresa stiffened. "What do you mean?"

"You're probably already planning our first angle for when war breaks out here. I can't say I blame you. It'll be like the old days in Bosnia."

She hoped not, but said nothing. Ever since they had crossed the border, unease had spread through her like oil poured into a frying pan. With the recently sighted Ansari, the oil had now begun to crackle and spit. She had no intention of covering any war here. She had only come for this one story. The sooner they were out of Iraq, the better.

Fifteen minutes later they arrived at the cave and quickly bedded down for the night. For the fourth night in a row, Theresa chose not to take her medication. It made her sleep too deeply and, even though Barham and Massoud were taking turns keeping watch, she wanted to stay alert.

THE ANSARI

(Northern Iraq—August 25, 2002)

In the light of dawn, Theresa stood at the mouth of the cave and brushed her hair out. She sprayed a fine mist of perfume on both sides to hide the smell from four days of hot travel without a shampoo. Peter knelt beside a nearby stream, one of many that fed a large, glistening lake down below. He filled the canteens while the guides packed up.

As they loaded the horses, Theresa used binoculars to scan the area below. She could clearly make out the village of Halabja not far from the lake. Bamuk, Jalal's smaller ancestral village, lay a few miles to the west.

It was his family's tale of horror and death that had pulled Theresa and Peter over the border. Jalal's relatives in Turkey had urged her to seek him out in Northern Iraq, and she hadn't been disappointed. But she wondered again if it was worth the risk. In case they were stopped at a checkpoint, the two journalists wore expired press credentials in Arabic looped around their necks. They had kept them from an earlier shoot in Jordan. The tags would be useless if they were examined closely by anyone beyond the regular Iraqi army. So far, they had been lucky. She scanned the valley again for any signs of Ansar or Republican Guard. Nothing but a few herds of sheep here and there.

"Ready?" Peter handed her a full canteen.

Barham approached as she clipped it to her belt. The striking Kurd in his traditional baggy pants looked more like a fighter than a guide this morning. He had strapped an AK-47 around his back one way with a bandoleer full of bullets crisscrossing the opposite direction.

Her scalp prickled. "Are you expecting trouble?"

"It is best to be prepared. My father says we should go now. The way is clear."

Peter helped Theresa onto their horse and climbed up behind her. They broke apart a loaf of rough-grained mountain bread for breakfast as they headed down the trail. Barham took the lead once they descended to the foothills, with Massoud bringing up the rear. Nervous, Theresa wrapped up in her khafiya again. Peter put his on, as well, to hide his blond hair. As the trail widened, Jalal came abreast and Theresa began questioning the older man in Arabic to rehearse the details of their story and focus her mind on something beside the danger in this no-man's land. Satisfied with the thrust of the Kurd's tale, she switched to English to test his ability to handle on-camera questions. If necessary, she would use Barham to translate, but she knew Americans paid closer attention when the subject spoke English.

The hardy Kurd's description of his family's loss was punctuated by occasional sighs and angry gestures. His English was fair. He only stopped Barham once to translate an elusive Kurdish saying. Half an hour later, Theresa nodded to Peter. Both were satisfied Jalal would provide a strong, emotional taped interview once they reached his village.

Barham clicked his horse to the right and slowed, waiting for Theresa, Peter, and his father to come along beside him. He spoke without taking his eyes off the surrounding hills to the left.

"Do not look around, but we are being watched and followed."

Theresa's face froze. "By Ansar?"

Barham smiled and nodded as if pleasantly conversing. "I first noticed them twenty minutes ago. Careful. We do not want them to know we know."

Jalal leaned forward to look across Theresa at his son. "How far?"

"Two or three kilometers. Off in the hills to your left. I cannot be sure how long they have been tracking us."

The elder Kurd feigned checking his saddle strap to look. Theresa pretended to follow his movements and caught sight of two riders on a ridge in the distance. Both carried rifles.

"Should we tell Massoud?" Peter turned around to see how far back the younger brother lagged.

Barham considered, but clicked his tongue. "*La.* It might look suspicious. The Ansari have not moved closer. If we stay to this side going to the lake, they may not bother us."

Jalal nodded. "But no eat at lake. We hurry to Bamuk."

Spurring his horse ahead, Barham picked up the lead again, as well as the pace. Fifteen minutes passed. Theresa sneaked another glance at the hills on her left. Empty. They had gone. Relieved, she reached for her canteen and unscrewed the lid to take several swallows. The group was coming up on the lake now, and she marveled at the lush green of this part of Iraq. She had always thought the country brown, dusty, and dry. This area almost reminded her of Scotland. She raised her canteen for another sip.

Before it reached her mouth, gunshots clipped the air above their heads from each side. Their horse reared and Theresa's scarf slipped back. She dropped the canteen to pull the khafiya up again. Peter kept both of them from falling off, but she saw that Barham had dismounted. He tried to use his horse for cover as he held up his hands in surrender. A dozen Ansari, fully armed, had emerged from the tops of nearby hills. They swooped down on Theresa's group, yelling and firing their guns in the air.

Five of them swarmed Barham, stripping him of his gun and ammunition in seconds. Screaming in a mixture of Kurdish and Arabic, the men knocked him to the ground and began kicking and beating him. Others pulled Jalal and Massoud from their horses.

"Down. *Yalla.*" A bearded fighter with bloodshot eyes pointed his Kalashnikov directly at Theresa and Peter.

They obeyed without speaking. They had been held at gunpoint before and knew better than to argue. Besides, the Ansari were paying little attention to Jalal's protests and Barham's grunted explanations. And Theresa was not about to reveal her knowledge of Arabic. She clenched her jaw as the fighter moved closer to squint at their Jordanian press passes.

Peter whipped off his khafiya, stepped between her and the gunman, and removed the expired ID from around his neck. He held both hands high in the air, clutching the pass in his right with his thumb carefully covering the Arabic script so that only his photo showed.

"We're press. Reporters. We're just here to do a story. He's one of our guides." He pointed to Barham, lying on the ground bruised and groaning.

Theresa looked over to see Jalal and Massoud also disarmed and on the ground. The Ansari had opened a cut in the elder Kurd's cheek. They took turns driving the butts of their guns into his face. Twenty-four-year-old Massoud cowered nearby, curled up in a vain attempt to ward off similar blows.

Theresa clutched Peter's shirt from behind and whispered, "Don't say anything."

The fighter holding the gun on them appeared to be the leader. He barked an order in Kurdish. Three Ansari immediately went for the horses and began pulling off the packs, tents, and bedrolls. When one of them carelessly tossed Peter's bag of camera gear to the ground, the Canadian moved to save it.

"Careful. You're going to break…"

The Ansari leader cut him off with a vicious blow to his back, using the butt of his AK-47. Theresa sucked in a breath as Peter crumpled to the ground, still clutching his ID. He groaned and rolled over to see the gun's muzzle now inches from his nose.

She started forward, but another Ansari grabbed her, pinning her arms. The leader's eyes glared hate. His focus danced back and forth between the Westerners as he kept Peter frozen on the ground with his gun. He said something in Kurdish, pulled Theresa's khafiya off to reveal the length of her hair, and spat in her face. The others sneered as the spittle ran down the side of her nose, but she kept her face a blank. This seemed to anger the Ansari more. Aiming his gun between her and Peter, he let loose a spray of fire, kicking up the grass and dirt around them.

She couldn't help jumping back and Peter rolled over and away from the spray, which only made the fighters laugh more. The leader's mouth curled up as he took another step toward the Canadian and shoved the end of his gun into Peter's cheek. Theresa bowed her head and tensed.

At that moment, she heard a car engine accelerate and she lifted her head to look. A Land Rover roared into view around the base of a nearby hill and the Ansar leader kept his gun on Peter as he pivoted to watch its approach. The vehicle jerked to a stop several yards away, and an Iraqi officer emerged, followed by two other soldiers. Theresa stifled a groan when she recognized their Republican Guard uniforms. This wasn't getting any better.

He walked briskly toward the group, yelling in Arabic to release the prisoners. The man holding Theresa's arms let go, and she wiped the spit off her face with her sleeve. Slowly, the fighters backed off. All but their leader.

The Iraqi drew his pistol and shouted at the defiant Ansari. The officer was tall, at least six feet two by Theresa's estimate, and he used his height to intimidate the shorter Ansari. The fighter glared and finally lowered his AK-47, but still refused to give ground. Inches apart, the two argued and gestured in Arabic for several minutes. Theresa caught Peter looking at her for some kind of hint as to whether this development made things better or worse.

The dialogue was fast, but Theresa caught snatches here and there. The Ansari wanted at least one foreigner as a hostage, but the officer wouldn't give ground. The Iraqi mentioned "the colonel" several times without effect. But when he invoked Saddam Hussein's name, the militant spat on Peter, turned aside, and barked an order in Kurdish. He and his followers took to their horses and headed back to their camp in the hills with the Kurdish horses, guns, and ammunition as bounty. After they rode off, the officer turned to Peter and Theresa, addressing them in English.

"I am Captain Tariq al-Awali of the *Mukhabarat*. I apologize for your treatment. We allow them to live here, but they are sometimes difficult to control."

Peter staggered to his feet, clutching his injured back. "Never mind our treatment. Look what they did to our friends." He pointed to Jalal and his sons.

The officer glanced their way and pursed his lips. "I'm afraid the Ansar don't look kindly on Kurdish *pesh merga*. In any case, I'll have to see your passports."

Peter managed to stuff the expired press ID in the back of his jeans before he fished his passport from his breast pocket.

Theresa had stiffened at the word "Mukhabarat." Iraq's secret police. At least he spoke English well. She walked over to her pack, unzipped a small pocket on the side, and pulled out her U.S. passport. After handing it to the captain, she folded her arms to stop her hands from shaking. She knew about the Mukhabarat from her years with Human Rights Watch. The Ansari were bad, but this could be worse.

Before examining their documents, the captain directed a subordinate to gather the identity papers of the captured Kurds. Jalal and Massoud could barely get up, let alone empty their pockets. Barham lay unconscious, so a Republican Guard searched him on the ground.

The officer opened Peter's passport. "Peter Cranston. Canadian?" He flipped through the pages. "Where is your visa?"

Peter swallowed and handed him the piece of paper issued by the Kurdish authorities up north.

The Iraqi tipped his head back. "This is for the northern area. Why did you come south?" Without waiting for an answer, he folded the paper, enclosed it in the passport, and put it in his uniform pocket, before opening Theresa's.

She began to talk as he turned its pages. "We're journalists. Harmless. We just came in to do a story, then get back out. We didn't have time to get the regular Iraqi visa."

"You should have taken the time." He continued to leaf through her passport.

She knew it was critical to turn the situation now, before they were hauled before someone less sympathetic. "Please, just let us go. Escort us to the border if you like."

He looked up, cocked his head and examined her more closely. He reached for the expired Jordanian press tag hanging from her neck, read it, and let it drop. She noticed that, unlike many Iraqi men, he was clean-shaven. There was no Saddam mustache.

"I'm afraid that won't be possible, Miss Fuller. You'll come with me. The others will ride in the truck."

He yelled an order in Arabic and, immediately, a soldier ran to the top of the hill and signaled. Theresa heard the squeaking and grinding of gears. A minute later, a truck rounded the base of the hill and pulled up. Barham began to stir.

Other soldiers got out. Following orders, they threw the captured gear onto the covered truck bed, and shoved Jalal and his sons in after. They tossed Theresa's pack into the back of the Land Rover.

Peter pleaded with the officer as he, too, was led to the truck. "Wait a minute. Let me go with her. We're a team. I'm a journalist just like her."

The captain shook his head and took Theresa by the arm, gripping her firmly. He walked her to the Land Rover, cuffed her hands in front, and placed her in the back seat. She heard Peter yell before the truck started up.

"Theresa, don't worry. We'll be fine."

She watched the Iraqi pull out a cell phone and punch in a number. He spoke in Arabic for several minutes, standing almost at attention. From his posture and manner, she assumed he addressed a superior officer as he described the incident with the Ansari. When she heard her name, followed a few seconds later by the words "Tripoli" and "Libya," she closed her eyes and bowed her head.

The captain finished his conversation, slammed her door shut, and walked around to slide in next to her on the other side.

"I have to blindfold you."

Theresa swallowed and looked directly at him, trying to memorize the details of the last face she might ever see. The dark eyes set off by high cheekbones and a strong nose. He pulled out a black hood and drew it down over her head.

TO BAGHDAD

(On the road south—August 25, 2002)

Thirty minutes into their trip, after she had grown used to the silence, she overheard the driver beg a cigarette off his comrade in front. The click of a lighter was soon followed by the unmistakable smell of burning tobacco. The nicotine smoke caught in her throat and Theresa couldn't help coughing. She swallowed and turned away, but when she inhaled she coughed again.

"Does the smoking bother you?"

The captain had said nothing until now and Theresa weighed how best to respond. Should she remain silent or try to keep him talking? She chose the latter.

"I'm not used to it."

"After all this time in the Middle East?" He told his men in Arabic to roll down their windows and keep their cigarettes outside.

She recalled the captain's quick glance at her passport, and wondered if he was guessing or had a photographic memory. Either way, she was impressed and steeled her mind for a subtle interrogation. But instead of more questions, she felt him lean into her. She tensed.

He touched her bandaged left hand. "What happened?"

She hesitated. "My horse took a stumble and I fell. I cut my hand on some rocks."

"Do you mind if I have a look?"

Without waiting for an answer, the captain slid nearer and began undoing her bandage. Through the hood, she caught a brief scent of sandalwood soap mixed with sweat brought on by the unrelenting Iraqi summer. His closeness unnerved her and her mind raced to gauge his real motives. Was he making advances, or would he use the hand against her? She knew these people were trained to look for any weaknesses.

The handcuffs made his examination awkward, but she was grateful he took care not to touch the scrapes and cuts. After a minute, he re-wrapped the hand without comment and moved back to his side of the vehicle.

"It's nothing serious," Theresa said. She wanted him to know she could deal with pain.

"No, but we don't want an infection. When we stop for gas, I'll get a local doctor to clean and disinfect the wounds."

"Where? In Tikrit?"

He said nothing. She wondered if he had smiled or scowled at her attempt to learn which direction they were heading. He didn't seem the surly type and she decided to try and keep him talking.

"I'm impressed with your English, Captain. The accent's only slight and you even use contractions."

A moment of silence lapsed and Theresa tried to think of something else but, before she could begin again, he cleared his throat.

"I spent some time in America."

Somehow she wasn't surprised. His English was too good. "Where in America?"

"Are you always this curious, Miss Fuller?"

"Of course. That's why I'm a journalist. Are you afraid to answer because your comments may be reported?"

"To whom? The world?"

Again, she wondered if this was harmless banter or an attempt to learn her employer. Theresa decided she had to measure this man in some way, test his loyalty to Iraq's regime before they got any closer to it. She also needed to know if anyone else in the car spoke English before going any further. It would be risky, but she felt safer trying something here and now.

She swallowed before speaking. "I meant to your superiors. Will the smokers up front report what we say?" She cleared her throat. "Will my life end immediately if I tell you I think your president is one of the most despicable men on earth?"

She flinched, half expecting to be struck, but nothing happened. There had been no reaction from the front of the car, either. No gasp or sudden outburst in Arabic. Nothing.

The captain finally broke the silence, his voice smooth and even. "I don't think very highly of your president, either. As for the two in front, their English is very poor. I am the only one who can report what we talk about, if you still want to talk."

She breathed out. "Do you?"

"Where were you trained as a journalist?"

Theresa thought she detected sincere curiosity in his tone, almost as if he yearned for normal conversation. Perhaps she could make an ally of this man. Wherever they were going, Theresa sensed she would need help. From any quarter. But she also realized she would have to give him something first.

"UCLA. I received my degree there more years ago than I care to remember."

His voice warmed with pleasure. "I studied at San Diego State. I'm afraid I couldn't get into UCLA."

Theresa smiled underneath her hood. A smile of relief and hope. "When were you there?"

"Like you said. Too many years ago." His tone seemed sad, almost longing.

She shifted toward his voice. "What did you study?"

"History. A Master's degree."

They talked for what seemed like hours to her, comparing university experiences and sharing memories of

Southern California. Theresa was careful to reveal only her college years. She gave him nothing before or after. And she sensed his caution, as well. They finished by discussing favorite movies and film actors, and discovered a common appreciation for the works of Lean and Scorcese. For a few brief hours she almost forgot she was handcuffed and hooded, heading no doubt toward Baghdad.

When they stopped to refuel, the captain was true to his word. He located a doctor who attended to her hand. While she was being re-bandaged, she heard the captain make another call on his cell phone, but this time he walked away to talk so that she couldn't hear him.

Upon his return, he was an officer again. Using Arabic, he ordered the soldiers to go back to the truck and bring the old Kurd and his younger son. She wondered if he had reported her comment about Saddam Hussein.

Once the soldiers left, he leaned through her open window to speak. "Miss Fuller, there will be a slight change. I'm afraid you're going to be a little crowded here in the back seat. I will move to the front for the duration of the trip." He paused. "I enjoyed our conversation, but from this point there must be no speaking at all. I'm sorry."

The regret in his voice did little to alleviate her alarm for Peter. Why were they leaving him in the truck with Barham? Before she could question, the car door opened and two bodies were shoved in next to her. She thought she made out Massoud's breathing, heavy with fear, and the calming "Ssshh" of his father, Jalal. The silence that followed in the ensuing hours was almost as stifling as the heat.

COLONEL BADR

(Outskirts of Baghdad—August 27, 2002)

Her head throbbed with the dull pounding ache of hunger. She wanted an aspirin but they had denied her access to her personal effects; she guessed any particular request would be scoffed at since they were obviously trying to weaken her. The spindly peasant who came to sweep the cells had made clucking sounds of pity and returned later with a plastic pitcher of water and a tea glass. But the pitcher was dirty and the glass stained and chipped. Theresa didn't want to chance diarrhea, so the water stood there unused and warmed from the August heat. If it remained much longer, she would be risking malaria. At least, the cuts on her left hand were healing. She had taken the new bandage off last night. Scabs had formed, so she decided to leave it off.

Theresa rose slowly from the thin, grimy mattress, checked for roaches, then stepped barefoot onto the cool mud-brick floor of the cell. She thought about putting her shoes on again but the idea of enclosing her feet in this heat oppressed her. Wherever they had brought her, the cool mountain breezes had been left far behind. With the air stale and static, all she could smell was her own sweat, mixed with a combination of urine, excrement, and dry clay. She assumed a man had occupied the cell before her because of the stain patterns on the back wall. He must have been denied the bathroom privileges she had been given. What had happened to him? What was happening to Peter? She squeezed her eyes shut, fear slicing through her belly again.

Stepping to the pitcher of water, Theresa examined it closely for dead flies and mosquitoes. Finding none, she poured some into her cupped right hand to splash on her face. Though warm, the water still made her feel cleaner. She repeated the process a few times before combing wet fingers through her straggled hair to make it lay down better. Her tan cargo pants had wrinkled from being slept in day and night. Dirt and sweat stains marked her favorite pale blue cotton shirt. Worse, Theresa had endured the same underwear now for three days and it was beginning to stick up her crotch. She crossed back to the mattress, eased herself down, and lay there thinking.

She had phoned her friends and family a week ago, telling them she would be on assignment and out of reach for a few months. When her mother pressed for details, Theresa was purposely vague, not wanting to worry her. Now she wished she had provided an itiner-ary or, at least, a more specific timetable. Why had she been so careful about some things and then reckless about this? No one who cared about her would suspect anything amiss for some time. Since she was often gone for months on a story, her mother likely wouldn't begin worrying until Thanksgiving.

The searing air was at least clear of dust storms. And for once, the compound slept quietly. From the play of light on the wall she guessed it was near noon. Perhaps the guards had gone for their midday meal. Despite her hunger, she relished the peace.

So far, the only English she had heard was directed at her by her questioners, so she had been unable to tell if Peter was even in the same facility. She knew he would be worried about her and hoped his concern would keep his mind occupied. He disliked isolation, even in the normal world. Not like her. She thrived on solitude. And each time the cell door opened, the interruption unnerved her, only ballooning her fear.

Since their arrival two days ago, she had been inter-rogated every three hours. And when the Iraqis weren't questioning her, they were laying into her Kurdish friends. Loudly and with a good deal less deference. Theresa had heard the sounds of blows, followed by grunts and cries. She wondered when the screams would start.

Her interrogations had not varied since the first ses-sion. During her first night here, a pair of guards un-locked her door. Alarmed and confused, she followed them down an ill-lit hallway to a windowless room furnished with a short wooden table and two chairs. A cheap tin tray with a scratched flower design lay on the table, holding cups and an old brass coffeepot. One guard pushed her inside, following and closing the door, while the other remained outside to stand watch. Theresa's heartbeat accelerated. Was he going to rape her? The unshaven man scratched his neck and gave her a sidelong look, but stayed by the door.

After several minutes, two officers entered. She recognized the face of the captain immediately and exhaled. Tariq al-Awali. No longer hooded, Theresa could now match the man with his voice. The voice in the car that had lifted the nightmare for a few brief hours. He stood even taller than she remembered, but perhaps the more official setting stiffened his back. Taking in his black hair without any flecks of gray, she judged him to be in his mid-thirties. He looked ill at ease in uniform, despite his posture and the two medals and numerous bars pinned to his chest. She wondered if he had earned them on a battlefield or in an interrogation room like this one.

Tariq had smiled upon entering, and her eyes warmed in response. But his greeting faded when he turned to introduce the balding Colonel Farouk Badr. At least three inches shorter and wearing thick large-rimmed glasses, the colonel said nothing, but dipped his head slightly and walked to the other side of the cat. They chilled Theresa.

Tariq gestured toward the table. "Please sit down,
Miss Fuller."

Theresa complied warily and was relieved when
Tariq took the seat opposite her and began to pour
from the coffeepot. She inhaled the strong aroma of
the thick, dark brew and tried to corral her nerves. Had
they drugged it? He extended a cup toward her.

She brought her hand to her chest in the Arab way,
shook her head, and lied. "I'm sorry, but I'm allergic to
coffee."

"You are?"

She swallowed and nodded.

The captain's left eyebrow rose, highlighting a thin
inch-long scar she hadn't noticed before. "But it's the
middle of the night. We need you to be alert."

"I'll do my best. I'm a night owl anyway."

He persisted. "Americans love coffee. I've never
heard of anyone being allergic to it. Are you sure? I
could arrange for tea?"

Theresa hesitated. She didn't want caffeine keeping
her up all night, but her throat was so dry. She licked
her cracked lips and her thirst overcame any resolve.
"An herbal tea would be nice."

Lemon tea became her staple at every ensuing interrogation. As she sat and sipped that first time, the
young officer spent several minutes discussing allergies

and the finer points of Arabic coffee. Although coffee was a staple in Arab hospitality, she had never liked the thick pitchy brew offered throughout the Middle East.

"How could Allah make such wonderful coffee plants, yet make you unable to enjoy its fruits?" He clicked his tongue. "It's really a shame. Believe me, there's no coffee like Arabic coffee. And our tea, too. Even our real tea is beyond imagining. Much better than this *hamudth*." He gestured toward her cup of lemon tea.

Theresa wondered when the real questioning would start but, in the meantime, she masked her anxiety with humor. "Lemon tea is better for my breath. I wouldn't want to kill you with my answers."

With the colonel behind him, Tariq cracked a smile. "We're still examining your personal effects. You'll get your toothbrush as soon as we're finished."

Colonel Badr cleared his throat, and Theresa saw Tariq stiffen. The younger officer's smile disappeared and she realized that the chitchat, enjoyable but strange in this setting, was over. Tariq stood and moved aside as the colonel stepped forward to begin the true interrogation.

"I hope you are comfortable in your cell, Miss Fuller," he began in a stiff British accent. "It is the only one with a mattress."

"Yes, thank you. But I would be willing to let Peter have my mattress. Is he here?"

The colonel gave a slight smirk, but said nothing.

"I'm an American citizen. At least, allow me contact with someone who can get in touch with my government."

He smiled and asked, "Is there anything else you require?"

His smile and stiff, formal manner chilled her bones, shutting down any resolve to ask for aspirin. She shifted in her chair and shook her head. Theresa couldn't read this man. Both officers were obviously well educated. Tariq spoke English like an American, relaxed and soft on the consonants. Badr, on the other hand, came off cool, precise, and detached in his British intonation. She thought about complimenting him on his English when he pulled a black fountain tip pen from his pocket and asked the guard at the door to fetch some paper. The tap of his pen against the table echoed in the room until the guard returned with a note pad.

Theresa glanced at Tariq but the captain stood at attention, his eyes focused beyond her on the back wall. Badr sat down to write. She had barely deciphered her name in the upside down Arabic script before he looked up. Shifting her gaze quickly to avoid suspicion, she looked again at Tariq. This time his eyes were locked on her. The captain had been watching her as she read. Her heart pinched.

"Is Theresa Fuller your real name?" the colonel began.

He wrote while he asked questions, looking up to regard her face when she answered. Despite the pen and paper, his manner became less threatening the longer he questioned her. Theresa might have thought him bored by the process, were it not for the way he paused every now and then at an apparent inconsistency and flipped back through his notes.

She had nothing to hide about the present. She was a free-lance correspondent hoping to sell a good story to MSNBC, FOX, or CNN. She had gone into the Kurdish area of Northern Iraq with her cameraman to follow up a promising lead. Her contacts had invited the pair back to their ancestral village to report on ongoing birth defects caused by Iraq's use of chemical weapons on Kurds in that area several years ago.

"It was a war," Badr interrupted. "We only used such weapons against those fighting us. The Iranians used worse. They were attacking with a cyanide gas. We retaliated with mustard gas. We were only doing our duty as soldiers."

"And I'm only doing mine. As a journalist, I can't ignore a good lead."

"*If* that is what you are." Badr put his pen down, pulled her passport from his pocket and dropped it on the table. "Even journalists must go through the proper channels. Why did you sneak across the border?"

"I didn't. I got a visa to cross into Kurdish-controlled territory."

"But you wandered beyond that territory."

"It was an honest mistake. That area is a kind of no-man's land anyway, as you well know."

Badr picked up his pen again to write. "I know no such thing. As far as I can tell, you crossed illegally into Iraq. Your passport indicates no special validation from your government. Where is your reporter's permit?" Badr challenged. "Maybe you are a spy."

Theresa felt the hairs on her arms tingle and stand up straight, but she held his gaze and said nothing.

"And I find it curious that your American passport indicates you were born in Tripoli, Libya," he continued. "Would you not find that strange? After all, the Americans are not known to be friends of the Libyans."

"Exactly. Don't you imagine that, if I were a spy, the CIA would have given me all the proper documentation—the permit, the special validation…and a more normal birthplace like Akron, Ohio?" Theresa immediately regretted her sarcasm and bit her lip. Fatigue, mixed with tension, had made her less careful.

The colonel opened her passport and shuffled through the many stamped pages. "You have been in Jordan, Lebanon, Egypt…and even Syria?"

"I'm a reporter. I was doing stories."

He tipped his head back and crossed his arms, saying nothing.

"Look, if I had gone through the proper channels, your government wouldn't have given me access to this story. You know it and I know it. Yes, I was born in Tripoli. But it was before Ghaddafi. I was born on a U.S. Air Force base that was bombed into oblivion by

Reagan. Why does Libya matter? I was only there for a few weeks."

"It interests me. Why Libya?" he demanded, his eyes narrowing. "Was your father in the Air Force? If so, why were you there for only a few weeks?"

This necessitated a careful explanation of her father's public affairs duties in the Mediterranean area while attached to the Department of the Army. She didn't tell him they had later lived in Baghdad for five years after he changed careers. If Libya had aroused the colonel's curiosity, her past in Iraq would certainly send up alarms.

"Did you visit any other Arab countries as a child?"

Theresa wasn't comfortable lying, but she told only part of the truth. "We lived in Lebanon during my high school years and did some traveling to neighboring countries during that time."

"Did you ever visit Israel?" he asked with a raised eyebrow. "Israel is a neighboring country."

Each time he asked about Israel, she shook her head firmly, truthfully. The interrogation usually ended shortly afterward. Denied her passport or any access to an official of the U.S. Interests Section at the Polish Embassy, she was returned to her cell to await the next session. So far, there had been no roughness. Only denial of food and sleep. Theresa hoped Peter wasn't facing worse treatment.

Lying on the mattress now, she concluded it was only a matter of days, perhaps hours, before they would somehow find out this wasn't her first visit to Baghdad. How would they react then? What would she tell them? How much could she even remember? She had only been nine, almost ten when they had left Iraq in 1965. Her memory produced scattered pictures from that period. Occasionally, when her family reunited to celebrate a birthday or anniversary, talk would turn to those early years, and scenes began to focus in her mind. Still, much hovered beyond her recall. If many more days passed without her medication, her epileptic "episodes," as the neurologist called them, were sure to return. Perhaps they might bring the recollections closer.

She stood again. Weak from hunger, she paused until the dizziness passed, and then walked to the only window in the cell. Located in the east wall and six feet up, it was barred to prevent escape and too high to provide a direct look at her surroundings. Still, she could see something. Part of a tall, stately palm tree, heavy with ripening fruit. With no breeze, the Baghdad air lay thick in her nostrils and she closed her eyes and stood there, baking in the heat and reaching for her past. She remembered the day her family had first stepped out of the plane and into the oven of an Iraqi August forty-two years ago in 1960.

She recoiled, surprised at the heat's force. At six in the evening, with the temperature dug in at 118 degrees, Theresa reluctantly followed her family down the ramp. The stairs wobbled slightly and she gripped her older brother's hand more tightly.

"Don't be scared. I've got hold of you." As the oldest, her seven-year-old brother, Jimmy, took his job as assistant parent very seriously.

Ahead of them, her mother, Ruth, held baby Laila in her arms while her father, Nate, hefted two-year-old Angela. That left Theresa, almost five, in the care of Jimmy.

"It's hot here." Theresa wondered if the heat bothered him as much as it did her.

"Yeah, be careful not to touch the railings."

She looked at the metal railing, considered a second or two, and reached out her right hand tentatively before immediately regretting the move. The pads of her little fingers felt as if they had been sliced.

"Ow!" Her eyes squinted and started to water.

"I told you not to touch it. Don't cry, just blow on your fingers."

She blew hard as she descended, taking care not to miss the last step. Once on the tarmac, they caught up with their parents. Her dad was speaking to a portly man in that new language he had been studying back in California. He called it Arabic but to her ears it was a mix of "bil's" and "wa's" and "al's" and "id's."

Dad's work with the Army had taken them to Greece and Turkey. She hardly remembered Greece. Turkey had been full of fleas. She hoped there weren't any here. After Turkey, they had returned to the land of milkshakes and hamburgers. They had lived on savings while he finished his Master's degree at Stanford. Now they were embarking on Dad's new dream—teaching at a university in an exotic country. A hot, exotic country.

"Jimmy, Theresa." Her father beckoned them forward. "I want you to meet the Chairman of the Political Science Department at Baghdad University, Dr. Ahmad Adhami. Dr. Adhami, allow me to introduce my two oldest children, James and Theresa."

Dr. Adhami smiled broadly and leaned down to shake both their hands. "It is pleasant to meet such well-behaved young children. How do you like Baghdad?"

"It's very hot here." Theresa got a jab from Jimmy's elbow and winced.

"My sister means it's nice and warm here. We're used to being warm since we came from California."

Laughing heartily, Dr. Adhami addressed the whole family. "Do not worry about the summers. You will get used to them. Besides, in the summer we sleep during the worst heat. It is at night that we have our enjoyments."

Her memories of the rest of that first day were jumbled like building blocks that had fallen. She worked to reconstruct the scene, placing one block on top of another, but many were missing.

Dr. Adhami led them through passport control and customs. She saw men in long shirt dresses she later learned were called dishdashas. Women wore black abayas with snatches of color peeking out here and there. Theresa had never seen so many packages and parcels. *The unpleasant smell of hot and sweaty crowds jostling for position made her hold her nose.*

Somehow they ended up in two cars heading for the Hotel Baghdad downtown. Her dad rode with Dr. Adhami and the luggage in the first car.

The ride from the airport was fast, presenting a quick slide show of the city. With the taxi windows down, she squinted through the hot breeze to glimpse shopkeepers putting away their wares as women with children in tow argued to make one last purchase. On the outskirts of the city, anywhere there was an open lot, houses squatted close together, built of mud bricks or cinder blocks and topped by roofs thatched with palm fronds. Everywhere, bright-colored clothing hung on lines, baking in the sun. She and Jimmy pointed and giggled at young children, often half-naked, standing in the doorways of these primitive shacks. Women bustled along the sidewalks, balancing incredible bundles on their heads without breaking stride.

Closer to downtown, traffic thickened and slowed. Buildings in the center were modern, containing markets and stores of all sorts. Theresa began to notice pictures of a man posted on building after building. Gray at the temples, he was sharply dressed in uniform and smiling broadly with white even teeth. Upon reaching the hotel, she approached her father to ask about him.

"Oh, that's the leader of Iraq. Colonel Abdul Karim Qasim. He took over in 1958, isn't that right, Dr. Adhami?"

"Yes. We call him 'Al Ca'id al Wahid'—the Sole Leader. You see we used to have a king, but he was killed and Qasim is trying to get rid of all imperialism. He is trying to bring everyone a good life."

Theresa thought this Colonel Qasim must be as powerful as a king to have so many pictures displayed. Even inside the luxurious air-conditioned hotel, his images were on every wall. His smile, highlighted by a thin moustache, was set widely in a strong square face; but the smile beamed excitement, not warmth. Qasim's dark eyes, overhung by thick brows, seemed predatory. They followed her every move. She slept fitfully those first few nights in Baghdad.

A sharp prick on her lower left arm startled Theresa's thoughts back to the present and her eyes swept down from the window view. She waved the small winged insect away and blew on the bite. Too fast to be a mosquito. Despite the heat, she rolled her sleeves down and buttoned them. Without access to medicine, she couldn't afford fever or infection.

A key sounded in her cell door and she turned as it swung open. Theresa groaned silently at the sight of the two guards. She couldn't take another session with more lemon tea on a full bladder.

"May I use the bathroom first?"

They glanced at each other, confused by her English.

"Toilet? *Hamam?*" She used the wrong word intentionally, but they understood.

"*Hamam, na'am*...yes, this way toilet," the older guard nodded, motioning her out. He gave instructions to the other guard in Arabic about informing the colonel of the delay as she bent over to put on her shoes. The younger guard headed toward the interrogation room while Theresa was led in the opposite direction toward the bathroom.

A curdling scream froze her a few feet from the bathroom door. The pained cry pierced the air full-throated and strangled in sounds of cursing and struggle. It seemed to come from the direction of the interrogation room. Theresa started to turn, but her guard shoved her into the bathroom and locked the door.

A PIECE OF HELL

(Abu Ghraib Prison—August 27, 2002)

Peter woke before dawn when the warm wetness spread down his right pant leg. He closed his eyes again and cursed silently. At least he wouldn't have to brave the toilet drill upon rising. Within seconds the warmth turned cold and the pungent smell of his urine added one more layer of fetidness to the packed hall. He estimated that eight hundred men and boys were being held in this foul fifteen by four-meter corridor. Wedged in to sleep between others on the dirt, he could do little but reflect until the guards came to roust them.

He hoped Theresa wasn't locked up elsewhere in this hell. After their capture, the commanding officer had deliberately separated them. Why? He had placed Peter and his equipment with Jalal and his sons in the back of a truck holding seven other Kurds. Peter had last glimpsed Theresa being forced into a car with the officer. Later in the day when the convoy stopped to re-fuel, soldiers had come to the back of the truck to re-move Jalal and the younger son, Massoud.

"Where are you taking them? Where is Theresa?" Peter was insistent.

The soldiers ignored him.

"You'd better take good care of her," he yelled as they led the two Kurds away. When Peter lifted one leg over the truck's tail onto the bumper and leaned out to look, a guard rapped him sharply with the butt of his automatic. Barham pulled him back in.

"Stay back. They will shoot."

"Don't you want to know where they're taking your father and brother?"

"Of course. But we can't help them if we are dead."

Peter raised his head now to see if Barham was still asleep. Despite the beatings of the last two days, the re-silient Kurd snored evenly, hardly moving. Peter longed to stretch out the soreness in his muscles, but another prisoner's head lay only centimeters beyond his feet. He would have to wait.

He had thought they would put him in the Foreign-ers' Section but they had marched him directly here with Barham. Now he wondered if he would ever have a chance to protest, and if he should. They were probably better fed, but he had heard they were kept in small iso-lated cells. People were far more essential to Peter than food. While his job often took him off the world's beaten paths, he had always thrived on the company of others.

The man above him kicked out in his sleep, knocking Peter's head. He certainly wasn't alone here. This was a well-beaten path and the bruises were showing. At the very least, if he got out of here alive, he would have a much better story to tell.

He only wished he knew Theresa was safe. Peter closed his eyes and tried to picture her lying there curled up with her back to him. He had imagined it a hundred times but never in these circumstances. It was difficult to supplant the present stench with the perfumed smell of her silky hair. Riding behind her on the horse after sunrise had been intoxicating.

Peter thought back to the evening on horseback before that morning. They were the most intimate moments the two had yet shared in their five years working together. Once she took off her khafiya, he had imagined combing her long strands between his fingers. When she began to doze, he leaned closer and wrapped one arm around her waist as if to keep her from falling off. He was certain she must have felt his longing when he whispered in her ear. That was why she had tensed and claimed to be okay. The following morning, she avoided his eyes and sat straight in the saddle. He wondered now if she would ever allow him that close again.

After all this time he still knew very little of her background. She had wandered from one aid organization to another after college, searching for just the right fit. She said she was looking for a way to give back more than she was taking. He had been teamed with her after she left Human Rights Watch, frustrated at all the inequity in the world and the willingness of people to turn a blind eye. Convinced she would have a better platform as a journalist, she had pitched her way into a job with CNN. After doing grunt work in Atlanta for a few years, the network sent her to Bosnia and him. They had been paired ever since, filing stories on the war, the tentative peace, and finally breaking off to go free-lance. Still, her life before college was a black hole.

Once, in Los Angeles, he had offered to drop her off at her mother's home, hoping for a chance to meet her family, unlock her past.

He had tried to sound casual. "I'm on my way to meet an old friend in Century City. I can give you a lift. I'm pretty sure it's on the way."

Her refusal was polite, but firm. "Thanks, but I've already rented a car."

He persisted. "Why waste the gas? I can take you there and pick you up when you're done."

She had given him a very clear look, as if to say *I know what you're after. It won't work.* Instead, she said, "Peter, I like you. But I keep my work separate from my personal life. It's just less messy that way."

He couldn't help feeling hurt. "I'm only offering a ride. Aren't we friends?"

"Of course we're friends. I said I like you." She looked away.

Peter decided not to push. A month later in Beirut, she presented him with a gold friendship ring. The outline of a Canadian maple leaf had been custom cut into the surface. He supposed she had felt guilty after their conversation, but it touched him all the same, and he never took it off.

The conversation hadn't deterred him from trying to investigate on his own. All he gathered were rumors that she grew up overseas and saw conflict as a child. Nothing concrete. He was tempted to track down her mother, but he knew Theresa would never forgive him, so he decided to let it go.

The haunting call of the muezzin broke the stillness. For a moment the melodic phrases of the chant urging all Muslims to prayer comforted the miserable prisoners as they awoke. Many used their blankets as prayer rugs, placing them to face in the direction of Mecca. Others slept on. At seven a.m. the guards charged in with sticks, metal rods and batons to punish those still clinging to their dreams. Another day of torture was beginning.

Barham had roused himself before the guards could. He now stood before Peter looking down at the stain on his friend's pants.

"I guess I couldn't hold it," Peter shrugged.

His friend smiled. "Not to worry. I am sure everyone will have soiled pants before we are out of this place. It is a mark of distinction."

He glanced toward the end of the hall. Guards armed with plastic pipes were forming two rows facing each other. He coughed, hitched up his baggy Kurdish pants, and said, "Let the games begin."

Peter watched as Barham joined the line heading to the toilet. The daily routine never varied. Prisoners could only relieve themselves between seven and ten-thirty in the morning. To get to the toilets they had to pass between the two rows of guards, five on each side. As they walked by, the guards flailed away. If a prisoner tried to protect himself from the blows, the guards only swarmed him more viciously. Peter's bruises began to throb at the sight.

A few feet from the gauntlet, Barham swiveled his head, caught his friend's eye and flashed a thumbs-up. Then he turned to face the blows. Peter marveled at the Kurd's sure and steady pace as stroke after stroke found his shoulders, head, and back. Since they had arrived, Peter had yet to see him flinch, let alone cry out. At last, Barham was through. He could enjoy a brief respite before having to return through the same sadistic beating. Peter decided he would wait until closer to ten before using the toilet.

The routine for food and drink was similar. A single drink of foul, brackish water was allotted each day between ten-thirty in the morning and two in the afternoon. The detainees received their only food—a piece of bread—between two in the afternoon and eight in the evening. To get these they had to endure the same ritual battering. Since he would have to use the toilet later that morning, Peter planned to get his water at two and his bread at seven. That way he would have a while to nurture his cuts and bruises before having to lie down on them for the night.

When Barham returned, he pulled out a pair of men's trousers from under his shirt. "I found these in the toilet. There were others, but these looked like a good fit."

Peter held them out. They were dirty but not soiled. "Whose are they?"

"Not to worry. The man who had these will not use them again."

"Are you sure?"

Barham looked down. "In the night, every night, they take some back to the toilets, strip them, and take them to another place for torture. Most do not come back."

Peter looked at the pants again and started to hand them back, but his friend insisted.

"They are only pants. They are not the man. We must do everything we can to survive. I see the guards looking at your jeans. Calvin Klein, yes? They cost maybe fifty dollars? We can get many *dinars* for them. The money will help us survive. We can bribe the guards with it."

Peter nodded and changed out of his jeans to put on the dead man's pants. They were a bit tight but that was good. In prison he was losing weight daily. Even the ring from Theresa, once snug, hung loosely now. His friend took the soiled jeans, approached a senior guard and, after a bit of haggling, returned with a smile and twenty-five thousand dinars—the equivalent of fifteen dollars.

That evening, the two sat slowly picking apart their chunks of hard brown bread. Peter had almost lost his when one particularly savage blow on the walk back cracked his left hand. As it began to slip from his fingers, his good right hand frantically pushed it in to his body, catching it against his hip.

"Is your hand broken?" Barham had seen the blow from behind.

"Could be. It hurts like hell and it's starting to swell."

Barham chuckled. "You are a poet, yes? But let us be practical. If it is broken it should be fixed. And they will not fix it. I will ask others tomorrow. There must be a doctor among all these prisoners—probably several. So not to worry, I will get you the best."

Peter smiled and looked directly into his new friend's solemn black eyes. "I'm glad I'm with you. To be honest, after my first day in here I almost asked to be moved to the Foreigners' Section."

"I would not blame you. You still should. Maybe they would fix your hand."

Peter shook his head. "No. Theresa told me enough about this place to know you don't get medical care no matter where you're from. At least in here I'm not alone."

Barham snorted. "Alone? I should say not. Look at all these men."

"You know what I mean. Even in a crowd you can feel alone. But I'll have to admit this crowding is kind of getting to me."

"I have noticed." His friend's smile had faded.

"Thanks for helping me out in here."

Barham pulled him close in a rough hug. "Hey, you are as important to me as I am to you. A Kurd alone in here is a dead man. But a Kurd, even a pesh merga, with a Westerner has a chance."

"Why did you become a pesh merga?" It struck Peter that he knew very little about the Kurds. Because of Theresa's expertise, he hadn't bothered to read up much on Iraq or its people.

Barham pulled off another small crumb, placed it carefully between his teeth, and looked away for a moment before speaking.

"A Kurdish man is born a fighter, a pesh merga, one who is prepared to die. We have always fought. We have fought for thousands of years. Sometimes I wonder what we would do if we ever achieved a free Kurdistan."

"You mean here in Iraq?"

Barham looked at him directly. "Kurdistan is not only in Iraq. There are Kurds in Syria, Turkey, Iran…even in parts of what used to be the Soviet Union."

"But surely you don't mean to make a country out of…"

"Why not? If the British and other colonial powers could come here and lay down imaginary lines, saying 'This is Iraq, this is Syria, this is Iran, and we will leave this part to Turkey,' why can we not say, 'This, this, and this is all Kurdistan?'" Barham's expression dared Peter to argue.

"I had heard that your people have been abused over the centuries," Peter offered quietly.

His friend snorted. "Abused? That word is too polite for all they have done to us." He blinked several times and looked away.

Peter probed cautiously. "What happened to your family? I know Theresa has talked with your father, but I never heard your story. You were from Halabja, right? What happened there?"

The proud Kurd swallowed deeply and began slowly: "We lived in a village not far from Halabja called Bamuk. I was sixteen in 1988 when Saddam began the '*Anfal*,' the campaign to round up and kill all Kurdish men and boys. Massoud was ten. The other village elders thought it was going to be prison again, but my father knew better. He had been in prison and he knew the next time would be worse. So he took Massoud and me and loaded all our guns and ammunition, and we went to the mountains to hide in the caves. He left one loaded rifle with my brother, Rizgar, to protect my mother and three sisters."

"How old was Rizgar?"

Pain etched lines around Barham's angry mouth. "He was only seven—a baby."

Peter set his bread down and placed his good right hand on his friend's shoulder.

Barham shook off tears and continued. "We should have all gone to the hills. More than one hundred thousand men and boys were killed in the *Anfal*."

Peter gasped. "They took your seven-year-old brother?"

"We don't know. We never saw him again. But even if they had not taken him he would have died with my mother and sisters in the chemical gas attacks in March. Our whole village was wiped out. The only survivors were those who ran up into the hills. In Halabja alone more than five thousand died."

Barham paused and looked up. "That is why I am a pesh merga. Because no one else will fight for us."

They finished the last of their bread in silence. Peter wondered how he could have taken so many photos over the years, taped so many minutes of video, and still missed so much of the big picture. He marveled that his friend would endure all this for a piece of land. Was it worth it? Why not just leave, walk away? Of what value was a family, homeland or country in the face of such death and suffering? The questions kept him awake long after the lights were out.

In the middle of the night, Peter awoke to the sounds of guards cursing in Arabic and started to raise his head.

Barham reached over to hold him down. "Ssshh. Stay down and pretend to sleep. Whatever you see or hear, do not make any sound," he whispered.

Peter did as he was told, trying to peer through half-closed eyelashes. A guard approached, walking between the rows of sleeping bodies and swinging a long stick. He stopped next to Peter's neighbor, a sickly man in his seventies. Peter recognized the guard in the moonlight as the one who had bought his jeans, and sucked in a breath.

The guard heard, looked his way, and smiled as if he knew Peter was watching. A moment later he used the stick to gouge the older prisoner in the stomach, startling him awake. The man doubled up in pain. He hardly knew what was happening as he was yanked up and led away.

The guard threw the old man against a wall into a line of twelve others who had also been singled out. Some wept and babbled in fear, while others stared dully, resigned to their fate. Peter watched as they were marched out in a direction opposite the toilets. Long minutes passed. He heard a distant command in Arabic. A volley of gunfire followed and Peter flinched. He looked at the space now open next to him for several minutes before making up his mind. Slowly, taking care not to hurt his left hand, Peter rolled halfway over into it until he was on his other side, looking at Barham.

His friend regarded him a moment, nodded, and closed his eyes to sleep. Peter laid his aching hand on his right hip and tried to forget the old prisoner for the rest of the night.

BREAKING POINT

(Outskirts of Baghdad—August 27, 2002)

Theresa stayed in the filthy roach-infested bathroom as long as possible, using the extra minutes to think. This interrogation session would be different, and she wanted to be ready.

Who had screamed? Was it Jalal or Massoud? She couldn't recall if it had been only Arabic she had heard after the scream. Maybe it was Peter. The thought made her more frantic, and she sat back down on the stained ceramic toilet to calm down and plan her next steps.

If they were torturing her friends to get information about her, there was little she could do. Peter and the Kurds knew nothing of her prior years in Baghdad. Would they torture her next? Torturing Kurds was one thing, but an American woman? Theresa felt sure her Western citizenship would save her, as it would Peter, from anything too terrible. She decided to hold out for as long as possible. She felt mentally strong, despite her lack of sleep.

A sharp rap on the door interrupted her thoughts. "Miss, you come. *Bi sura.* Now."

The door was unlocked and opened. Theresa left the security of the bathroom and nervously followed the guard to the interrogation room.

At the entry she stopped. Her eyes bulged at the pool of blood on the table where the tea service usually lay. Before she could ask, the door closed behind her and she was alone. As she tracked the spatters on one wall, the drops on the floor, and the overturned chair by the table, her nerve dissolved. She noticed a large pot full of a thick, black liquid standing in a corner. It gave off the smell of a newly paved road. The trail of blood seemed to lead in its direction. What had happened here, and to whom? Her eyes pulled back to the crimson liquid in the middle of the table, and she swallowed to keep her stomach out of her throat. She stepped closer. The sickly, metallic smell filled her nostrils, making her head swim.

Abruptly the door opened, and she whirled to see Colonel Badr with Tariq on his heels. The younger man avoided her eyes and retreated to another corner of the room. Theresa's heart raced. There would be no niceties this time.

"You look quite pale," Badr began as he pulled out the upright chair for her to sit in. "Please sit down and excuse the mess. We have not had the time to clean up."

Theresa hesitated, but his look compelled her to sit. Now she was inches from the blood. Rather than righting the other chair to use for himself, the colonel began walking in a slow circle around her and the table. He fired questions as he walked.

"Tell me about your family."

"I...I'm not married." She took a breath to control her stammer.

"I mean the family you grew up in. How many brothers have you? How many sisters?"

"I have an older brother, two younger sisters, and a younger brother." Theresa's mind raced. Had they found out? Did they know about Mitchell's birth in Baghdad?

"And where were they born? Each of them," he barked.

Her heart sank. "Well, Jimmy was born in Germany. Angela was born in California." Should she lie or would that make it worse in the end? Now that the moment had come, her mind refused to think.

Badr was impatient. "And the others?"

"Uh, my sister Laila was born in Ankara, Turkey." She reached down to retie a shoelace in a bid to buy seconds and stop her hands from shaking.

"What year was that?"

"Oh, it was…1959." She searched out Tariq, her eyes pleading as Badr circled behind her. He saw her desperation, but turned away.

"And the youngest? What is the full name of your youngest brother?"

Her heart turned cold and she responded dully, "Mitchell Owen Fuller." She lowered her head and started to add, "He was born…"

But Badr interrupted her. "Never mind. I want to know more about your father. His full name?"

"Nathan Adams Fuller." Theresa could hardly believe her luck. She exhaled and slumped in the chair. But her relief was short-lived.

"Where is your father now and what is he doing?"

She didn't answer.

"Answer the question. Where is your father?"

Theresa looked into the colonel's eyes and whispered, "He's dead." Her response seemed to throw him off balance, and he turned away for a minute. She prayed the session would end here.

But Badr resumed circling. "When did he die?"

She tensed again and, after a brief pause, said, "1965."

At this, his left eyebrow raised. "He died a relatively young man?"

She nodded.

"How did he die? Was it a heart attack? Where was he?"

Theresa's mind and heart were struggling to stay in control. "I would rather not say."

The colonel opened his mouth, stopped, and moved behind her. He leaned over to whisper into her right ear. "I realize it's difficult to talk of the death of a loved one. I, myself, have lost family members." Then, straightening, he yelled, "But you are in no position to deny me the information I seek!"

Theresa shuddered, but remained mute.

Badr came around to the other end of the table to face her head-on and pointed to the pool of blood. "Do you want this to happen to you?"

She looked from the blood to his contemptuous eyes. A reckless anger welled up, vanquishing her fear. "You can't treat me like this. I'm an American citizen and right now the networks I've contracted with are working to find me." It was an outright lie, but she didn't care.

His flared nostrils relaxed and the thin, tight line of his mouth curved into a sneer. "Networks? You have been missing now for two days and there is no news of you on CNN. You are not news. That means nobody knows you are missing. We can do anything we want with you and no one will know."

A cold fear clutched her insides. She had lost this challenge. She wasn't strong. Not strong enough for this.

"So, one more time, how did your father die and where was he when he died?"

"I don't know how he died," she said limply.

Her face stung with the colonel's sudden backhand. A gold ring set with a ruby on his third finger left a vicious welt across her left cheek. Terrified, she looked up to see Tariq approach the colonel and whisper something. Badr rubbed the back of his left hand and nodded. The captain stepped outside.

Theresa began to panic. What instrument of torture would he bring back? "I'm telling you the truth," she yelled. "I don't know how he died!"

The door opened and Tariq entered, followed by two guards and her friends. The first guard held a bloody butcher's cleaver in his right hand, while dragging Jalal behind him with his left. She could see the old Kurd had been badly beaten. His right eye was swollen shut and his whole face was a reddish purple mess laced with cuts. When she caught sight of Massoud behind the other guard, she gasped. Black tar covered the end of his left arm where the hand used to be.

Looking back at the pool of blood and the pot in the corner, she now knew who had screamed and why. She had suspected the pot's purpose, but seeing the results of such a primitive method for cauterizing an amputated limb shook her nonetheless.

The colonel was matter-of-fact. "They could not give me the information I wanted about you…and so they suffered. Do you want them to suffer more?" He gestured toward Massoud. "After all, he has another hand to give."

Theresa set her mouth grimly, but tears pooled as she looked into Jalal's pleading eyes and the terrified face of his younger son. She knew how much they had already lost as a family. It tore her heart to know she had brought them even more anguish.

She rose from the chair and spoke calmly and deliberately. "I will tell you everything you want to know, but only if you release them into his care." She pointed to Tariq. "I trust him to arrange for their safe return to the north. It's useless to hold them any longer. I'm certain you've gotten everything you can out of them. And there's no point in killing them."

"I beg to differ," Badr began to argue. "They might alert other reporters to your disappearance."

Theresa cut him off. "Do you think they'll have anything to do with foreign journalists after this? Let them go. I won't talk unless you do."

The colonel considered this and relented. "Very well. They are not important. But first, you must answer my question fully. How and where did your father die?"

Resigned, Theresa sat down again. "I told you the truth. I don't know how he died...only where."

"Where, then?"

"In a Baghdad prison."

THE SWING

(Outskirts of Baghdad—August 27, 2002)

Hours after her Kurdish friends were taken away, Theresa left the bloody room and Badr's grilling, returning to the comforting solitude of her cell. Had Jalal and Massoud been sent north to freedom? She hoped so.

She had explained about her father and his position at Baghdad University. She gave the names of their cook, maid, and houseboy—all Assyrian Christians. Badr had begun a list of their Iraqi friends during those years, at least the names she could remember. She hoped she wasn't bringing new trouble into their lives.

Under the colonel's constant pressure, she recalled more than she ever imagined possible. Still, he found glaring holes in the tale she had slowly woven.

He refused to overlook the biggest. "Why was your father put in prison? Was he a spy? How was he caught? Where was he arrested?"

Theresa could only respond blankly, "I don't remember."

"That is ridiculous. You are a grown woman. Surely, you have spoken of this with your family. How does your mother explain it?"

"She won't talk of it. All she ever says is that it was all a mistake, a terrible mistake."

Badr's patience looked as if it were wearing thin.

Theresa insisted. "We don't talk about it. We talk about everything but that. When the others used to bring it up, Mom and Jimmy always changed the subject." Her eyes fixed on the bloody wall and she didn't hear his next question.

"You expect me to believe when you get together with your family, you talk about everything in Baghdad but your father?" he repeated.

Theresa pulled her eyes from the wall and considered. "No. We talk about Dad. All the good times, everything until…"

"Until what?" he prompted.

She shook her head, exasperated. "I can't remember the last months. Believe me, I've tried. It's as if one day Dad returned from classes as usual and the next we said goodbye to him for the last time at the prison."

"You visited him in prison?"

She nodded. "A few times."

"Was he executed?"

"I don't know. I only remember Mom telling Jimmy and me he died in prison. She didn't tell the others until we got back to California."

Badr leaned forward. "How soon did you leave after he died?"

Theresa shrugged. "I can't be sure because I don't know if Mom told us immediately. But we left exactly one week after she told us. I remember because it was a Friday after church, and we left the following Friday morning when all the mosques were full. We didn't go to church that day. Mom thought it would be safer leaving on a Friday." Theresa laid her head down on her arms.

The colonel paused, looked at his watch, and rose from his chair. He indicated to Tariq the session was over. On their way out, the captain asked him something in Arabic and Badr nodded, replying briefly. Theresa was too exhausted to try and translate mentally.

Several minutes after she was deposited back in her cell, the old peasant entered, carrying a tray laden with rice and brown flat bread, as well as a generous portion of *baba ghanouj,* an eggplant dip. A meatless stew filled with tomatoes and carrots had been ladled onto the rice. The aroma of garlic mixed with tomato filled the dim room. Tears rimmed her eyes as the old man carefully placed the tray beside her on the mattress.

She thanked him in Arabic. "*Shukran.*"

"*Afwan*," he replied, dipping his head politely before leaving.

As hungry as she was, Theresa reached first for the cold bottle of soda. She had talked for hours and her throat felt like a desert. She gulped down a third the lemon-lime drink before tackling the food. Cold rice, stew and stale bread had never tasted better.

She had just scooped up the last of the baba ghanouj when Tariq entered. Theresa stopped, holding the dipped bread in midair.

He smiled. "Please, continue eating. The stew is called *marga*. Do you remember it from your childhood here?"

She shook her head.

"No matter. I am sure you were very hungry."

She put the bread in her mouth, chewed, and swallowed before responding. "Yes, I was. Thank you."

"Well, you've had a long and difficult day." He seemed apologetic. "The colonel said you could have bread and water, but I didn't think a full meal would hurt. Just don't let him know, okay? Besides, you're talking now. Cooperating."

Theresa nodded and said again, "Thank you." She suspected he had intervened purposely during the interrogation to keep Badr from hitting her again. This favor only confirmed it. He was different from the colonel. She tilted her head and examined his fine eyes, recalling his look of anguish and embarrassment at the sight of Jalal's face and Massoud's arm. How had such a mild man come to be enlisted in the state's repressive security apparatus?

Tariq grew uncomfortable under her scrutiny and shifted his feet, making a show of examining her cell. "Well, I'm going home. Is there anything else you require?"

Theresa thought about her medication but didn't want to get him in trouble. Besides, she had only been off her pills for about a week now. It usually took two weeks for the phenobarbital to clear her system, but these were not usual circumstances. She had no idea what effect this kind of stress might have on her condition. He looked anxious to leave. She shook her head and he turned to go.

But as he started to close the cell door, she asked a final favor. "May I use the bathroom again before the lights go out?"

"Of course. I will inform the guard. Good night."

Her cell door closed. She listened to his departing footsteps until the outer steel gate creaked open and clanged shut behind him.

Returning to the mattress, Theresa lay down, satisfied by the food, but still horrified by the day's events. Anguish for Massoud and Jalal nagged her conscience. She thought she could trust this Tariq to see them safely home to the north, but what if Badr had countermanded his orders? Were they indeed on their way or lying dead in a ditch somewhere?

Her thoughts turned to her father. Had prison been like this for him? Her only memories of him in prison were the few visits in the dusty courtyard. His clothes were wrinkled and dirty and his look hollow, but her mother did her best to make a picnic out of each occasion. Theresa even remembered the brightly embroidered red tablecloth they had spread on the ground and the amused looks it elicited from the guards patrolling nearby. Her father had wolfed down the egg salad sandwiches, stopping only to reach out and gently wipe away an occasional tear from her mother's face.

All Theresa could recall of their last visit together was how much his moustache and grizzled face had tickled and scratched when he held her close and kissed her goodbye. What had he said after hugging her? He had spoken so quietly. Did he know he was going to die? Or was he simply worn out from all the questioning? She had looked up at him as he spoke, but the sunlight glared all around his figure, blinding her to the words his blistered lips formed.

Theresa continued to puzzle over the memory after the lights went out. As she lay in the dark with eyes closed, her heart began to beat hard and the old tingling from years ago gathered at the base of her neck, then spread upward to fill her head. Her throat felt warm and constricted, her tongue swollen with a sour garlic taste. The pulsing began. She was having an episode.

Lying there, unable and unwilling to move, she opened her eyes. Fixing on the dark corner of the ceiling, Theresa's eyes beheld her and her father in the side garden of their home in Baghdad. It was daylight and they were alone. She watched herself mount their new swing set. She blinked and, finding herself in the vision now, she began to swing.

Back and forth. Back and forth. The rhythm was soothing but she wanted to go higher...high enough to see over the wall.

"More, Daddy, push me more," she demanded.

"Okay," he said. "Just hang on. You're not gonna jump, are you?"

"No, I just want to see the village. Keep pushing. I can almost see over."

He gave one more big push and she pumped her legs out as she rose. She strained her neck and caught the glimpse she had worked for—the dried mud huts of the poor peasants on a small plot of land across the street on the left side of their house.

"Did you see it?" Her father gave another big push to make sure.

She looked again. "Yes! Thanks, Daddy." As she swung back toward him, Theresa leaned way back to look at him upside down. Her blonde hair brushed the dirt and grass as his figure raced toward her. She approached his shoes, rose past his belt buckle to his grinning face framed by the bushes behind him. He kissed her forehead and she sat up and pumped her legs back and forth to ascend again.

This time she didn't bother to look beyond the wall. She laid back for another upside-down look at her father, but when her hair once more brushed the ground, she noticed the view had changed. There were no shoes, only the rose bushes. Her father wasn't there.

He was gone.

The colors in the vision faded to black and the tingling died away. With the last beat of the pulse between her ears, her eyes relaxed. Again, she found herself bathed in the moonlight of her cell. Alone.

LOOKING BACK

(Mansour—August 27, 2002)

He yearned to be home. Away from all of this. Tariq
merged onto the Airport Road, gunned the motor of
his Land Rover, and headed toward Mansour, east of
Baghdad. He punched on the radio, leaned back, and
let the air conditioning and lilting Arabic music ease
the knots in his neck and shoulders. By the time he
had exited at Um al-Tabul Square to head northeast on
Junub Street toward his neighborhood, he had almost
forgotten the pleading of the old Kurd, the terrified
eyes of his son, and the blood.

He shoved the images behind him as he rounded
Qahtan Square and continued past the hospital on the
right. He was almost home now. West of the Tigris, Mansour drew most of Baghdad's elite, and Tariq's family felt
fortunate to own a modest villa there. His mother would

have dinner warmed and waiting for him. He pressed a bit harder on the accelerator.

Cruising down Dimeshq Street, he glanced to the left at the hulking complex of Iraqi Intelligence Headquarters with its lights still on. His hunger died in a swallow and he turned off the music. A few minutes later, he pulled into his driveway.

He parked, but was unable to turn off the engine or his thoughts. Why live in all this comfort, cut off from the daily lot of average Baghdadis, if he had to witness and take part in such scenes of torture and horror? He had done what he could for the American, but his conscience still seared with guilt. At age thirty-six, how had he come to this?

He had wanted to teach. After earning his degree from San Diego State, he had seriously considered remaining in America. He wanted to apply for citizenship, pursue a doctoral degree at UCLA, and maybe start a family once he found the right woman.

But his mother needed him. Shortly after Tariq's birth, his father had abandoned them, so he had always been the man in the family, notwithstanding his grandfather's formidable presence. His grandfather would never leave the Iraq he had helped build, and his mother could not leave the old man to fight his cancer alone, so Tariq had to return.

He came back in the spring of 1990 when Saddam was actively building up his army after suffering over a quarter of a million casualties in the eight-year conflict with Iran. Tariq soon found his personal ambitions sacrificed on the altar of the Ba'athist state. He was more fortunate than most. His family's stature in the party had, at least, ensured the young man a solid position in the Republican Guard.

With the rank of Lieutenant came responsibility; and when Saddam ordered the invasion of Kuwait, the Gulf War followed in January of 1991. Tariq, under the command of Colonel Badr, led a platoon of crack Republican Guardsmen near the border town of Khafji in one of the few engagements where the Iraqis weren't immediately overwhelmed. He fought well, keeping his men on the attack for three days. They managed to inflict several casualties before a bullet grazed the left side of Tariq's forehead, just above his eye. With their lieutenant wounded, his men folded. The whole platoon was captured and held as prisoners for over a month in Kuwait.

But Badr had passed on word of the young officer's daring. Before the colonel left to join the Mukhabarat, he made certain that, upon Tariq's return to Baghdad, the young man received two medals and a promotion to the rank of captain over a company based in Northern Iraq. Once more, the military defined his life. Instead of teaching history, he taught discipline, order, and how to kill. He felt a part of him dying each time he ordered his soldiers against rebelling Kurds. And so it continued for years.

Then two years ago, his life turned inside out. He had been unexpectedly called to serve in the dreaded Mukhabarat, Hussein's Security Services. His services had been particularly requested by Colonel Badr and signed off by Saddam's son, Qusai. To refuse the assignment would have been suicide. Tariq endured the odious eighteen months of training, learning how to torture and maim. He became particularly adept at cauterizing amputations. Others in his class took to torture as if they were scientists, exploring the limits of man's nervous system. But each night when he returned home, Tariq ate dinner without speaking and threw it up later after his mother and grandfather had gone to bed.

When the training ended, and he had lost twenty-five pounds, Tariq convinced Badr to assign him to surveillance and capture. Thus, he had avoided carrying on with the uglier tasks. Until today.

Tariq closed his eyes and weighed the day's events. He had witnessed both physical and mental torture. He was surprised to find the latter the worst. However painful, physical torture had an end. The prisoner talked, passed out, or died. At least, at some point the pain stopped. But mental torture opened up other wounds in the psyche and spirit. Injuries he doubted could ever heal. Long after the prisoner returned to the cell and the questioning ceased, the mental lacerations continued to fester. He saw it tonight in Miss Fuller's eyes as Badr grilled her about her father. He noticed it again later through the cell door window before he had interrupted her meal. Even while seeming to relish the food, her gaze had been hollow, tormented, and distant.

A sudden tap on the window tensed his body. He turned to see the familiar face of Ghassan, peering in at him. Tariq relaxed and rolled down the window.

"Are you all right? You have been sitting out here for some time. Your mother thought perhaps something was wrong." The gardener, now in his sixties, had served the Awalis since long before Tariq's birth. He had taken care of much more than lawns, gardens, and trees. He had also served as houseboy and chauffeur. Indeed, he had been the father Tariq had never known.

"I'm only tired, Ghassan. It was a difficult day and I wanted to rest a moment before coming in." He turned off the headlights and the engine, and stepped out of the vehicle.

The old man glanced down at Tariq's uniformed pant leg. He gave the young man a searching look and suggested, "You might want to change before you see your mother. I will have it cleaned."

Tariq looked and saw the dried blood stains for the first time; he nodded, thankful the night hid his blush of shame. Somber, he walked into the house, called out a greeting to his mother, and went in the opposite direction to his room to change. Once in pajamas and slippers, he handed the soiled uniform to Ghassan and padded his way back to the kitchen.

His mother turned from the sink as he entered, a smile creasing her lined face. "You're later than usual."

Still lovely at fifty-seven, she gave him both cheeks to kiss and heard his sigh as he sat down at the table. "Is anything wrong?"

"It was just a very long day. There were some... difficult interrogations."

She brought him a plate heaped with rice and *kubba*, minced meat with nuts, raisins, and spices. It was his favorite dish, but when Tariq recalled the way Theresa had devoured her food, the memory turned his stomach sour.

He pushed the plate away. "I'm sorry, Mother. I'm not hungry. Perhaps just some tea, please."

She frowned, but began to prepare a cup of tea, flavored with a wedge of lemon. Her back was still turned when she spoke. "You know, I could speak to your grandfather and perhaps he could arrange for a reassignment. He still has influence in the party."

"No." His tone was firm. "I don't want any more favors. I don't think it's safe. The less we call attention to ourselves, the better."

She turned, set the cup and saucer before him, and seated herself nearby. "You say the interrogations were difficult?" Her uneasy eyes surveyed the face of her only child. "It was not anyone we know, was it?"

He quickly reassured her. "No, no. Just two Kurds and an American journalist."

Her eyebrows raised. "An American? But there has been nothing of an American on the news. Was he arrested today?"

"Two days ago. And it's not a 'he,' it's a 'she.'" He sipped the hot tea carefully, weighing whether or not to confide in his mother. His fatigue and disillusionment tipped the balance in her favor. "There has been no news because nobody knows she's missing. At least not yet. She and her cameraman crossed over the border from Turkey illegally."

"Illegally?" His mother turned her head to the side in disbelief.

Tariq nodded. "She had not even applied to her own government for permission."

Her eyes narrowed. "Is not that unusual?"

"Yes. That's why Colonel Badr thinks she might be a spy."

"Do you think she is a spy?"

Tariq took another sip before responding. "I'm not sure, but I believe she just wanted to get in and out fast with a story. She took a risk and got caught."

"And the cameraman…is he American too?"

Tariq sucked some juice from the lemon wedge before answering. "Canadian. He's being held somewhere else." He finished his tea, and his mother took the cup and saucer over to the sink for rinsing.

"Why was her interrogation difficult?" His mother had tossed the question delicately over her shoulder. He wasn't sure how to respond.

She turned around to look at him. "Surely Badr did not hurt her?"

"Oh, no." Tariq looked down as he added, "He didn't have to."

She picked up his plate of uneaten food and offered it to him again. But Tariq shook his head, so she pulled out some plastic wrap to preserve it for another day.

"You will probably let her go soon, yes?"

"No, I don't think so. It's a little more complicated than that. We found out it's not her first trip to Baghdad."

His mother moved back to the sink to finish washing the dishes. "Well, I would imagine not. After all, she is a reporter and…"

Tariq cut her off. "She was here as a child."

His mother turned with the water still running. "What?"

"The reporter was here with her family during the years of Qasim and after. Come to think of it, maybe you can help me. Didn't you study at Baghdad University before you went to the American University of Beirut?"

His mother paused a moment before answering. "I was there in '64 and '65. But how can this connect with your reporter?"

"Her father was a Visiting Professor at Baghdad University. That's why they were here. He taught Political Science."

Tariq's mother turned back to finish the dishes, saying nothing.

Tariq persisted. "Do you remember an American professor by the name of Fuller?"

She began scrubbing the bottom of the rice pot. "Fuller? The name is familiar. Of course, I would have to look back in the university annual."

"Could you? His name was Nathan Fuller."

She started to rinse off the pot. "And what is the daughter's name? This reporter?"

"Theresa," he answered. The pot clanged against the sink enamel and his mother swayed slightly. He rose and moved to her side. "Are you all right?"

She smiled and brushed her bangs back with her wrist. "Yes, but I think I have been on my feet too long here in the kitchen. And I was tending to your grandfather most of the day." She dried her hands on a towel. "Could you ask Ghassan to finish up here? I think I should go to bed."

"Of course. Good night."

Tariq kissed her cheek and watched her hasten down the hall to her bedroom. After her door closed, he turned back to the sink and set the pot in the dish rack, rubbing his finger over the mark it had left on the enamel.

A BARGAIN

(Abu Ghraib Prison—September 18, 2002)

Barham's head, once held so proudly by a firm neck and broad shoulders, now drooped against the sweat on his bare chest. He had been strapped to a chair, blindfolded, and handcuffed behind his back. Peter saw electrical wires extending from his friend's armpits to a machine set up on a nearby table.

Daily interrogations had begun a week ago. Questioned separately, the two had held up fairly well. They even made a contest of it by comparing their bruises and cuts each evening. Of course, Barham was winning. The guards beat far more sadistically on a Kurd.

Until now they had only been blindfolded, stripped, and beaten with plastic pipes. It proved particularly painful for Peter, who had nothing but a makeshift splint with rags protecting his broken hand. Each day the number of interrogations increased.

Over the past two days, the guards had introduced a new form of torture. They called it *falaqa*. The prisoners were forced face down on the filthy floor, and beaten on the soles of their feet with a cable. Yesterday, Peter had come close to passing out.

No response seemed to satisfy their questioners. Peter had begged to know what information they wanted so he could give it to them and end the pain. The guards merely snickered and struck him harder.

Today, all that had changed.

Handcuffed and stumbling on sore, bleeding feet, Peter entered the interrogation room; his blindfold was yanked down. First, he saw Barham in his sorry state. Before he could make sense of the scene, a Republican Guard officer he had not seen before stepped forward. The older man, dressed in a colonel's uniform, beckoned him to the empty chair a few feet from his Kurdish friend.

Peter hesitated, but the guards thrust him forward. He sat with a thud. Barham made no move as the chair scraped the floor.

"Barham?" Peter leaned toward his friend and was immediately thumped on the back with a pipe. He flinched and stifled a groan.

"I believe your friend is rather tired of my questions."

Peter was surprised at the colonel's English accent.

The officer turned to a guard with a dripping hose. "Wake up the pesh merga. He has a visitor."

The guard aimed the hose at Barham and squeezed the nozzle, letting loose a blast of water. The Kurd barely moved his head.

"Again," ordered the colonel in his clipped style.

After the second soaking, Barham moaned and turned his head away. Peter could see he had been badly beaten around the face, and blood was dripping from cuts near his mouth and left ear.

The officer snapped on a rubber glove, approached the Kurd, and jerked his head up by the hair. Peter guessed he was leery of lice or fleas.

"A friend has come to visit you. You must be attentive." The colonel released Barham's hair and carefully peeled off the glove, handing it to a guard.

The officer turned his attention back to Peter. "Go on, talk to him. Tell him it would be wise to cooperate."

Peter complied. "Barham."

The Kurd's body tensed at the sound of Peter's voice.

"Remember? You're no good to your family dead. Hang in there."

The colonel snorted. "Every man has a limit. Shall we see where your friend's limit lies?" He nodded to the guard with the hose and the man sprayed Barham again.

"Wait a minute," Peter interrupted, "what do you want to know? What have you been asking? I could answer your questions."

"Your turn will come." The colonel gestured to the guard at the machine who flipped a switch. Immediately, Barham's body arched. His head jerked back; the pupils of his eyes rolled up so that all Peter could see were the whites of his eyeballs. For eight seconds, fifty thousand volts of electricity coursed through Barham's body. When the current broke, he collapsed with a shudder.

The officer leaned in to the quivering Kurd. "Tell me about Theresa Fuller. Why did she come to Iraq?"

Peter interrupted. "Theresa? I can tell you why she came. She's a reporter. I'm her cameraman. We only came to do a story."

"Is that so?" The colonel took a few steps towards Peter. "Why did you not follow the usual procedures and obtain the necessary permits?"

He nodded again at the man with the hose. A second time the guard drenched Barham to maximize the pain of the electric shock that followed.

Peter yelled. "Stop it! I'm talking to you. I'll tell you what you want to know. We didn't go through the right channels because we knew your government wouldn't let us get the story we wanted."

The colonel turned his back on him. "You are not telling me anything I have not already heard."

"But it's the truth," Peter argued. "We're only journalists doing our job. And Barham was our guide."

"One of your guides," the officer corrected with his back turned.

It dawned on Peter that this officer likely knew where the others were. How could he convince this man to let him see Theresa, as well as Barham's father and brother?

"If you take me to Theresa, I can help you get the information you need. Is she here? Is she in the Foreigners' Section?" Peter tried not to sound desperate.

"And how would you do that?"

"We're close friends."

Badr turned. "That is interesting. How close?"

"We've worked together for…" Peter stopped, realizing the dangerous turn this conversation was taking.

The colonel smiled. "If I were you, I would be more concerned about your own welfare. Miss Fuller—if that is her real name—is in capable hands."

The word "capable" conjured ugly pictures in Peter's mind. A dread filled him and it led to an anger that he found difficult to control. "You had better not be hurting her. If you've laid one finger on her…"

"Enough!" The colonel issued orders in Arabic.

Immediately, a guard unlocked Peter's handcuffs only to cuff him again behind his back. He knotted one end of a rope around the cuffs and threw the other end over a hook hanging from the ceiling. Pushing Peter back, he took the free end of the rope and pulled. Peter cried out as his arms extended behind him like an iron cross gone wrong. Slowly he was hoisted off the floor a few inches, his straining arms holding the full weight of his body. Shoulder muscles and ligaments began to tear.

He screamed. His joints popped out and he heard and felt the sinew stretch and rip.

"Now," the officer resumed, "perhaps you will tell me what your friend would not. What do you know of Theresa Fuller's childhood? Why was her family here in Baghdad?"

Peter tried to keep his mind clear despite the stabbing pain lancing his upper torso. "I don't…know… what you're talking about. She was here…as a child?"

"I am asking the questions, not you. What do you know of her childhood here in Baghdad? Specifically, what do you know of her father? Was he working for the CIA?"

Peter's mind started to cloud. "She doesn't talk… about her past."

"How long have you known her?"

The agony threatened to overwhelm him and he barely got the words out. "Since Bosnia."

"Bosnia? You must know her rather well. Come now, you must have exchanged childhood stories over drinks. Why are you protecting her? Are you CIA too?"

"CIA? No. I don't…I don't know anything. She won't talk about it."

As he said the last words, everything in his view—the colonel, Barham, the floor—grew white. His head rolled down and his body went slack.

The officer barked another order in Arabic and the guard pulling on the rope let go. Peter collapsed in a heap. The guards lifted him up, set him in the chair, and slapped him back to consciousness.

Peter moaned and opened his eyes. He felt a numbing burn from his armpits to his fingers.

The colonel stepped directly in front of him. "You cannot be CIA," he barked. "You passed out too easily. It is all too apparent you have not had the training."

"I told you. I'm a journalist," he mumbled.

"And you know nothing of Miss Fuller's prior experience in Baghdad? Nothing of her father?"

"No. I swear to God."

The colonel pursed his lips, nodded, and gave one last order in Arabic before exiting the room.

Despite his wooziness, Peter's heart beat faster. His eyes roamed from guard to guard to ascertain his fate. The one who had been drenching his friend set the hose down, approached Barham, and began to remove the electrical wires. Once disconnected, the blindfolded Kurd was lifted from his chair to stand. The other guards grabbed Peter roughly by his aching arms and yanked him to his feet, as well. He had no strength to object. What little remained was used to focus on staying conscious.

Saying nothing, the guards replaced his blindfold and pushed him ahead. He stumbled. The guards veered him down a corridor, but he couldn't tell which one. He shook his head to try and regain some sense of direction, straining for familiar sounds. He heard screaming in the distance. Was it getting louder?

They turned another corner and he began to hear the familiar sounds of the large hall. Ten paces on they pulled Peter up short, and removed his blindfold and handcuffs. He swallowed in relief. Barham was beside him. They had been returned to their original holding place. Supporting each other, the two shuffled to their old familiar spot against the wall. They hugged the cool concrete, taking their time before sliding carefully to the floor. Peter knew his arms would never be the same.

Later that night, the guard who had bought Peter's jeans—Barham and Peter called him "Pants"—sidled up and crouched next to them.

He spoke to Peter in broken English. "You live? One thousand."

Peter looked at Barham. "Is he guaranteeing we won't be killed if we pay him a thousand?" The Kurd nodded and Peter turned back to the guard.

"One thousand dinars?"

Pants spat. "Dinar no good. One thousand dollar."

Peter realized he wasn't in much of a position to bargain and gestured for Barham and himself. "Okay. You keep us alive until we get out and you'll get one thousand dollars."

The guard squinted, looked at Barham, and pointed at Peter. "You—one thousand. He and you—two thousand." He held up two dirty fingers.

Peter, too tired to haggle, nodded. "Agreed. The day we walk out of here, you'll get two thousand dollars."

Pants smiled and stood up. "No worry. You safe now."

Peter waited until the guard left before adjusting the bandage on his hand to better cover the glint of gold. Barham had advised him to hide his ring and the dinars under the wrapping for safekeeping. He felt the outline of the ring now and thought of Theresa. Was she safe?

FRIENDSHIP

(Outskirts of Baghdad—September 19, 2002)

Theresa averted her eyes from the bloodstained walls and sat down. The table had been freshly scrubbed in an attempt to conceal the horror of weeks ago, but she could still see the outlines. They hadn't gotten around to repainting the walls yet. Or was Badr leaving them smeared as a less than subtle form of intimidation? She heard footsteps and steeled herself for another frustrating grapple with her memory.

The door opened and Tariq appeared...alone. He dismissed the guards and closed the door. The captain smiled as he crossed to sit opposite her. Where was Badr?

He greeted her in Arabic. "*Marhaba.* How are you?"

"I'm fine. *Marhabtain.*"

"So you do speak Arabic."

"*Shwaya, shwaya.* A very little."

Theresa had decided it would look more suspicious if she didn't use a phrase here and there. After all, she had been working and traveling throughout the Middle East for over a decade.

"I don't suppose you will take some coffee or tea?"

She smiled, but shook her head. "*La, shukran.*" Tariq nodded approvingly at her accent and Theresa began to relax before catching herself. Badr was sure to walk in any moment. "Where is the colonel?"

"Colonel Badr is away on other business for several days. He has asked me to continue your questioning in his absence." He watched her eyes for a reaction. "I hope you don't mind."

She wondered if Badr was gone or simply lying in wait somewhere. Perhaps this was their version of a good cop, bad cop routine. In any case, she spoke the truth. "I don't mind it being you."

Tariq's face flushed and he looked away. He seemed to be staring at the spatters on the wall and deliberating. After a minute, he stood up abruptly.

"I think it wouldn't hurt if you had some fresh air. Would it be all right if we talked outside for a change?"

"Outside...the prison?"

He nodded.

Surprised, Theresa seized the offer. "That would be wonderful." She had been captive for three weeks. Other than the view of sky and part of a palm tree through her cell window, she had seen nothing but dingy walls and a dirty bathroom. Tortured screams and clanging doors obliterated any sounds of nature. She had, in a sense, lost the world.

The captain led her out of the room, turned left, and headed toward a guarded door at the end of the corridor. At Tariq's command, the guard unlocked the steel door and pulled it open. Bright sunlight burst on Theresa's face and she squinted in the glare. Tariq made way for her and she stepped down into a garden area ringed by lovely flowering oleander bushes. Blue periwinkle mixed with yellow and red zinnias dotted the ground all around. Fragrant rose bushes lined a far wall. The sudden beauty contrasted so violently with the past several weeks that she buried her face in her hands and began to sob.

Tariq came to her. "What's wrong?"

She took a deep breath, exhaled, and wiped her tears. "Nothing. I just never expected the outside of this prison to look this way." She waved her arm around. "This is the Baghdad I remember." Her eyes teared up again.

His smile was kind. "Come, let's walk. I'm sure you could use the exercise."

Theresa hesitated. "Are you sure it's all right?" She worried about Badr. Along with that, she feared being alone with this man. Something in his manner disarmed her and she wasn't yet sure he could be trusted. Was the kindness in his eyes a ruse? What did he want from her?

"Of course. I've sent the guards to eat. All except for that one." He cocked his head back to the door where they'd exited. "And he won't tell."

Her desire for some sense of normalcy cast aside her doubts, and she followed his lead. They crossed the garden area and rounded a corner facing the back of the prison. Rows of stately palm trees, bordered by irrigation ditches, stretched for miles. Her eyes swept the horizon.

Tariq gazed with her. "Impressive, isn't it? Today Iraq is still the largest exporter of dates in the world. Have you ever been on a date farm before?"

She nodded, looking off into the distance. "When I was a child. We went to one outside Baghdad for a picnic. I didn't like the flies. But it was fun to see the worker climb to the top of a palm, cut a bunch of ripe dates, and drop them to us for our dessert." The memory warmed her.

"The prophet Muhammad said, 'There is among trees one that is pre-eminently blessed, as is the Muslim among men; it is the date palm.'"

Theresa turned, surprised. "You don't strike me as the religious type. Are you trying to convert me to Islam?"

He held both hands up and smiled. "I'm only talking about dates, something I know about."

Theresa hesitated. "Where is this conversation leading?"

"What do you mean?" His smile wavered.

"Why are we talking about dates? I'm a prisoner. Are you trying to pretend I haven't seen the things I have? Or did Badr tell you to bring me out here?"

Tariq looked back at the prison, his mouth grim. "The colonel knows nothing of this. If he did, I might be shot…or worse."

"What could be worse than being shot?"

Tariq turned to look directly in her eyes. "Seeing your family shot first."

Theresa took a step back. "Badr would do that?" When Tariq didn't answer, she turned back to the prison. "You don't need to take this risk. I can pace my cell."

She felt his hand take her arm, then let go. "Please. If I didn't think it was safe, I wouldn't have brought you out. He won't know."

She whirled and her eyes bore into him. "Why are you working for a man like that?"

"He wasn't always like that. In the Army, he was a good commander."

"Is he the one that gave you those medals?"

He glanced down at his chest and nodded.

"What were they for?"

He shrugged. "Getting wounded while I was trying to be brave during the Gulf War."

Theresa moved closer to inspect them. "Let me guess. The wounded medal is this one here with the red crescent." She pointed to a gilt five-point star set on a maroon background. In the star's center, painted into a white circle, lay a maroon crescent.

"How did you know?"

"My mother belonged to the Red Crescent Society here in Baghdad. It's the Middle Eastern equivalent of the Red Cross, right?"

He nodded, impressed.

"Is that scar from your wound?" Theresa pointed to the thin white slash above his left eye.

"Yes. It could have been serious, but it wasn't."

"So if Colonel Badr used to be such a good commander, what happened?"

Tariq sighed. "You must understand there are forces in this country...forces we can't control. This is not America. Fear rules this country."

"You mean Saddam Hussein."

Tariq shifted and lowered his voice. "Him. And others like him."

"What's going to happen to me?" She searched his eyes for an answer.

Tariq paused, looked beyond her to the prison, and then back at Theresa. "Hopefully nothing. But you must keep talking. Even if you have to make things up, you must keep talking. Because if you have nothing to give, you become expendable."

Her eyes grew wide. "But I'm an American. Badr wouldn't dare kill me when my government is looking for any excuse to attack."

"Are they?"

"Absolutely. Bush and his advisers are itching for a war."

"I agree. Many here think that America will attack regardless. Even if we show Bush there are no more nuclear or chemical weapons, he will attack. But what happens to you is not up to Badr, anyway."

Theresa's stomach turned over and she stared hard at the ground. She had hoped for release in a matter of weeks. Tariq seemed to be telling her to forget about freedom and worry about staying alive...at least until the war.

She spoke to the ground. "But the invasion is likely months away. I'll run out of things to say..."

Tariq interrupted. "I can help you. Badr trusts me. If I convince him that you have information but you will give it more easily to me, then he may allow me to conduct your questioning. I will keep you from getting hurt."

Theresa's hopes rose again, but the look she gave him was guarded. "Why do you want to help me?"

"Because of all this." Tariq waved his arm back toward the prison. "I never wanted any part of this. There will be a war. I am counting on it. And America will win, though the cost will be higher than they suspect. When they enter Baghdad and liberate the city, the first ones to be detained and punished, after Saddam and his sons, will be those of the Mukhabarat. Men like Badr...me." His eyes lowered.

Theresa shook her head. "You're not like Badr."

"No. Perhaps not yet. After work, I don't join the others when they go out to drink or celebrate. I go home to be with my mother, my grandfather."

She noticed he said nothing of a wife or children.

"But Badr is pulling me in deeper," he continued. "And if I don't do something to fight against all of this, I will lose my mind or become just like him." He raised his head and fixed her with a look of pleading. "Let us help each other."

"What things can I tell you?"

"Little things. Things from your childhood here. Like the picnic at the date farm. I can make them look important to Badr. Whose date farm was it? Where was it?"

She thought for a minute. "It was about an hour outside the city, but I can't remember which direction. I believe we went with the Abashi family. I don't know if it belonged to them but… wait. Yes, it was their farm. But it was smaller than this."

"That's good. You have remembered a new name. Each name you provide takes weeks to track down."

Theresa stiffened. "And what happens to these people once you track them down? By naming them, am I sentencing them to prison and torture? Are they dying?"

"In all likelihood, no. These are names from forty years ago. Many have died already…or left Iraq. Thousands left in the years after Saddam rose to power."

"You don't like him, do you? When you didn't react to my comment in the car, I knew that you hated him as much as I do. Probably more."

He didn't reply.

"You didn't tell Badr what I said about Saddam, did you?"

Tariq stuffed his hands in his pockets. "Of course not. But let's not talk of unpleasant things. Tell me more about your childhood. I wonder how different or similar it was to mine."

Theresa smiled in agreement. "What did you do as a child?"

He gave her a sidelong glance. "Are you interrogating me now?"

"Maybe," she teased. "I find it intriguing that someone educated in history would take the time to learn about dates, for example."

He rose to the challenge. "You don't believe I know about dates? I will prove it to you. Come, sit down." He led her toward the shade of a nearby palm.

Theresa seated herself and looked up. "*Tayyib*, okay. You have a captive audience."

Instead of beginning his explanation, Tariq leaned over, seeming to examine the top of her head. "So you are not a brunette?"

Theresa had forgotten about her hair dye. After three weeks, her natural color was clearly showing at the roots where her hair parted.

"I thought I'd be safer with dark hair."

He stepped back, nodding. "A good decision. It's strange to think of you now as a blonde."

She held up her hand. "You're changing the subject. I'm still waiting to be impressed, and I don't impress easily."

"Very well." Tariq cleared his throat, held his hands behind his back, and began to pace as he threw out facts. "The first cultivated dates grew here six thousand years ago. In Ancient Mesopotamia. The date palm can grow thirty meters high. Unripe dates are green. As they ripen, they turn yellow and end up reddish-brown. Each tree produces…"

Theresa held up her hand to interrupt him. "Okay, you've convinced me. You know about dates."

"Wait, there is one more interesting fact. Only female palms produce fruit."

"That doesn't surprise me."

"But one male tree has enough pollen to pollinate fifty females."

Theresa shifted, now uncomfortable with the male-female talk. "How is it you know so much about dates?"

"My uncle owns a date farm. Not nearly as large as this one, but good-sized. As a boy, I worked on it in the summer and during school holidays." He sat down beside her. "Now, I believe it's your turn. What did you do as a girl in Baghdad?"

She looked off in the distance. "Let's see. My life here revolved around school, the Alwiya Club…"

Tariq interrupted, a broad smile on his face. "I swam at the Alwiya Club all the time. Did you see the open air movies at night there on the big screen out on the lawn?"

"Yes! That's where I first fell in love with films."

"Me too."

She couldn't help smiling at his boyish delight.

Embarrassed, he cleared his throat. "I'm sorry, please go on."

Theresa continued. "I started kindergarten here. A.C.C. was in the old building when we first arrived."

"A.C.C.?"

"The American Community Center. That was the name of our school. I don't have a clear memory of the old building… except the day my first boyfriend saved my life."

Tariq feigned surprise. "A boyfriend in kindergarten?" He shook his head in mock disapproval. "You American women are so fast."

"Fast? Did you pick that up at San Diego State?"

"Don't you say 'fast' anymore?"

She laughed. "I'm almost too old to know. Anyway, I remember the classroom was huge and kind of gray. It was free time, and Ryan and I were playing with the blocks. He was building something and all of a sudden he looked up and stopped. He told me not to move, so I froze while he picked up one of the biggest blocks and smashed it down on the floor just inches from me on the right."

"Did he scare you?"

"Of course. And I was plenty mad until he showed me the dead scorpion."

"Ah. From that moment on he was your first true love, your hero."

"At least until I met up with him again in college. He didn't turn out to be that impressive."

"No scorpions to kill?"

"Not of the Baghdad variety."

"We do have many dangerous scorpions," Tariq allowed.

"What bothered me most as a child here were the cockroaches. I think I remember some of them flying, too. They were huge—two inches long, maybe even three. I notice they still are. Anyway, I would be up in my room playing, and catch sight of one scurrying along the wall."

Tariq snickered.

"I'd scream and run from the room and you should have seen our maid, Asil. She would go running in, whip off her slipper and chase after the roach, all the time cursing in Arabic. By the time she whacked it to pieces it was probably already dead from fright."

He bobbed his head. "In my house I was the designated roach killer. Whenever Grandmother would start screaming, Grandfather would calmly hand me his slipper and say, 'Tariq, do your job.' Roaches here are fast. I can easily picture your maid chasing and screaming at the same time."

"I can smile about it now," Theresa said, "but it wasn't funny at the time. They scared me to death as a child. I hated kneeling by my bed at night to say my prayers because I was sure one was going to climb right up on my bare feet."

"So now that you're back, are you having difficulty saying your prayers again?"

She looked down. "I stopped saying prayers a long time ago."

When he didn't respond, Theresa turned back. The merriment had left his eyes. She reached to touch his arm, but stopped, clenching her fist instead. "Long before all this, you understand."

Neither of them spoke. After a few minutes, Tariq rose and helped her up. "Come, let's walk over and visit the caretaker and his family. You must be hungry, and they may still be sitting at their afternoon meal."

Theresa followed, grateful he hadn't pressed for more. Had he thought her religious? If so, her comment about prayer must have puzzled him. Still, he said nothing, respecting her privacy. They walked around the side of the complex, away from the guards' lodgings. A small concrete hut squatted in the shade of three tall palms. Beneath the palms stood fig and pear trees, and a black rooster strutted after a few hens that were scratching for food in front of the hut. Nearby, a slight, curly-haired girl in a tattered shift fed palm leaves to a tethered goat. As the pair approached, she ran barefoot into the hut. Seconds later, a man emerged to welcome them and Theresa recognized the old peasant who had given her the pitcher of water in her cell.

After an exchange of greetings, they were invited in to a meal of rice, lamb, tomatoes and cucumbers. The family of six had already eaten, but crowded around to watch their guests dine. As soon as Theresa had cleared her plate, the old man's grown daughter offered a second helping.

Theresa looked to Tariq for help. "I can't possibly eat any more. Besides, this is a poor family. I don't want to take food from their mouths."

He smiled indulgently. "If you are full, just refuse. They are obligated to keep offering more. It is the Arab way. Surely you remember this."

She nodded and politely declined the woman's proffer. But when the caretaker's old wife produced a basket of apples, figs, grapes, oranges and pears, Theresa's resistance faded. She hadn't eaten fruit in weeks, and she tore off a small bunch of grapes.

Tariq raised his eyebrows. "You're not afraid of Baghdad Belly? Surely you remember that too."

She did. Every third world country had its own name for the diarrhea and stomach cramping that came from drinking the local water, or eating the home-grown produce. Theresa remembered how her mother used to wash the fruits and vegetables purchased from the open-air markets with laundry detergent so that the family wouldn't suffer the effects of Baghdad Belly. Still, the fruit looked too good to pass up.

"I'm willing to risk it. May I take them back to my cell to eat later?"

"Of course."

They rose to leave and she slipped the grapes into a pocket made looser from loss of weight. When Theresa thanked their hosts in Arabic, the old man and his wife and daughter smiled broadly. The grandchildren giggled behind covered mouths. Tariq lingered at the door, and Theresa saw him press several folded bills into the old man's hand.

Halfway back to the compound, she spoke. "Did you pay him for the food?"

"Of course not. The food was a gift. This is one of Saddam Hussein's farms, you see, so they will never starve as long as he's in power."

"Then what was the money for?"

"I paid him to keep his mouth shut. After all, you're supposed to be eating only bread and water." They arrived in the garden area, and he stopped. "I also arranged for you to have a weekly bath."

"A bath?" Her eyes brightened.

"There will be a small tub of hot water set out for you in the bathroom tonight after the guards change shifts. And a change of your clothes. I hope you won't mind my going through your bag to select appropriate items."

The thought of him handling her underwear made her uneasy, but she shrugged it off. "Not at all. Thank you very much. For a while today I almost forgot I'm a prisoner." Tariq checked his watch. "We have a few more minutes before the guards come back on duty. Tell me more of what you did for fun as a child here." He walked her to a stone bench in the corner near a pink oleander bush. "Come, sit in the shade a while longer."

As she turned to seat herself, a strange feeling of déjà vu swept over her. Had she been here before—with him? Almost immediately, the tingling began in her throat. Her heart beat quickened. Another episode. She'd been averaging two or three a week since the vision of her father. So far, that had been her only vision. Would this episode bring another? Theresa sat still, mouth open, and stared at the roses against the far wall.

Tariq waited. When she didn't speak, he looked closely at her. "Well, didn't you have any more fun in Baghdad?"

She heard him, but said nothing. Concentrating on forming words while experiencing the waves of sensations felt like swimming against the tide. Too fatiguing. In the periphery of her sight, she saw him approach the flowers on which she seemed so focused.

His voice grew fainter. "They are pretty, aren't they? Shall I cut some for you? They might make your cell a bit more hospitable."

He pulled out a pocketknife and proceeded to cut off several of the red and yellow blooms. As he cut, Theresa swallowed twice. Instead of roses, she saw her fourth-grade classroom at the new A.C.C. school building.

A bell rang for recess and she watched herself join the others filing out into a spacious dirt yard enclosed by high cement walls. Bushes lined the side and rear walls, interrupted by an occasional flowering plant. Four huge palm trees formed an approximate diamond. She ran over to her brother and their friends at the base of the "home" palm tree for their daily game of kickball. The teams were rapidly organized and Theresa was up to kick. Jimmy rolled the ball fast and bouncy, but it didn't matter. She timed her kick carefully, aiming for the left side of the school building. The abundance of bushes on that side would make it difficult to field the ball. While her brother screamed at his teammates to hurry, she was already rounding the third palm tree, heading for home base. Hot and sweaty, she tagged the big palm just ahead of the ball, relishing her team's cheers.

A touch on her shoulder closed the vision and brought her back to the garden. She looked up into Tariq's worried eyes.

"Are you all right? You didn't seem to hear what I was saying."

"I was… just daydreaming." She saw the long-stemmed roses in his right hand. "How beautiful."

He held them out to her. "I thought they might brighten your cell."

She thanked him and breathed in their sweet fragrance. Theresa had not wanted to mention her epilepsy for fear Badr would use it against her in some way. But now it occurred to her that Tariq might be able to help her without the colonel's knowledge. She was not yet concerned about the episodes. While the aura had come with little warning, it had been pleasant and comforting. The only true seizure she had ever suffered was the one in eighth grade—the one that brought about her diagnosis. She had not had so much as an episode for decades...until now. But, given her current circumstances, she thought it best not to take chances.

"Captain, I wonder if you could provide something else with my bath?"

"Your medication?"

She nodded in surprise, but realized he must have seen it while going through her things. Indeed, she had begun to wonder when Badr would ask her about it. Now, she looked on the man before her with new eyes. Perhaps the captain had decided to keep this discovery from his superior.

Tariq sat beside her. "What is it for?"

"Epilepsy." She peered into his eyes, wondering how he would react.

He did not flinch or draw back. "You weren't merely daydreaming, were you?"

"No, I was having a seizure, although I don't like to use that word. My first neurologist suggested I call them episodes. Seizure connotes a loss of consciousness and control, and that's not what happens in my case."

"What does happen?"

Theresa described the tingling, the sensations, and the visions. She told him about the seizure in Junior

High, but emphasized that nothing like that had occurred again. He asked about her supply.

Theresa sighed. "That's the problem. I only have enough for three months. I hadn't counted on being held prisoner for an indefinite period. What happens if I run out of medicine before I am released?"

"Let me worry about that. Medicine is difficult to come by in our country because of the sanctions, but I may have some connections. In the meantime, I will get your prescription to you. Keep it in a pocket. While you aren't searched regularly, your cell is." He paused. "Is there anything else you haven't told me? Anything I should know?"

She started to shake her head, but stopped. A trust had developed between them, now that she knew he was willing to defy orders.

"I speak and read Arabic."

Tariq's lip curved up on the left. "I thought so. You had better keep that a secret. You mentioned that visions sometimes come with your episodes. What did you see this time?"

Theresa smiled. "Kickball."

"What?"

"I saw the time I kicked a homerun off my brother's pitch in a kickball game here in Baghdad. It was glorious. He fumed for days, as I recall."

Tariq shook his head. "I'm afraid I don't know this game."

She teased him. "You mean they didn't teach you about kickball at San Diego State?"

He was about to answer when the door opened and the guard said something in Arabic. Tariq nodded and got to his feet.

"I'm afraid the other guards are on their way back. We'd better get inside."

Reluctantly, she stood and followed him into the dirty corridor to her cell. Tariq watched her place the flowers in the pitcher of water, then turned to go.

She called to him as he reached the door. "Captain."

He swiveled to face her.

"Thank you."

He smiled. "Thank *you*. Have a good evening." He locked her in and was gone.

Later that night after the guards changed shifts, Theresa was let out to go to the bathroom. The guard who accompanied her was the same one who had witnessed their outing that day.

As he unlocked the bathroom door, he spoke in broken English. "You take all time you want. Captain say." He winked and sprawled on a chair in the hall.

Theresa entered the cramped and dirty room. Flipping on the overhead bulb, she hardly noticed the roaches scurrying for the corners. In the middle of the floor sat a tin tub full of water. That, alone, brought tears to her eyes. She turned and saw the bar of soap on a towel hugging the corner of the sink to her left.

A fresh set of wrinkled clothes and underclothes had been pulled from her confiscated bag and placed on top of the toilet. When she checked the pants pockets, Theresa discovered her plastic bottle of phenobarbital. She closed the door and undressed.

After soaking for several minutes in the warm water, she reached for the soap and began to scrub. She winced as she ran the soap over her lower left arm. Taking a closer look, she noticed a sore just above her wrist. Theresa rinsed it off to better examine the raised whitish bump in the shape of a circle, surrounded by sensitive red skin. Was this from the bite three weeks ago? She recalled scratching it for the first week, before forcing herself to leave it alone. It must have become infected. She finished her bath, taking care to avoid the strange skin lesion.

TARIQ'S GRANDFATHER

(Mansour—September 30, 2002)

Tariq's grandfather, for once, felt well enough to eat with them, so they would be eating in the formal dining room. As Ghassan escorted the frail old man to his seat at the head of the table, Tariq shot a quick glance at his mother. She nodded without speaking. Her father, bald from the chemotherapy and stooped by age, would not be with them much longer.

Once settled, Ibrahim al-Awali looked up, coughed, and addressed his grandson. "Tariq, I have not seen you for some time. You have been working hard?"

"Yes, Grandfather. How are you feeling?"

The seventy-nine-year-old man waved the question away. "It does not matter. I am still alive and that is an accomplishment in this country."

His daughter's eyes grew wide and she brought her index finger to her lips. The old man's comment had frozen Ghassan in his steps toward the kitchen. Fear gripped Tariq in the stomach. Over the past week he had discovered two listening devices, one in the kitchen and another in the sitting room. As far as he knew, their house had never been bugged before. Who knew how many more lay hidden throughout the various rooms? He had passed a note to alert his mother and Ghassan, but they must have failed to tell his grandfather.

The old man took a sip of water. "What? Surely, an old man can complain about the lack of adequate medical care." He smiled slyly as he added one more comment for the benefit of any state security official listening in. "Can I help it if the American imperialist Bush continues to step on our neck with sanctions, denying us the food and medicines we lack?"

At this, they all smiled in relief, echoed his sentiments loudly, and Ghassan proceeded to serve their meal.

Once the food was brought, Ghassan retired to the kitchen to eat his portion. Lately, he had been eating with Tariq and his mother as one of the family. But the grandfather held old-fashioned views about servants and wouldn't countenance his presence at the dinner table.

Tariq watched his grandfather guide a trembling spoonful of warm pomegranate soup to his mouth. The stew contained lamb, vegetables and rice, as well as the paste that gave it its name. Flavored with mint, cinnamon and pepper, it had long been his grandfather's dish of choice. But swallowing seemed difficult tonight. The cancer was in the lymph nodes now. Tariq was glad his grandmother, one of Iraq's best female doctors, hadn't lived to see her husband struggle with a spoon. This Ba'athist, who had once addressed thousands at political rallies, could now barely speak above a whisper. Ibrahim al-Awali had helped establish the original Arab Ba'ath Socialist Party in Iraq in 1952. Opposed to the corrupt monarchy and the growing Iraqi Communist Party, his group sought for a renaissance, a *ba'ath* of Arab heritage. They sought to bridge the chasms of religion, tribe and class by promoting Arabism before and above everything. Following the ideology of its avowed Syrian architect, Michel Aflaq, the Ba'ath mixed passionate Arab nationalism with a less stringent socialism.

But Awali had talked more moderately than most of his fellow party members, certainly more than the up and coming young Saddam Hussein. A true intellectual and Arab nationalist, Awali had counseled against killing Qasim in the February, 1963, revolution. He worried that it might invite tribal retributions in a country defined most of all by clans.

He was ignored. The other party leaders chose not only to kill the general, but also to broadcast his bullet-ridden corpse live on Iraqi TV. For the first time, the moderate began to doubt the movement he had helped establish.

He buried his reservations nine months later when the Ba'ath was displaced. He hoped that the loss and resulting imprisonment of several Ba'athi leaders might humble them and moderate their approach. But in 1968, when the party took complete control of the country again, Awali felt disappointment and doubt creep in again. The new Ba'athist president, Ahmed Hassan al-Bakr, hailed from Tikrit, an area north of Baghdad. Perhaps shaken by their earlier failure to hold power, the new Ba'ath determined to ignore their original ideology and rely on tribal loyalty and terror. Bakr chose as his vice president a fellow Tikriti and relative—his thug of a cousin, Saddam Hussein. Purges and public hangings of suspected Zionist spies in Baghdad's Liberation Square soon followed.

Before long, the government reached beyond Iraqi Jews and began arresting and killing Muslims and Christians, as well. By the time Hussein took the reins of power in '78, Tariq's grandfather no longer doubted. He knew. The Ba'ath had become a curse, not a blessing to his people.

Awali learned to keep his mouth closed and his head down. He served when asked, but never volunteered because he sensed ambition would doom him. On the evening of August 8, 1979—"the night of the long knives," as it came to be called—Saddam Hussein had twenty-one members of his own government executed for treason before his eyes. Included were the deputy prime minister and the ministers of education, industry, planning, and health—all friends of Awali. Still, he said nothing. When he was awarded the Ba'ath Party Medal a decade later as a badge of honor and service, he bowed his head to the "Butcher of Baghdad." Thus, he survived. Cancer, not Saddam, would kill him.

Tariq's mother broke the silence at the table. "Son, you are so quiet. Is the food not to your liking, or is your mind wandering?"

Tariq took his eyes off his grandfather to acknowledge the excellence of the meal and thank his mother for her special efforts. Along with the soup, she had prepared rice with saffron, almonds, and raisins, and the *kubba* he loved. Taking another bite of it now, he recalled their talk the last time he had refused his favorite dish.

"Mother, did you have a chance to look through your university annual about that professor?"

His mother blinked, her smile gone.

"What professor?" asked his grandfather.

She answered before Tariq could. "Oh, he just asked me about a professor I knew at AUB. Son, would you please help me select another bottle of wine in the kitchen?"

"But Ghassan can help you."

"We only have two bottles left. I would prefer you to make the choice."

Baffled, Tariq followed his mother into the kitchen where Ghassan sat at the kitchen table eating his dinner and listening to a CD of Arabic music.

Tariq spoke as the door swung shut behind him. "Why did you say AUB? He was a professor here at

Baghdad University, not in Beirut. And the colonel would appreciate anything you might know about the case."

Remembering the hidden microphones, she turned up the volume on the CD player and spoke in a whisper. "Ssshh. I don't want to upset your grandfather. Promise me never to talk about this reporter or her father in front of him. All right?"

"Why?"

"Those years were difficult for him. They will only bring bad memories." She pulled two bottles of wine from a cupboard and set them on the counter. "He was in and out of prison. I do not want him to dwell on those times."

Tariq disagreed. "But he loves talking about the old days. He's told me all about his stays in prison. He said they gave him a chance to read, study more, and culti-vate his political philosophy."

She cut the argument short. "Well, there were other things going on, too. Please, I do not want you bringing it up. Do you understand?"

He shrugged, unconvinced, and opened the bottle of Bordeaux while she retrieved wineglasses from an-other cupboard.

As he poured the red wine into three glasses, he re-turned to the subject of Theresa's father. "So what can you tell me about Professor Fuller? Did you find his pic-ture? Badr hasn't shown me the file yet and I would like to see what he looked like."

She glanced at Ghassan, took one of the glasses and sipped. "I could not locate my annual. I think I must have thrown it out. As I recall, he was of average height, with light-colored hair. I believe he had one of those American military haircuts. I mean, it was flat on top."

Tariq gave this some thought. "He used to be with the military. I suppose it's not surprising he would continue wearing that style." He looked sideways at his mother. "But I'm impressed you even remember him without looking at his picture."

She took another sip. "True, I had not thought of him for years. But once you mentioned his name, some memories began to come back. He taught one of my classes. He was a popular teacher, as I recall. Foreign teachers generally were."

She started toward the door to the dining room, but he called her back. "Wait, Mother. Were you able to find out or remember why he went to prison?"

She stopped and turned. "I believe he was charged as a spy."

"Was he executed for that reason?"

"What?" She blinked in confusion.

"Theresa said he died in prison, but she wasn't sure how or why. Was he executed?"

His mother stood there, mouth open. She had gone quite pale. "He died?"

"Yes. You seem surprised."

Her tone was hollow and she spoke without looking at him. "I never heard. In those days, foreigners were never killed. I just assumed he was let go and...." Her voice trailed off. She took another sip of wine, licked her lips, and filled her glass again. "I am finished with my dinner. Will you help Ghassan here get your grandfather settled down for the night?" She still wouldn't look at her son.

"Of course." He moved to kiss her cheek, but she had already turned to head down the hall to her bedroom. Tariq started to follow, but he heard his grandfather call. He looked back at Ghassan, leaned over to turn the volume back down on the CD player, and picked up the remaining two glasses of wine to return to the dining room. As he sat down to finish eating, he heard her bedroom door close.

RELEASE

(Abu Ghraib Prison—October 20, 2002)

Pants sidled over to Barham midmorning after the ritual toilet beating. He whispered in Arabic and flashed a smile at Peter.

As soon as he walked away, the Canadian turned to his Kurdish friend for an explanation. "What was that about?"

"He said there will be news today. Good news."

Peter's eyes widened. "Are we getting out?"

"I don't know. Maybe. He just said to stay close to him, whatever happens." Barham's mouth slowly widened to a smile.

"They're letting us go, aren't they? That's why Pants wants us to stick close—"

"I know, I know."

"So he'll get his money."

Peter rubbed his bandage yet again. He had taken to stroking the bulge made by Theresa's friendship ring every morning and night, and particularly when anything good happened. Barham kidded him about it, but he was now more convinced than ever that the ring brought him luck.

The Kurd noticed. "Money has kept us alive. Not that ring. It is money that is buying your freedom."

"What do you mean my freedom? What about you?"

Barham shrugged. "There is no guarantee I am going free. He only said good news. And he smiled at you."

"Yeah, but I promised him two thousand for both of us."

"*Insha'allah.*" Barham looked heavenward. "It is in the hands of God, not a guard. Pants can only keep us alive. He doesn't decide who leaves this place."

Peter knew his friend was right. His excitement tempered slightly, he tried to pass the time as if this was any other day, but the waiting seemed interminable. He noticed, though, as the hours wore on, that a noisy murmuring was growing among the prisoners. Had word spread?

In the afternoon, Peter began to hear cars honking in the distance. He knew Abu Ghraib was about twenty miles west of Baghdad. But it also lay on the way to Saddam International Airport. Was something happening at the airport? The honking grew louder as cars drew closer, but he noticed they didn't continue on. They stayed. And now all the prisoners heard new sounds... the beating of drums and chanting and singing. What was going on?

Barham pointed to the guards conferring in anxious whispers. At one point, Pants broke away from the others, and headed straight for Peter and the Kurd.

His smile was wide as he spoke in Arabic to make sure Barham understood the full story. The Kurd's expression changed from an aloof skepticism to unabashed joy.

Peter waited eagerly for the translation. "Well? What's happening?"

Barham paused to kiss Pants on both cheeks and turned to his friend. "Saddam has declared a general amnesty. Throughout the whole country. All prisoners are being released. Pants says there are thousands outside the gates right now, waiting to see relatives who have been locked up."

Before Peter could ask another question, they heard a huge roar. The main steel gate had been forced open and a flood of people descended on them at a run. Pants grabbed Peter, who, in turn, clasped hold of Barham by the shirt, and all three sprinted ahead of the crowd out a door at the back and down a corridor.

Everywhere they turned, screaming mothers and wives hugged long lost sons and husbands, while others, with children in tow, frantically searched cells and corners for their loved ones.

Peter stopped and turned to Barham. He had to yell to be heard. "Wait a minute. We've got to find Theresa and your family. They might be here."

Barham nodded and screamed in Arabic to the anxious guard. Pants wanted them out of there but he listened to the Kurd and replied while shaking his head. He waited as the Kurd translated his reply.

"He says there were no women in the Foreigners' Section."

Peter didn't want to believe it. "How can he be sure? Maybe she's being held separately."

"My friend, I described her. Pants is one of the chief guards here. He would know of an American prisoner. She's not here."

His heart sank. Pants started pulling him, but he held firm and looked at his friend. "What about your father and brother?"

"They could be here," Barham allowed. "But he insists on getting paid first. How are you going to pay him, by the way?" He looked down at Peter's bandaged hand. "You only have enough money there for a taxi to Baghdad. And he wants dollars."

"Don't worry. This is breaking news. There are bound to be reporters out there. If they want my story, they'll have to pay for it. I'll make them pay for both of us."

He nodded for Pants to continue and the guard led them away from the crowds into a deserted corridor. At the end of the hall, they turned left and began passing cells that were still locked and occupied.

Peter thought he had grown used to the depravity of this place, but what he saw now sickened him more than ever. The men in these cells were naked and covered with sores, their ribs pushing out beneath dirty skin. The gaunt prisoners hardly looked at them, their hollow eyes fixed on the floor, the walls, and the bars.

He tried to get Pants to stop. "What about these? Aren't they free?"

Pants squinted their way and shook his head. "Spies. No free. Hurry, this way."

They rushed out of the concrete building into bright daylight and were almost overtaken in the panic. Tens of thousands of Iraqis were storming the various prison blocks. The people used steel tubing and anything else they could get their hands on to break down the cinder block walls and free their loved ones. Guards beat them back just to control the frenzy.

Pants had stopped. Throngs of people blocked the way out through the prison's main gate. He stood for a moment, unsure of their next move. He looked toward a building off to the northwest and began steering them toward the isolated warehouse.

As soon as Peter stepped inside, he realized they'd entered at least one of the prison's execution chambers. He grimaced at the dozens of rusty-looking butchers' hooks extending from the ceiling. Each five-foot hook held a rope. Hundreds, if not thousands, had been hung here. A raised platform ran the length of the building with square holes every four to five feet. Peter understood its meaning at a glance. The ropes were placed around the victims' necks, a metal lever pulled, springing the trap doors open and leaving the bodies to strangle over gaping holes.

Barham poked him. "See how the floor slants to the middle of the room. See the drain."

Peter nodded slowly. Fluids spilled before or during the throes of death could more easily be washed away.

Barham closed his eyes. "Iraqis have always been excellent engineers." He muttered a phrase in Arabic that Peter couldn't decipher, except that it included their word for God, *Allah*.

Peter wondered if it were a prayer or a curse, but didn't ask. They had come to the other end of the chamber and Pants unlocked a door. They passed through and suddenly found themselves outside Abu Ghraib. Peter and Barham looked at each other, blinking back tears. They were free.

Pants wanted his money. He made it clear he wouldn't hand over Peter's passport or Barham's identity papers until he had the two thousand in hand. So Peter headed for the crowd still surging through the main gate, hoping to glimpse a Western reporter somewhere in all the confusion.

He got lucky. Kissing Theresa's ring with gratitude, he veered toward the familiar blond locks of BBC correspondent Daniel James. He had shot film for Daniel when the Brit was still a free-lancer. Peter shouted to no avail, but a slap on the back turned James around.

"What in bloody hell?" James' mouth opened and his eyes squinted to make sure. "Peter?"

"Yes, it's me, you old goat. Have you got any money on you?"

"You look terrible."

"Well, this prison doesn't do much for your health."

James' eyes went wide. He almost salivated. "You were here? There's been nothing about you in the news. You were a prisoner here? You've just got out?"

Peter needed to hurry this up. "You catch on fast. Listen, this guard here helped us stay alive...for a price. Two thousand dollars. You pay him off and I'll give you my story."

James pulled his head back. "Come on, Peter, we're mates. I'd pay him off regardless." He pulled out a wad of bills, and counted out twelve hundred dollars into the outstretched hands of Pants. He asked his cameraman to make up the difference.

Peter watched him pay off the last of their debt. "Thanks, Daniel."

"Don't mention it. You did say I'd get an exclusive, right?"

Peter snorted and glanced Barham's way. "An exclusive will cost a bit more."

James protested. "What do you mean? I've already shelled out two grand. How much more do you think I've got on me? We're only allowed so much, you know."

"I know the rules. But I also know you. An exclusive of my story—and it's a good one—will cost you five hundred more…payable to him." Peter pointed to Barham.

"Him? Why him?"

"Because he also kept me alive. He has to find his family and get back up north."

James pursed his lips. "Were you tortured?"

"Yes. Do you want the exclusive or not?" Peter began looking around for other Western reporters.

James made up his mind fast. "Of course I want it. Hold on." He bent down to pull out more bills secreted in his right sock. He counted five hundred into Barham's hand and looked at Peter. "Okay, now start talking."

The Canadian held up his hand. "Wait a minute. We've got to get our papers from Pants here."

A word from Barham sent the guard digging into his uniform pocket until he pulled out Peter's passport and an identity card with the Kurd's picture on it. He handed them over and kissed the former prisoners on both cheeks. When he didn't leave, Peter smiled and shook his head. Whatever he was, Pants knew a good deal when he saw one and the sight of all that money was keeping him around. Peter guessed he would prob-ably offer a private personal tour next…for the right price.

James prompted his cameraman to start shooting and turned back to his old colleague. "Now, then. Are you ready to tell your story?"

Peter had one final stipulation. "Only if, afterward, you promise to send my friend, Barham here, up north in a taxi and take me straight to Amman for a bath and decent meal."

James huffed in exasperation. "But I'm at the Rashid here in Baghdad. Why do you have to cross into Jordan for a hotel?"

"I want to avoid being arrested again. I entered illegally, without a Press Permit. I promise, we'll be back in Baghdad as soon as I have the proper credentials."

James looked put out but agreed. "All right. But it won't be easy for you to get back in. Are you even sure you want to return?"

Peter shouted over his shoulder as he led them, pushing through the crowds, back into Abu Ghraib.

"Definitely. I've got to find someone."

A CHANGE

(Outskirts of Baghdad—October 20, 2002)

Tariq pressed the accelerator harder. Driving to the farm, he had been singing along with a Simon and Garfunkel classic—"Mrs. Robinson"—on Voice of Iraq FM. Shortly after noon, the song was interrupted by the unmistakable voice of Iraq's Information Minister, Muhammad Said al-Sahhaf. Cutting into the lyrics, the minister read a statement from Saddam Hussein.

"Prisoners, detainees will be set free immediately," Sahhaf declared.

When Tariq heard the amnesty applied to "anyone imprisoned or arrested for political or any other reason," he immediately began passing cars. This meant Theresa would be released.

He turned off the highway, avoiding the logjam of cars heading for Abu Ghraib, and fifteen minutes later pulled up to the small prison facility on the farm. He practically ran into the building. Tariq wanted to break the news personally. He beamed as he imagined her reaction. Her eyes would stare in disbelief, slowly flicker with hope until, convinced, they'd fairly dance. He was striding past the interrogation room when Badr's voice stopped him cold.

"Captain. Come in here."

Tariq entered the room. The colonel was alone, seated, and doodling with his pen on a pad of paper. A tray with two cups of tea lay in the middle of the table's scrubbed bloodstain. He beckoned the younger man to sit in the other chair and offered him a cup.

Tariq thanked him and took a sip.

"You are slightly early today."

"I just heard the news over the radio and thought I had better get here as soon as possible."

Badr sipped from his cup and set it down. "Ah, you are referring to the amnesty."

Tariq leaned forward. "Yes. Have you told Theresa yet?"

The colonel's eyes narrowed. "Theresa? No, I have not mentioned it to Miss Fuller. It does not concern her."

Tariq blinked. "But the announcement said it applied to all prisoners."

"Well, Sahhaf often says things that will make the people happy. That is his job."

Tariq's heart sank. "Do you mean it's not true? There is no amnesty? But why would they announce..."

Badr cut him off with a wave of his hand. "Of course there is an amnesty. Our beloved leader was very happy with the results of last week's presidential election. He surprised everyone. If you ask me, he is generous to give all these criminals a second chance. Perhaps they have learned and will now make wiser choices."

Tariq was confused. "Certainly. But why would..." He stopped himself before using her first name again. "Why would Miss Fuller not be released?"

Badr smiled and took another sip of tea. After placing the cup back on the tray, he folded his arms and leaned back. "I neglected to pass the word down to you. This amnesty excludes those held as spies."

Tariq shifted in his seat, worried that he no longer held the colonel's trust. He had to choose his words carefully. "But is she a spy?"

Badr's eyebrows rose. "Do you doubt it? What is your assessment?" He rose from the chair and walked behind Tariq. "Has she confessed anything to you on one of your walks around the farm these past few weeks?"

Tariq tensed. "I am sorry, Colonel. I only thought she might speak more freely if her surroundings were less...restrictive."

"And I applaud your thinking. I do." Badr circled back to face the captain again. "Did she... speak more freely?"

"Yes. We talked of many things about her childhood."

"Did she explain why she concealed her true hair color?"

"Oh, that. She only felt she would be safer, not attract so much attention."

"Yes, a spy certainly wouldn't want to attract attention."

"But, I don't…"

Badr cut him off. "Have you learned more about her father?"

Tariq searched his memory. "Well, they were close at one time. She talked about the family outings they took in and around Baghdad. Even up to Samara."

The colonel sat again, leaning forward. "And what about his imprisonment? What have you learned about that?"

"Nothing. She truly can't remember."

He sniffed. "You believe her?"

"Yes." Tariq decided to press her case. "Colonel, if she knew anything…if she were guilty of anything, she would have broken by now. She would have talked. I can't believe she's a spy."

"Even if she were not a spy, there is still the matter of her father."

Tariq's voice pitched higher. "But she can't remember."

"Then obviously your walks in the countryside are not enough."

Tariq stiffened.

Badr stood again. "She will be moved tonight to a facility where I can keep a close eye on her. A modern facility equipped with a wider range of persuasive methods. These daily drives out here are a waste of my time... and yours."

Apprehension filled Tariq's mind. "Where are you taking her?"

"Intelligence Headquarters. That should make your life simpler. After all, you only live five minutes from there. I want you to spend more time with her. I believe she trusts you. The question is, can I?"

Tariq rose and stood at attention. "Of course, Colonel."

"Do you know why I brought you into the Mukhabarat, Tariq? To help you, and protect you. From the days of the Gulf War when you came under my command, you interested me. Can you guess why?"

Tariq shook his head, bewildered.

"You reminded me of myself. Like you, I was studying abroad when I was called back to Iraq to care for my family. My father died when I was young. In that, too, we are not so different, yes? But I had an uncle who stepped in, adopted me, as it were. He saw my promise and sent me to study in England at Cambridge." Badr began to circle around the room as he talked.

Tariq watched him carefully. He had sensed the older man's personal interest in him for years but, until now, he never understood it.

"I had plans." Badr turned to face him. "You did, too, did you not?"

Tariq swallowed, unsure where this was leading and how honest he should be. But he couldn't dissemble to the colonel's face in the moment his honesty was being questioned.

"Yes, I had plans. All young men tend to dream."

Badr nodded. "But we both had to return. For you, it was your grandfather's cancer. For me, my uncle's death. We had to give up so much for our families…our country. The way life is in Iraq cannot be changed. It is we who must change. I saw your courage on the battle-field…"

Tariq interrupted. "I was as afraid as the next man."

"But you didn't panic. You led. Still, I could see that you were not hard enough yet to survive in this Iraq. And I want you to survive. You are like a son to me. So I brought you into the Mukhabarat to make you strong. Are you strong enough for this?

Badr came within inches and looked directly into Tariq's eyes. "We are approaching a crucial time in our country's history. The world's superpower is almost at our door. Can I count on you?"

Tariq's heart hammered, but he pulled himself up straighter and saluted. "You can count on me, sir."

Badr smiled. "Good. You are a credit to your family and your president."

The colonel turned to pick up his pen and note pad on the way out. At the door, he swiveled to look back at Tariq. "By the way, how is your grandfather doing these days?"

The question threw him off-balance. "My grandfather? He's…fighting the cancer. We don't expect him to live much longer."

"What a pity. I was hoping to talk to him."

"About what?" Tariq's stomach tightened.

"I have discovered our Professor Fuller was acquainted with several founding Ba'athists. I imagine your grandfather might shed some light on that, but…well, if he is dying, I won't bother him. At least, not at this point."

Tariq swallowed. "Thank you. He's not well."

Badr dipped his head slightly. "You are dismissed for the rest of the day. But be back here at midnight to oversee Miss Fuller's transport."

"Yes, sir." Tariq saluted again and Badr returned the formality. He hoped the colonel would leave, giving him a chance to see Theresa and prepare her for the change. But Badr stayed there, waiting, so Tariq walked past him toward the door leading back out to his car.

As he reached the door, Badr called out one last command. "Captain. Make certain she is cuffed and blindfolded for the trip."

A MIDNIGHT DRIVE

(Outskirts of Baghdad—October 21, 2002)

"Theresa," her mother called. "Get out of the pool now. The chips and drinks are here."

She splashed Jimmy one last time, sucked in air, and dove under the clear water. Pulling with her arms and legs, Theresa swam for the wooden ladder, painted sky blue, at the shallow end of the Alwiya Club's medium-sized pool. Jimmy raced to beat her, but she reached the ladder first. As she clambered up the steps, he grabbed her left ankle.

"Let go." She kicked at her brother to shake free, but he held on. "Mom, tell Jimmy to let go of me!" She had to yell to be heard over the shouts from the crowded pool.

Her mother looked up. "Jimmy, let go of your sister right now. And you get out now, too. I don't want these snacks going to waste."

Jimmy released her ankle, and Theresa took the final step up and out, turning around to stick out her tongue. In that instant, she was struck by a gigantic splash, courtesy of her brother.

The spray went too far and splashed Mom, who was in no mood for games. "Jimmy. You're getting us all wet. Now, stop it and get out."

Theresa ran to towel off, then dug into a plate of potato chips with ketchup, while her brother sullenly left the water. He grasped his towel and dried off. But as soon as Theresa put the plate of chips down to grab a Seven-Up, he moved to her plate, and started stuffing his mouth.

She turned around with her drink to find the chips half gone. "Hey. Who ate my chips?" She saw Jimmy's bulging cheeks and yelled. "Jimmy! Those are mine. Get your own plate."

He acted nonchalant. "Okay." He strutted over to take another plate of chips.

But Theresa wasn't about to let him win the war. She took four long sips of his drink as his back was turned. When she saw him swivel back, she turned to shield the soda bottle from him and continued drinking.

He grabbed her by the arm and shook. "Give me my drink."

She tried to cast him off.

He shook her arm again.

"Theresa. Theresa, wake up."

She opened her eyes to blackness and realized she hadn't been swimming at all. She was still in prison. Tariq knelt beside her in the cell.

She mumbled. "What...what time is it?"

"It's after midnight." His tone was apologetic.

"What's going on? Am I being questioned?"

"I'm not supposed to say."

Her eyes and mind worked to focus. In the moonlight, she could see the wrinkles lining his brow, and she heard the anxiety in his voice. She sat up slowly, making out the figures of two guards at the door. One came forward and handed something to the captain.

Tariq stuffed it in his pocket. "You'd better put your shoes on. We're going somewhere."

"Where?"

"Please, just put your shoes on."

She reached in the shadows, and shook her sneakers out for roaches; deftly she laced them up and stood.

Tariq turned her so she faced the window. "I have to blindfold you. But I'll be with you every step of the way."

He shook out a cloth. The next moment it covered her eyes, and everything was black. He tied it firmly, and turned her around again.

His voice was in her right ear. "Okay, we're going to leave the cell now and turn left. Just hold on to my arm and I'll tell you how and where to walk."

He took her right hand and hooked it onto his left arm, holding it with his hand. Despite Tariq's reassurance, Theresa's heart raced as she imagined everything from torture to execution. What if their walks and talks around the farm had been a ruse to lower her defenses? She argued both sides as she took halting steps and, gradually, she began to calm down. The sense of help-lessness in total darkness had nearly paralyzed her. Yet she felt surprising confidence in this man who was guiding her by the arm. She found his touch strangely liberating.

When she heard and felt the crunch of gravel under her shoes and sensed a cool breeze, she knew they were outside. A few more paces and they stopped. She heard Tariq give orders in Arabic. A car door opened. More Arabic followed, but nothing to give away their destination. Then, Tariq brought her hands together in front of her.

"I'm sorry, but you have to be cuffed for the trip."

The cold metal pieces encircled her wrists and snapped shut. He put one hand on her shoulder and the other on her head. "Okay, I'm helping you into a car now. Just stoop down a bit and I'll ease you into the seat."

She turned back to his voice. "You're going with me, aren't you?"

"Of course," he reassured her. "After I help you in, I'll come around to sit beside you."

She felt for the seat with her hands and backed in. As she lifted her legs and swiveled, she heard the driver open his door. Her door slammed shut and the two passenger side doors opened and shut again. True to his word, Tariq was sitting in back with her.

He leaned over. "Are you okay?"

"I suppose so."

He directed the driver to get going. "*Yalla.*"

The car started and they drove on gravel for several seconds before hitting a paved road. Soon they turned, and sped up, as if merging onto a highway. They traveled in silence. Occasionally Theresa heard the roars of semis passing in the opposite direction. Was she heading away from Baghdad to the border? Maybe she was going to be released. Her heart fluttered at the thought.

But ten minutes later she began to despair. Traffic was increasing. They were approaching a city, not the desert. Baghdad. She sensed it. She wasn't sure how much time had passed, but before long they pulled off the highway and traveled briefly down a city street.

As the car rounded what appeared to be one of Baghdad's circles, she lost her balance. Unable to right herself with cuffed hands, Theresa leaned into Tariq. In a second she sensed his rigid posture become accepting, almost tender as if he realized why she could not sit upright.

"Sorry." This close, she could not help but breathe in his scent of sandalwood mixed with some spice she couldn't place. Cardamom?

"Not at all." He put his hand on her arm to steady her, holding it there a minute before withdrawing.

A moment later, they turned left and pulled up at some kind of checkpoint. A voice outside the car spoke in Arabic. The driver replied and drove on, slowing and turning sharply as if into a parking place. The engine stopped, doors opened and shut, and she heard foot-steps running around behind the car to her side.

Her door opened and Tariq told her they had ar-rived. He eased her out and took her left arm to guide her.

"Can you take these handcuffs off?"

"Not yet, I'm afraid. It won't be long now. Come."

He led her inside a building. She strained for any identifying sounds, but heard only the squeaking of her sneakers on a smooth polished floor. He pulled her up short and, after waiting a moment, she heard elevator doors open. They entered and she sensed it moving down. She counted to seven before it stopped. As the doors opened, she heard distant weeping and moaning to the left. A sudden chill clamped her heart like a vise. *What kind of place was this?* Theresa started to ask. But she knew.

Tariq turned her away from the sounds, stopping briefly to converse in Arabic. She heard her name in the midst of the dialogue. Tariq was asking about the cell. He wanted to know if it had been made ready. The guard assured him all had been put in place, including the hidden camera and microphone. But he added they were not yet functioning. Theresa showed no expres-sion outwardly, but alarm and unease grew within. What little privacy she had enjoyed would soon be lost.

They proceeded slowly down a long hallway. When they stopped, she heard a steel door unlock and open in front of her. Tariq flipped a switch, and light teased the edges of the blindfold. He led her in, closed the door, and removed the cloth.

Theresa brought her hands up to block the sudden brightness. "Where am I?"

"I can't say. But I live close by and I will check on you every week. I promise."

Her eyes widened in alarm. "Only once a week?"

"It's all I'm allowed for now." He brought her hands down to remove the cuffs. As he unlocked them, he accidentally pressed against the sore on her arm and she winced. She tried to pull her arm away but he held on.

Tariq unbuttoned her sleeve and pulled it up. "How long have you had this?"

"About a month. Something bit me and it seems to be infected."

His mouth set. "A sandfly."

"What?"

Tariq examined the sore closely in the light. "You were bit by a sandfly. This looks like the beginnings of leishmaniasis, a kind of skin boil."

"You sound like a doctor." She pulled her hand back.

"My grandmother was a doctor. She took me on some of her rounds in the hospital and explained the different maladies to me. I saw many of these growing up. It's not uncommon in Iraq."

Theresa frowned. "Is it bad?"

"Not if it's just a skin lesion. Have you had any fever or vomiting?"

She shook her head.

Tariq relaxed. "Good. It's just a skin disease. It will grow into an ulcer."

"Sounds ugly."

He smiled. "It will take some months to heal, but I'll bring you something to put on it. It will heal."

Theresa looked at the whitish mound. It had grown bigger over the last month. "There's medicine for it?"

"Yes, but I can't get you the prescription. Besides, Badr wouldn't allow it. I'll bring a homemade remedy. There will be some scarring, but that's all."

She turned to survey her cell. It was newer and cleaner but somehow more depressing. A ripped foam mattress lay on the floor of the four-by-six-foot room. She noticed a small window in the door, as well as an opening at the bottom. Hatches that could be accessed only from the outside covered both. The cell contained its own dirty toilet, which meant one thing to Theresa. A person could live for months, even years, in this cramped space without seeing another human face.

Tariq sensed her despair. "Let me get you another blanket. They aren't careful about the heating down here. I'll be right back."

Theresa heard him walk down the hall. He had left her cell door open, but the guards stood watch. As she turned around to scout for roaches, she heard a high-pitched scream. It sounded like a woman. Had she been brought to a woman's facility? The scream repeated every three seconds, interrupted by male grunts, in a chilling kind of pattern. Theresa shuddered at the sounds. Was someone being raped?

Her breathing grew heavy. When she covered her ears to shut out the screams, the tingling began. She had kept her epilepsy at bay with the half-full bottle of pills Tariq had sneaked to her. But the pills had run out ten days ago and she had not yet been able to get her second bottle. Rather than fight the episode, she sat down on the mattress and gave up to it. Theresa stayed still and let it take control, heave up into her throat, and expand through her head. She swallowed once, twice, and then her cell seemed to spread out and away from her.

She climbed the ladder up to the high diving platform at the Alwiya Club. Though wet, the brown material covering the steps scratched against her feet. She scrambled up onto the small platform.

Her family was scattered. Jimmy played Marco Polo in the shallow end with two of his friends and her sister, Angela. Mom sat on the side of the nearby baby pool with three-year-old Mitchell in her lap. She was talking to another woman while watching Laila, five, splash around in knee-deep water. Where was Dad?

Theresa looked around for her father, turning back to the thatched roof of the snack bar. She recognized his crewcut and sunglasses and yelled out to him, but he didn't seem to hear. She wanted to show off the jackknife she had mastered, and called out again. But he had turned sideways to talk to a young Iraqi woman.

Theresa leaned over the railing to get a better look. She had seen this woman before at one of her parents' parties. The woman was wearing a bright sundress, her bathing suit strap showing on her left shoulder. Theresa yelled once more to her father but the screams and splashes around the pool swallowed her shout. She saw her father take a piece of paper out of his pocket and slip it to the woman. The Iraqi barely acknowledged it. Instead, she talked a moment longer, shook his hand, and walked away.

"Theresa?"

Tariq's voice brought the cell back into focus. She looked up at him and blinked. He was standing in the doorway holding a blanket.

"Were you having an episode?"

She nodded.

He closed the door, muting the distant screams, and knelt beside her to look in her eyes. "Have you been taking your pills?"

"Yes, but they've run out." She fumbled in her pocket and pulled out the empty bottle to hand to him.

"I will go through your things and get the other bottle. Have you had many episodes?"

She shook her head. "But I overheard what the guard said about the hidden camera and microphone. How can I take my medicine here without it being noticed?"

He stood and looked down at her. "That is not important. If you don't take your pills it might get worse. What's to prevent you having a full seizure?"

She shrugged. "I don't know."

"What's your dosage?"

"One hundred and twenty milligrams each night. Two of those pills."

"But you only have one more bottle?"

She nodded.

"All right. I'll leave instructions. You'll get two pills with your dinner every night…at least till they run out. If Badr asks, I'll tell him it's for migraines." He walked to the door.

"What happens when they're all gone?"

Tariq turned and lifted his hands helplessly. "In that case, I will have to tell him the truth and hope for the best. Medicines are hard to come by in Iraq, so prisoners are the last to get it and usually don't. To be honest, I doubt he'll want to give any to a citizen of the country that pushed for the sanctions against them."

Theresa understood and nodded.

"But I'll do my best. Is there anything else?"

Theresa started to shake her head, but remembered. "Could you tell me what has happened to Peter and the others?"

"Peter?"

"My cameraman. Has he been moved here?"

Tariq considered the request. "I'll see what I can find out about him and the other Kurd. I did make certain his father and brother went home as you requested. Anything else?"

"Yes, what date is it? Without a watch I've lost all track of time."

"Of course. It's Monday, October 21st. In a few more hours the sun will rise and the lights will come on for the day. Try and sleep while it's dark, okay? I'll see you in a week. Goodnight."

He left, locking her in and flipping off the light. She took up both blankets, turned, and spread them out. As she lay down, she tried to commit the date to memory. She had been in prison almost two months. Tomorrow she would have to find a way to etch a rude kind of calendar into the wall or floor. For now, she closed her eyes and tried not to dwell on the roaches creeping around the toilet.

Shortly before dawn, she awoke cold and disoriented. As she lay there, trying to get her bearings, the tingling came back. The dimness of the cell brightened with each pulsing wave through her head and she found herself back at the Alwiya Club. After a full day of swimming and eating, they were getting set to change and go home.

Mom led nine-year-old Theresa and her sisters to the Women's Dressing Room. The bees and wasps were abundant that day and Theresa froze when she saw the wasp nest hanging directly above the thatched entrance to the changing room. Before she could protest, her mother pulled her past to safety. The whole time she changed, however, she kept a wary eye on their golden bodies hovering around the entrance.

Her anxiety spread to her sisters, Laila and Angela, who now both balked at going under the nest again. Her mother's tone was kind, but firm. "Now girls, there's nothing to be afraid of. Those wasps didn't bother us coming in, and they're not going to bother us going out."

Theresa wasn't convinced. "But there are more of them now."

Her mother glanced at her watch and addressed all three girls. "All right. I know you're scared, but your father and brothers are waiting for us. We can't stay in here all night. I'm going to take each of you out, one at a time, okay? I'll be protecting you. That way, if anyone gets stung, it'll be me."

Her mother's logic seemed right and she trusted her mother. It was the wasps she didn't trust. Theresa watched as her mom escorted Laila and Angela without incident. It was her turn. Fear knotted her stomach. She felt like throwing up.

Her mother pulled her toward the entrance. "Come on, Theresa. You saw they didn't hurt your sisters. You'll be okay. I promise you won't get stung."

She promised. Mom always kept her promises. Eyes closed, Theresa huddled in front of her mother and scurried for the steps beyond the entry leading to safety. Passing under the nest, she peeked up and saw two dangling wasp legs hovering closer and closer.

Her cry was as sharp as the sting, and the hurt inside almost matched the piercing pain in her shoulder blade. She felt *betrayed. Somehow, despite her mother's best efforts, the wasp had come between them and stung her on the back.*

The episode ended with the sting and Theresa lay there in the dark, remembering the lesson she had learned that day. There were things beyond a parent's control.

TORTURED

(Mansour—November 20, 2002)

Tariq clicked off the television as his mother came into the sitting room. They could hear Ghassan cleaning up in the kitchen. The clinking and scraping of glasses and plates punctuated the servant's freestyle harmonizing. Breakfast dishes had always called for the enchanting voice of Lebanese singer Fairuz on the CD player.

His mother eased into the recliner. "I never tire of hearing that song. Do you remember I used to sing it to you as a lullaby in Beirut?"

Tariq smiled. "Not only in Beirut. I don't think you stopped singing it to me until I was eight years old and asked you to." He sat down on the nearby sofa.

She pretended to pout. "Yes. You said you were too old for lullabies. So I would wait until you were asleep and then I would sing it to you anyway."

"I wasn't asleep."

"Oh, yes you were."

Tariq shook his head. "I was only pretending."

She reached for a sofa pillow and tossed it at him in mock anger.

"Pretending? For how many years did you pretend to sleep while I sang you that lullaby?"

"Oh, maybe two or three."

She smiled, but grew serious. "And how long will you go on pretending now to sleep?"

"What do you mean?"

"I hear you getting up at night. You are not sleeping well. What is wrong, my son?"

He rose from the sofa and turned around to look out the window at their garden. She watched him, waiting for an answer. At last, he spoke. "Nothing is the matter. Your new roses are doing very well."

"My new roses?"

He signaled with his eyes. "Yes, why don't you take me out and show me exactly what you planted." He offered a hand to help her up.

She understood. Outside there would be no listening devices. He could speak freely. She followed him into the garden where they settled into wicker chairs by the roses.

"Now, Tariq. Tell me what is bothering you."

He looked down at his hands and began rubbing the palm of his right hand with his left thumb. "I don't know how much longer I can do this kind of work. It is torture to see the pain in the prisoners' eyes. I feel like a monster. They are the ones who are being treated like animals. But I am the real animal." Tears welled in his eyes and she reached out to touch him, but he stood and started to pace.

"Until August, it was all right. I only had to watch people and make arrests. Of course, I knew things were going on. But I was on the outside, not involved. Now, ever since Theresa's arrest, I've been a jailer, an interrogator, a torturer…"

His mother interrupted. "But surely you can go back to what you were doing before. She is gone now. Ask Colonel Badr to…"

"She's not gone." His back was to her.

"What do you mean she is not gone? On the day of amnesty, was she not released?"

"No."

"But I assumed…You have been working at headquarters since that day. I assumed she was released and you were given a desk job."

He shook his head, turning to face her. "A desk job? Well, sometimes I sit behind a desk, yes. I sit there and badger and torment and yell and…"

"That is not like you."

He laughed without humor. "Mother, if I don't do those things, I will be the one in prison. It is this job that has assured us keeping this house, eating well, and getting Grandfather the few treatments he's had. I had to choose. Either I am a monster protecting my family, or I give myself and my family up to all the other monsters."

Her eyes widened. "An interrogator and a torturer? Have you tortured? Have you tortured Theresa?"

"No, mother, no. At least, not in the way you're thinking. Badr isn't there to watch when I meet with Theresa. I don't know his motives but, for some reason, he's leaving me alone with her. And with her, I can be myself, not a monster. But don't you see? Solitary can be the worst torment of all. She is tortured every time she is put back in that cell, locked up, left alone. I can see her only once a week. And who knows what Badr has in store for her?"

She rose and took hold of his arm. "What do you mean?"

He pulled his arm away and stepped back before answering.

"I have seen terrible things, Mother. I have seen a man's hand chopped off in front of me, the blood spurting everywhere. I have seen another stripped naked and made to sit on a broken bottle."

His mother held up a hand to stop him. "But she is a woman."

Now he grabbed her arms, almost shaking her. "Do you think that makes a difference? I have seen..." He choked on the words and let go.

"What? What have you seen?"

His voice was barely a whisper. "I have seen women raped in front of their husbands and sons to loosen the men's tongues."

She gasped, covered her ears, and turned away.

Tariq persisted, louder now. "Badr ordered all of this. Who knows what he will do to Theresa?"

His mother swung around. "Well, you work with him. Ask him."

"He doesn't trust me anymore. He says he does, but I think he knows I'm growing fond of her."

She pulled back. "You like her?"

He nodded, and his mother walked over to the yellow roses. She reached out to touch one. "And does she like you?"

"I'm not sure. She trusts me. And I think she's come to rely on me. But, given the circumstances..." He grimaced as though in pain. "I'm afraid if I ask Badr, if I push at all, he will shut me out entirely. Take me off her case, leaving her with no one."

She turned around. Her voice grew agitated. "But you must do something, Tariq. She should not be in prison. Why was she not released?"

He shook his head. "I don't know. At first, he thought she might be a spy, and spies weren't released. But I don't think he believes that anymore. He is focusing more and more on her father. He is obsessed with her father."

"But her father did nothing!"

Tariq looked directly at his mother. "How do you know? You said you barely knew him."

She looked away, exasperated. "That's right. I barely knew him, but everyone knew the charges against him were false. He never could have been a spy."

"Well, Badr doesn't know that. And he's digging into the past and finding out things. He discovered that Professor Fuller knew several of the old-time Ba'athists."

His mother folded her arms. "Well, he was a professor and I am sure they were invited to the various university functions, the cocktail parties. Of course he met some Ba'athists."

"But he also said Grandfather might be able to shed some light on Professor Fuller."

A fire came into her eyes. "I will not listen to this anymore. I have told you—and I mean it—you are forbidden to speak of this with your grandfather. Do you understand? I forbid it!" She turned abruptly and swept inside the house.

He called after her. "But how can I help her, then? I have to know about her father."

Frustrated, he collapsed in one of the chairs and buried his head in his hands.

A moment later Ghassan appeared. "What did you say to your mother? She went to her room crying."

"Crying?" Surprised, Tariq moved toward the house. "Never mind, Ghassan, it's not your business."

But the older man caught him by the arm and held him. "Yes, it is. When your grandmother lay dying, she charged me with the care of her husband, her daughter, and you, her grandson. I have never failed this family and I am not going to fail it now."

Tariq looked at Ghassan. "If you want to help, then convince my mother to let me talk to my grandfather."

"About what?"

"About any Americans he might have known in the past."

"He is not well. Why should you weigh him down with questions about the past?"

Tariq pressed. "Because he may hold the key to a woman's freedom."

The servant weighed the request. "Your mother knows best. If she says you should not talk to him, you should not. And you should honor her by obeying."

Tariq pulled his arm away in frustration and brushed past the servant. What were they keeping from him? How could he help Theresa if he didn't know enough about her past to clear her father? And how could he keep his sanity while watching Theresa slowly lose hers?

SEARCHING

(Al-Rashid Hotel—November 19, 2002)

Peter paced. He and Daniel James had been sharing a room at the Al-Rashid for a week and a half now. After slipping enough dollars to the right people, he had finagled a tourist visa to get back into Iraq. But a Press Permit had proved impossible and, without proper press credentials, he couldn't meet with anyone from the Ministry of Information. Fortunately, Daniel wanted another exclusive and offered to chase Theresa's story for him. All Peter wanted was the woman he loved, safe at his side. So while Daniel combed the city, accompanied by a Ministry-appointed minder, Peter wore out the hotel room's carpet.

Tomorrow his visa expired and they had yet to find any trace of her. He had even looked up Pants and offered him a thousand dollars to sniff around the numerous other prisons in Baghdad. Within weeks of

Saddam's general amnesty, many of the released criminals had been rounded up and re-arrested so that the
prisons were fast filling up again. As it turned out, Pants
had friends or relatives working at most of them, and
he had snatched at the chance for more dollars—particularly the promised two thousand-dollar bonus if he
found her. Still no Theresa.

He glanced over the list of checked-off prisons in his
hand: Makasib, located along the airport road and holding some ten thousand; Baladiat, the General Security
Service's main prison facility; Radwaniyah, located on
one of Saddam's large farms not far from Abu Ghraib;
Rashidiya, on the Tigris north of Taji; and Al-Haakimiya,
the main interrogation center for the Mukhabarat. For
this latter facility, he had even provided Pants with the
first name and general description of the captain who
had initially arrested them. The guard had come up
with nothing.

His eyes scanned others with more ominous nick-
names: Mahjar, "the Sanctuary," located on the Police
Training College grounds in central Baghdad; Sijn Al-
Tarbut, the "Casket Prison," where prisoners kept in
steel boxes are supposedly let out for only half an hour
each day until they confess or die; and Quortiyya, "The
Can," another version of the Casket Prison. The last two
purportedly held only male prisoners, but Peter had insisted on covering all bases.

The list nauseated him, and these were only the prisons he knew about. A reporter in Amman told him he'd

heard that one in five Baghdadis had probably been detained or imprisoned at some point during Hussein's regime. With a population exceeding five million, that meant a million behind bars. And how many ended up killed?

He heard the key in the lock and turned. Daniel looked at him from the doorway, shook his head and walked in to collapse on his bed.

"Nothing at all?" Peter's voice held little hope.

"Nothing. I've been to every hospital in the city. She's nowhere to be found."

Peter sank down on the other twin mattress. "Okay, she's not in the known prisons. She's not in some hospital ward. She's got to be in one of the palaces or some prison we don't know about. Can you approach Sahhaf again?"

Daniel turned his head sideways and glared. "Not if I want to keep my visa. He about tore my head off last week."

Iraq's Information Minister was usually approachable and responsive, but the strain of preparing for the arrival of Hans Blix and the UN Weapons Inspectors two days ago had put him in a foul mood. That, and all the talk of the coming war with the United States.

Peter had tried to get national coverage of her arrest and disappearance, but after brief mentions on the network and cable news stations and stories in the major papers, she had been cast aside for coverage of the building case for war. The timing was all wrong. His former colleagues at CNN sympathized, but told him to call when he had a real lead.

He sighed, crumpled the list, and tossed it at the wall.

Daniel sat up. "Peter, I know you don't want to hear this. But have you considered the possibility she might be dead? You were tortured. Who's to say she wasn't?"

Peter began shaking his head.

Daniel persisted. "I'm only saying perhaps she didn't have the stamina you did. If she died while being tortured, I could understand the Iraqis denying, trying to hush it up."

Peter rose from the bed, still shaking his head, and went to the window. "She's not dead. I would know it if she were." He turned to face his friend. "I'm telling you, she's still alive somewhere."

Daniel gave in. "I hope so. But, listen, chum. It's nearly suppertime. I'm meeting a couple of friends in the restaurant downstairs. Why don't you come along?"

"I'm not hungry."

Daniel leaned forward and whispered. "Look, the place will be packed with UN Weapons Inspectors. You could pass one of them a note about Theresa's situation. They'll have access to the palaces and lots of other places. They could keep an eye out for her."

The light returned to Peter's eyes. "Good idea."

Daniel shrugged. "It's worth a try, anyway. But you'll have to be sneaky. We can't have the minders picking up on it. Otherwise, I'm liable to get kicked out, lose my chance to cover this war when it breaks. Agreed?"

Peter smiled and went to the desk to get some paper. "Agreed. Give me ten minutes to jot this down, okay?"

Daniel waved at the air. "Take your time. I want to shower before dinner. It's a first class restaurant and I don't fancy smelling like a hospital."

While his friend showered, Peter wrote. He detailed the bare facts of Theresa's detainment and disappearance, describing the arresting officer as clearly as he could remember. He pulled a small photo out of his wallet. It was a close-up of Theresa he had taken during an interview in Amman two years ago. She wasn't looking at the camera, but her finely tapered nose and azure eyes were clearly visible even at an angle. He pressed the picture against his lips before wrapping the note around it. Finished, he stood, shoved the note into his right pants pocket, and changed his shirt for dinner.

The high-priced National Restaurant, decorated in an oriental gold and black, had filled with journalists and Iraq's elite by eight p.m. when Peter's group was seated. Waiters glided from table to table, taking orders, filling glasses, and delivering plates piled high with steaming rice, topped by kebabs, grilled fish and steaks. Peter scanned the menu, and began searching the room for likely Weapons Inspectors.

Daniel leaned over and whispered. "Not so fast. The night is young and you're bound to have a better opportunity after dinner."

Peter turned to him. "What do you mean?"

His friend looked the other way as he talked. "I saw the group when they arrived two days ago. A couple of the women expressed a particular interest in the Rashid's disco. They're sitting over there eating right now."

Peter turned around. "Where?"

Daniel looked at the ceiling. "Well, don't look, for heaven's sake. You're about as subtle as our London tabloids."

"Sorry."

Daniel laughed at the chagrin on Peter's face. Their dinner companions, Max Erling and Wanda Knight of the Associated Press, lowered their menus.

Max raised his eyebrows. "What's the joke?"

"Nothing," Daniel said. "I just find it hard to believe the Iraqis ever suspected Peter of being a spy. He has no technique."

"All right. You've had your fun." Peter wasn't amused.

The waiter came to take their order. After he left, the four launched into a discussion of the coming war.

"It won't make a bit of difference what the inspectors find or don't find," argued Wanda. "Rumsfeld and Cheney have Bush wrapped around their finger. War is on the agenda. And nothing's going to take it off."

Max agreed. "They're just going through the motions with all this UN maneuvering. Trying to legitimize the decision for war in the eyes of the world."

"Right," Wanda nodded. "But if the world doesn't come on board, it won't mean anything to this administration."

Daniel shook his head. "Not necessarily. I don't believe Bush will do it without broad-based support. Blair will rein him in."

"Blair? That's nonsense," she retorted. "This war is going to get him re-elected, with or without Blair. I think he's banking on it. Besides, Bush is a gut man."

"Pardon?"

"He goes by his gut. If it feels right, he'll do it no matter who's supporting or not supporting him." Wanda dared Daniel to disagree.

He couldn't. "I suppose you could be right. He does hail from your Lone Star State, doesn't he?"

Peter couldn't remain silent any longer. "It's all well and good for you three to sit here analyzing from a safe, cozy distance…"

Wanda put her glass down. "What do you mean by safe? We're sitting here surrounded by government agents, followed everywhere we go. Our hotel rooms are bugged and searched whenever we're out working. I wouldn't call that safe and cozy."

"As bad as it is for us," Peter said, "it's ten times worse for the Iraqis. Families have fallen apart because they're being made to turn on each other just to stay alive."

"What are you getting at?" asked Max.

"I've been on the other side of things. Seen the slimy underbelly of this regime. Something has to give in this country. But no Iraqi has the nerve, the clout, or the resources to change things. I'm not saying I think Bush should attack. It'll probably turn into an awful mess if he does…"

"When he does," corrected Wanda.

Peter nodded. "But I can understand why he would. And I can forgive him."

Daniel raised his glass for a sip. "The question is, will the American people?"

Talk turned then to the U.S. election in 2004 and the Democratic candidates most likely to challenge Bush. They continued discussing war, politics, and their dealings with the Iraqi Information Minister as they ate.

They were giggling over a recent Bush malapropism when Max glanced at his watch. "Hey, I hate to break things up but I've got an early appointment in the morning. I'd better call it a night." He pulled out his money clip and peeled off several bills to cover his share. "It's been fun and it was nice meeting you, Peter. Stay out of prison, okay?"

"You can count on it. Good night." Peter shook his hand.

After Max left, Wanda reached for her purse. "Let me pay for my share."

Daniel leaned forward. "Does this mean you're leaving too? Why don't you come over to the disco with Peter and me?"

She considered and nodded. "That does sound fun. It's been ages since I've gone dancing."

The three left a generous tip for the waiter and headed toward the throbbing sound coming from the other side of the lobby. On the way, Wanda spied a friend and told Peter and Daniel she would catch up with them in a few minutes. Walking on to the disco, Peter asked Daniel about the two female inspectors he had mentioned earlier.

His friend reassured him. "They headed this way half an hour ago. I'm sure they're still here." He scanned the room. "There they are. Come on, let's introduce ourselves."

They weaved their way between couples on the dance floor until his friend stopped in front of a table occupied by two sharply dressed women and a man with thick glasses.

Nearby hovered their three very obvious and nervous government-appointed Iraqi minders wearing black leather jackets.

Daniel had to shout to be heard. "Hello. I'm Daniel James with the BBC and this is my friend, Peter. We've got a bet going. He claims you're all scientists and I told him scientists don't have time for dancing in Iraq. They're too busy trying to prevent a war."

The women smiled and Peter jumped into the conversation. "So, we agreed the one who was right would get to dance with one of you. One of you women, that is. We're assuming, of course, that you understand English."

The taller one with long blond hair spoke with a German accent. "Are you asking one of us to dance?"

"If you're a scientist, yes. Are you?"

"I am a microbiologist. Will that do?"

Peter smiled. "Perfectly. Shall we?"

She stood to take his hand. As she did, her minder stepped forward, regarding Peter with suspicious and narrowed eyes.

Daniel intercepted the Iraqi. "I don't believe they'll require your services as a translator. This isn't interpretive dance, just disco."

The humor was lost on the sour man with the Saddam-style moustache. He ignored Daniel and tracked his charge in her pale blue dress bobbing up and down amidst all the dancers.

Out on the dance floor, Peter got right down to business. "What's your name?"

"Eva. Eva Hoffman. And you are Peter...?"

"Cranston."

"Peter Cranston? That name is familiar. So is your face."

"Perhaps you noticed me on TV." He saw recognition light up her eyes.

"Yes. You were released from a Baghdad prison not long ago. Abu Ghraib." She looked over at Daniel and back to Peter. "He was the one who interviewed you. But you were also on the news talking about a missing friend, weren't you?"

Peter nodded. "That's why I'm back. I'm looking for her. I've had no luck so far. She was arrested the same time I was. Only she wasn't released." The song was nearing an end, so he talked faster. "Look, I know you're with the UN inspection team. I've looked everywhere I could, but you'll be going places I could never check. If I pass you a note with her picture, can you keep an eye out for her?"

She seemed reluctant. "I don't know. I'm here for one reason. I could get kicked out if I were suspected of spying."

He pressed. "I'm not asking you to ignore your job. Simply keep your eyes and ears open. Please. She's been a prisoner now for two months."

She pursed her lips and nodded. "Of course."

As the music ended, Peter put his right hand in his pocket, making sure her minder couldn't see. He pulled it out again, with the note safely secreted in his palm and he took her left hand with his right. He pressed the note to her palm, but said nothing as they casually walked back to her table, hand in hand. Wanda had joined the group while they danced, and the older man with thick glasses was now leading her out to the dance floor.

The German's minder had glared at Peter the whole time, but once they reached the table and separated, the Iraqi relaxed and sat back down with his friends. He didn't see Eva slip the palmed note into her purse.

An hour later, she and her friend said goodnight and went up to their room. Peter and Daniel waited until the minders were gone before enjoying one last drink. Wanda and the bespectacled scientist had managed to find another table away from the crowd and his minder for a brief interview.

"Well? Are you ready to leave Baghdad?" Daniel took a sip of his whiskey sour.

Peter shrugged. "I guess so. I don't think I can do any more. Finding Theresa is in Eva's hands for now."

"I'll keep my ear to the ground, too. Where are you headed?"

"Amman. Then California."

Daniel put his glass down. "California? I thought you were from Canada."

"Theresa's mother lives in Santa Monica. She's been worried sick about her daughter since I called from Amman. I think I should give her an update in person."

"That's decent of you."

Peter looked away a moment. "I'm not being entirely altruistic. This gives me a chance at last to meet some of her family. Maybe I'll pick up something about her past that will help. The guy who interrogated me in prison showed a particular interest in her father."

Daniel raised his glass to his friend. "Well, good luck to you. Oh, and you redeemed yourself rather well on the dance floor. Nice hand-off."

Peter chuckled. "So I've got technique after all?"

"Let's just say there's hope for you. Cheers."

They clinked glasses, downed the last of their drinks, and headed upstairs to bed.

THERESA'S FAMILY

(Santa Monica, California—Thanksgiving, 2002)

The plane was delayed. By the time Peter finally arrived at the Fuller home, the turkey had already cooled in the oven for an hour. While Theresa's family had gathered to see Peter, everyone—including the guest of honor—wanted to eat Thanksgiving Dinner. So her sisters, Angela and Laila, dashed around the kitchen, reheating the food in the microwave.

Theresa's older brother, James, offered a blessing on the meal and his mention of Theresa in the prayer brought sobs, particularly from her mother. But once he finished, it was as if they had reached an unspoken agreement. There would be no more sadness during dinner, not while the children were present.

The combined aromas of dressing, mashed potatoes and gravy, peas, caramel yams topped with marshmallows, and homemade butterhorn rolls flavored the air inside the tidy home on Stanford Street in Santa Monica long after the adults had pushed themselves away from the dinner table. But once the pies had been cut and served, Mrs. Fuller sent the younger grandchildren outside to play in the backyard. It was time to talk of Theresa.

Peter and James sat in the two wingback chairs opposite Angela, Laila and Mrs. Fuller on one of the living room sofas. Older grandchildren filled another.

Peter swallowed as he looked at Theresa's sisters sandwiching their mother. He cast a look sideways at James. The resemblance was undeniable. They all had Mrs. Fuller's blue eyes, but Theresa, more than any of them, looked like her mother. The nose, strong and straight, was the same.

Mrs. Fuller surveyed her family, looked to the ceiling, and closed her eyes. A moment later, she looked at Peter again, her eyes swimming. "I'm sorry for the tears, Mr. Cranston."

"Please. Call me Peter."

"Peter. It's just so strange to have Thanksgiving without her. She always spent this holiday with me. No matter where her assignments took her, she always arranged to be here for Thanksgiving. I can't imagine where she is or what..." Her words trailed off and Angela pulled her into a silent embrace.

James spoke up. "You'll have to excuse us, Peter."

"Of course. I understand."

Composed again, Mrs. Fuller leaned forward. "I'm certain you have other things you could be doing, but we just wanted…"

Peter cut her off. "No, I wanted to come, Mrs. Fuller. I miss her too."

She smiled. "Please, call me Ruth. I'm so glad to finally have the chance to meet you. Theresa's told me all about you." She looked at the others. "He's a prize-winning photographer, you know. That's why Theresa could never bring him by. He was always too busy."

Peter stayed silent. Is that what she had told them? True, he had won awards. But those were for assignments with Theresa. When the assignments ended he had breaks like her. Peter felt James watching him.

"So, what did Theresa tell you about us?" Her brother thrust his chin out as he asked.

"Not much. She's rather private, you know. At least, with me. But I thought she mentioned two brothers. Are you the only brother?"

"No. Mitch and his wife and kids are over in Belgium."

"Belgium?"

"He works for an international architectural firm with offices in several countries. He speaks fluent French, so they posted him in Belgium."

"How is it he learned French? I thought your family mainly lived in the Middle East."

Mrs. Fuller interjected. "He first learned a bit in Beirut. They speak a lot of it there. He didn't become fluent, though, until he went on a study abroad program in college."

James stood up and headed for the table to retrieve his glass of water. "So she never talked much about us? About our father?"

"Well…no."

James nodded as if he weren't surprised.

Angela broke the silence. "I'll bet they didn't feed you like this in prison, Peter."

"No, they certainly didn't." He saw the hesitation in her eyes and knew what was coming.

"Would you mind telling us what it was like?"

Peter swallowed. Of course they wanted to know. They yearned for some kind of connection. His experience could provide a clue to what Theresa might be facing.

"Of course, if you'd rather not talk about it…" Angela started to say.

"No, it's all right. You have every right to know what prisons are like over there. Just remember, there are all kinds. I was in one of the worst. Theresa wasn't at Abu Ghraib. I'm sure of that. She's likely in a woman's facility and being treated much better than I was. Particularly since she's American."

Mrs. Fuller teared up again. "But you said on the phone you checked everywhere. Didn't you look for her at all the women's prisons?"

"I checked all the ones I knew about. They could also be moving her around. Ruth, I promise you I'm going back and I will find her."

She squeezed the hands of her daughters. "Thank you. We don't know what we'd do without you. The newspapers and TV stations have stopped calling. I guess she's old news for the moment. Of course, the minute she's found they will be swarming us. But we need the publicity now to pressure the Iraqis. The State Department can't or won't tell us a thing, and they won't do anything."

James returned and sat down again. "They've got their hands full trying to counter the Pentagon's arguments for war." More than a touch of anger edged his voice.

"Believe me, Ruth, James...all of you. I share your frustration."

"So what was it like in Abu Ghraib?" repeated Angela.

Peter gave them a watered down version of his experience. Even toned down, they grimaced and covered their mouths at times.

When he finished, Angela turned to her Mom. "Was it like that for Dad?"

Mrs. Fuller looked down.

"Your husband was in a Baghdad prison?" Peter asked. "I was questioned about Theresa's childhood in Baghdad, but I had no idea your husband was imprisoned there."

The gray-haired woman looked him in the eyes. "She's never talked to you about it?"

Peter shook his head. "Until my interrogation, I had no clue she ever lived there."

James put his water glass down. "I'm not surprised. When we do get together and start reminiscing, she hardly says a word."

Angela rose to her defense. "That's because she can't remember."

"Well, you can remember and you're younger. I can remember. Why can't she?" James argued.

Mrs. Fuller interrupted. "Never mind. Angela, would you go back in the hall cupboard and get the photo albums from Baghdad?"

Two hours later, following conversation over old family photos and generous second helpings of pumpkin pie, Peter and Mrs. Fuller said goodbye to James, Angela, Laila and their families.

The door closed and Peter reached for his camera. "I should have taken a picture of all of you. But do you mind if I take your picture, Ruth? Your daughter shares your likeness and prison can… Well, her hair may have begun to gray. When I return, it would be useful to have something to show…"

"Say no more. Where should I stand? Or would you like me to sit?"

He looked around. The walls were crowded with family photos and art from the Middle East. Every square inch of the living room boasted telltale signs of their years abroad—ceramic figurines, brass trays, inlaid chests, ornamental daggers.

Peter indicated the sofa. She sat, brushed her bangs back and smiled. He framed the shot, focused and clicked. As soon as her lips drooped again, he surprised her with another quick shot.

"Oh, I wasn't smiling. I didn't know you were going to take two pictures."

"Sorry. I…Well, I always play it safe." He didn't wish to tell her he wanted a picture that would show what Theresa might look like under stress.

She patted the sofa next to her. "Come and sit down a moment longer. You don't have to leave just because everyone else did."

"Thank you." He sat down beside her, and put his camera on the coffee table next to the album. It lay open to a picture of Theresa, dated 1964. She stood in front of a ziggurat.

Mrs. Fuller followed his eyes. "That was Samara. She climbed all the way to the top with her father."

Peter touched the picture. "She looks happy."

"She was. It was one of the rare times she was able to do something Jimmy, I mean James, couldn't do. She and her father were very close. They spent a lot of time together."

Peter hesitated. "I hope you don't mind my asking, but was he a spy? Is that why he was in prison?"

Mrs. Fuller looked down at her hands. "No. They put him in prison for that reason, but he wasn't with CIA."

"How long was he held?"

She turned her head to look out the window. "Only a few weeks. Just long enough for them to kill him."

Peter drew back. "He died in Baghdad? They executed an American?"

"They claimed it was suicide. But I know better. You see, Nate's grandfather killed himself when Nate was just a boy and Nate could never forgive him. No, my husband wouldn't have done that."

"How did he die then?" Peter hoped it wasn't from torture.

"He was hung. The autopsy back here proved that much."

Peter tried to push Abu Ghraib's hanging room images out of his mind. "But how did you get his body sent back here for an autopsy? I can't believe they released it to you."

"You have to realize, Peter, that this was well before Saddam Hussein. Our government had an embassy there. We enjoyed good relations with the Iraqis. I don't know if I'll ever find out exactly what happened to Nate in that prison, but they were embarrassed. It didn't take much pressure from our ambassador to get his body flown back here. Our government arranged the autopsy. Besides the marks around his neck, there were bruises on his body and head. It was no suicide."

He fumbled for a response. "I'm...I'm very sorry. I...I never knew. Did Theresa know?"

She wiped her eyes. "I only told Jimmy at first because he insisted on knowing. Theresa never asked, and I've kept it from the others. They were so young at the time. They believe it was some horrible accident. I didn't want them imagining his murder." She got up and paced the room.

"Are you ever going to tell them?"

"I suppose I owe them the truth now, but I just can't bring myself to do it. Except for Nathan's death, their memories of Baghdad are happy ones."

"Is there anything else you can tell me? Any information you can provide that I might be able to use as leverage to see Theresa?"

Mrs. Fuller paused, thinking. "I don't know if he's still there or even alive, but one of our good friends in the Ba'athi government assured us after Nate's conviction that they knew he wasn't a spy but, to save face, the government sentenced him to a brief term. He promised me Nate would be released after a month."

"And this was before your husband was killed?"
She nodded.

"Who was this man?" He took out a pen and business card to write the information down.

"Ibrahim Awali. He and his wife, Muna, were good friends of ours. When Nate died, Ibrahim was almost as shaken as I was. But he helped us cut through the red tape in order to get our exit visas and return to the States as soon as possible."

"Have you been in contact with him since?"

She shook her head. "I couldn't bring myself to respond to Muna's letters. It was too difficult. I needed to put Baghdad behind me for a while. By the time I felt ready to write, they had moved."

Peter stood. "But if this man is still alive and well-regarded in the Party, he may be able to convince the Iraqis that your husband was no spy. Then, perhaps, they'll let Theresa go."

She rose from the couch. "Do you think so?"

"All we can do is try." Peter checked his watch. "I should probably be going."

He turned to leave, but Mrs. Fuller took hold of his arm. "Wait. The others... Theresa's brothers and sisters. They don't understand why she doesn't talk about it. But I do. My husband wasn't a perfect man, Peter. He was a good man, but he had his weaknesses. She found that out. It seemed to sour her on...Well, on everything. If you do see Theresa, please tell her how much we miss her. How much we love her. How much we want..." She broke off.

Peter put his arms around the grieving woman. "She's alive and, one way or another, I'll make sure she returns to you. I promise."

A NEW ROUTINE

(Iraqi Intelligence Headquarters—
November 22, 2003)

The hatch slammed shut, and Theresa scurried forward to grab the tin plate and cup. Stale bread again. Careful not to spill her day's allotment of water, she carried the breakfast back to her mattress. The water tasted foul, but she took a few sips and tore off half of the flat round loaf. She had learned to use the other half for lunch, since they didn't get any. Dinner usually consisted of a watery soup and another stale piece of bread.

Theresa ate the bread slowly, counting and picking off any bits of mold and tossing them to the roaches. She was lucky. Today, there were only two moldy parts. One morning she had found six. As she chewed, she lifted up the corner of her mattress and scratched a line with the edge of the plate to mark a new day.

She marked the days in rows of seven. Each time she started a new row, it meant it was Monday—time for her weekly session with Tariq. The visits with him had become a lifeline, as precious as the meager amounts of food and water she was allotted.

By her calculations, it was November 22nd. The date of President Kennedy's assassination. How strange. She had been here in Baghdad, a little girl listening to the BBC, when they heard the news. She remembered the stricken look on her father's face, the tears in her mother's eyes. Over the years that followed, Theresa had heard the refrain: "Where were you the day John Kennedy was assassinated?" Baghdad. How many Americans could say that? Now here she was again. She shook her head at the irony.

November 22nd. Had she missed Thanksgiving? She pictured her mother's dining room table laden with turkey, mashed potatoes, and dressing. But most of all, she thought of her mother's butterhorn rolls. Theresa closed her eyes and pretended to pick one up, pull it apart to reveal its doughy middle, and take a careful bite. She swallowed. All she could taste was the moldy saliva left from her prison fare. Opening her eyes, she cast all thoughts of her family's Thanksgiving celebration aside. She had to deal with her current situation, not the past.

Today marked her 32nd day of incarceration in this second prison...and Peter's 32nd day of freedom. She had smiled when Tariq broke the news of her friend's release. It lifted another burden from her conscience and gave her hope. Now her government surely knew of her incarceration. Peter would be doing all he could to find her and gain her freedom. But she had to concentrate on surviving until that moment. Tariq could help, but only to the extent that they could hide his assistance from Badr.

Key to their subterfuge had been locating the hidden camera and microphone. Theresa inspected every inch of the walls over the first several days in her new cell, but found no holes or cracks through which a lens might be aimed. Tariq clued her in to the camera's location during the following Monday's session in the Interrogation Room.

"Is your toilet functioning adequately?" He looked at her without breaking eye contact.

She nodded. "Yes, but it could use a good cleaning."

"Really? It was cleaned the day before you arrived."

Theresa rolled her eyes. "That can't be true. You smelled it."

"Believe me, it was." He gave the barest hint of a nod.

She understood and said no more about the toilet. An hour after she got back to her cell, Theresa pretended to be chasing a roach around the toilet's base while she scanned the bowl and the tank. She hardly paused when she noticed the tiny hole just under the tank's lid. Instead, she slammed her shoe down on the imaginary roach.

"Gotcha!"

Theresa had decided not to bother searching for the microphone. Tariq had found ways to pass her notes when necessary out of the camera's view. His occasional whispering also assured her the microphone wasn't very powerful.

Despite her loss of weight, she had begun a physical routine to stay strong and pass the time. Each morning and evening before her meals arrived, Theresa stretched out her muscles by leaning against the cell walls. She followed with sets of sit-ups and push-ups. The first day she had only managed ten sit-ups and two push-ups. But today she had counted off fifteen of each, thanks in large measure to the pieces of fruit or vegetable Tariq managed to sneak to her each Monday. She always kept his carrot stick or apple slice in her pocket until she was back in her cell. There she would begin one of her twice-daily oval walks. At the top of the oval, beside the toilet tank and well out of the camera's view, she would pull his gift out, take a nibble, and pocket it again. By keeping her bites as small as possible, Theresa could snack between meals for two, sometimes three days.

The boil on her arm seemed to be healing. True to his word, Tariq had returned with homemade poultices and instructions to change them daily for the first week. Made up of hollyhock, cardamom, and other herbs he had mentioned that she couldn't remember, each poultice gave off a smell that reminded Theresa of Mentholatum. After the initial week, she began to change the poultices every seven days. She was only too happy to do so because, over time, the aroma soured, becoming almost as foul as the stench around her toilet. The last time Tariq checked, he guessed the treatment would need another three months or so.

For the time being, her epilepsy was also under control. She had decided to stretch her supply by only taking one pill every other night. She knew it was risky but, so far, the episodes had not recurred. Strangely, she missed their relatively gentle pull from this harsh reality. But Tariq was right. The risk was too great and so she continued the medication. She slept lightly, however, under the lower dose. Often Theresa awoke in the night to the screams of men and women echoing faintly down the hall.

To keep herself entertained, she had taken to making up new lyrics for well-known show tunes. Her versions bordered on the macabre, but they suited her surroundings: "Any Food Will Do," instead of "Any Dream Will Do" from *Joseph and the Amazing Technicolor Dreamcoat* and "Don't Cry For Me, Colonel Badr," instead of the popular hit from *Evita*. She had composed her personal favorite fittingly from *Les Miserables*. Whenever the midnight sounds of terror would wake her, Theresa would close her eyes and begin singing "Do You Hear the People Scream."

She had not seen Badr for a month now. The colonel had last interrogated her on the day after she had been moved, reviewing all the names already given and pressing for more. Since that day, he had been strangely absent. From the way Tariq conducted her interrogations, however, she felt certain he was still watching somehow. The captain performed his part well, raising his voice at times, pacing back and forth, and always finding a moment to draw closer and belittle her or her country. She filled her role, as well, with tears and a voice that too often quivered for real.

Theresa revealed an occasional name or event from her past—enough to make the sessions with Tariq appear fruitful—but the real purpose of his interrogations was to pass her a note. Sometimes he secured it under her arm when he shook her, other times he subtly dropped the small slip of paper in her lap. Any feigned coldness in his verbal assaults dissolved in the warmth of his written words, regardless of the note's content. Whether the messages alerted her to Badr's whereabouts, provided news updates from abroad, or conveyed his reassurances, they never failed to pierce her growing sense of solitude.

Theresa had tried to vary her daily routines to fight these feelings of helplessness and isolation. Other than Mondays, she usually saw no one. So on Tuesdays she passed the time by reviewing aloud everything she could remember about American History and Government. Wednesdays were devoted to the poems of Emily Dickinson. Theresa had memorized several during a course in college and now she recited and tried to analyze a different one each day. On Thursdays, she turned to music. Not the dark knockoffs she had composed, but her favorite classical pieces. She would hum as much of a score as she could remember over and over again. Theresa always conducted interviews of famous people on Fridays. Saturdays were free when she would think about whatever came to her, and these days tended to seem the longest. Theresa reminisced about Baghdad on Sundays in preparation for her session with Tariq.

This being Friday, Theresa stood and began pacing the cell floor in her oval pattern. As she walked, she pretended to interview a well-known actress. She had learned to avoid anyone political, particularly from the current administration. Two weeks ago in the middle of a one-on-one with Dick Cheney, her cell door had been thrown open and she was dragged to the Interrogation Room. An official she had not seen before kept her there for over an hour, grilling her about her relationship with the Vice President. It might have been funny, had the interrogation not included some blows to the head. Only Tariq's delayed arrival ended the terror.

"Ms. Streep," she began, "when you take on a role that requires a foreign accent, do you find it difficult to let go of the accent once the film is finished?"

"Vell, I don't know vhat chu mean by a foreign accent. Zis is always za vay..."

She heard footsteps and stopped. Several pairs of clicks indicated at least two people, if not more. She held her breath until they passed her door. As she exhaled, the bolt on the door to her right slid open. Having never heard a sound from next door, she had assumed it was unoccupied. Theresa listened to the creaking of the heavy metal door as it opened. Were they locking someone up next to her?

Then she heard a hoarse male voice in Arabic asking, "What is it? What is happening?"

The response, also in Arabic, came in official tones: "Mahmud Wizak, on behalf of the Iraqi people and their beloved leader, Saddam Hussein—may his name be blessed—you are hereby sentenced to death for the crime of espionage against the state."

The prisoner said nothing and, a second later, Theresa heard a gunshot. She flinched. A second gunshot followed, then an order in Arabic and the sounds of a body being dragged past her cell.

Theresa forgot about Meryl Streep and sank to her mattress. She was still hugging her knees to her chest when unseen hands shoved dinner through her hatch hours later.

A CHRISTMAS PRESENT

(Intelligence Headquarters—February 10, 2003)

Christmas had come and gone, and still no sign of Badr. In a note the week before Christmas, Tariq had explained that the colonel had been called away to the north for a long-term special assignment. He added that, in Badr's absence, he had managed to disconnect the audio feed from her cell. She considered it one of her best Christmas presents that year. The other came Christmas day when Tariq paid her a surprise visit and gave her a book about San Diego—the kind with large glossy pictures for a coffee table. It was one of his souvenirs from his days at San Diego State. He told her she could keep it as long as it stayed hidden under her mattress.

She choked back tears. "Thank you, Captain."

"Please. Call me Tariq."

Since that day, he had conducted all their sessions in her cell. He sat on the toilet to block the camera's view. That way, they could look at the book together and reminisce about Southern California. He told her of his daily jogs through Balboa Park, the trips to Coronado Island. She ran her finger over picture after picture of sunsets on the Pacific Ocean. Of course, discussion of her past in Baghdad continued. Regardless of the colonel's absence, Tariq still had a written report to fill out each week.

Theresa told him of her family's particular friendship with the Jesuit priests who ran Baghdad's Al Hikma University.

"But what did you have to do with priests? Are you Catholic?"

She shook her head. "No, but we attended a non-denominational Sunday School out at the university. We were quite involved in the Christian group of American expatriates. Also, you have to understand my mother. She made friends with everybody. She was always inviting people she had just met over to dinner."

"How did she meet these priests?"

Theresa's brow furrowed. "I believe, as teachers there at the college, they were invited to our Easter sunrise service. I loved Easter every year because Mom and another lady always made homemade doughnuts to serve after the service. Anyway, I remember one priest, in particular. Father Dowling. I was convinced for the first few years that he was really Santa Claus in disguise."

"Did he have a beard?"

"No, but he had white hair and wire framed spectacles with rosy cheeks. Every time he visited, he pulled all kinds of candy out of the pockets of his cassock. He always had something for us kids."

She also told Tariq more stories about Asil, their maid. During the revolution in February, 1963, Mother had insisted that Asil stay over rather than risk traveling back to her part of the city after curfew hours. They taught her to play Charades and she helped their team win with her imitation of a camel. Jimmy claimed she cheated because she had bellowed out loud. But Dad gave her full credit anyway because it was so convincing.

"What ever happened to Asil?" Tariq asked.

Theresa shrugged. "We don't know. We didn't keep in contact with anyone we knew here. I did find out years later, though, that Mom helped save her life."

"What do you mean? While she was working for you?"

She nodded. "Asil wasn't married but she had a boyfriend. She used to pull out his picture and say, 'Handsome, yes?' Well, I guess she got pregnant. She was terrified that Shimone, our cook, would find out."

"Never mind your cook. What about her family?"

"That's just it. Shimone was a cousin. If he found out, she would have been killed for bringing such shame to the family."

Tariq nodded. "What did your mother do?"

"It wasn't easy, but she arranged for Asil to have an abortion. The way she saw it, there was no alternative."

Theresa shared other childhood memories—her membership in a Brownie troop, the Easter egg hunts on the lawn of the American Embassy, the trip by car to Jordan so Jimmy could be baptized in the Jordan River.

"And where were you baptized?"

"In the swimming pool at the Alwiya Club."

He had snorted, disbelief in his eyes. But she assured him it was true. They talked often about the club since it played such a big part in both their childhoods. Besides the swimming, there had been bingo parties, recitals, play readings and, of course, movies.

She carefully pulled Tariq's book out now and, hiding it behind her, approached the toilet from the side. Theresa sat down to block the camera and looked again at the photos of the marina, Balboa Park, Sea World, the beach. She closed her eyes and tried to visualize her mother on the sand near their home in Santa Monica. She saw her brothers, sisters, nieces and nephews there, as well. All gathered to celebrate the Fourth of July under a big portable canopy. Would she miss the reunion this year? Would she ever see them again?

Solitude used to be her friend. She had taken refuge in it, even shutting out friends like Peter. Now she cried for company. Tariq's half-hour visit each week was like a drop of water on a parched tongue. A single taste made her crave more. Any voices brought solace…even those of the guards speaking in Arabic as they walked past her cell. In the beginning, she had called out to them, trying to get them to stop and open the hatch in her door window. All she wanted was to see another pair of eyes. To connect somehow. But they never stopped.

In early December when her toilet overflowed, she had yelled and screamed for hours to no avail. And that night, as she lay close to the stench and sewage, she turned all her rage and frustration on God. She hadn't given Him a single thought for years. Certainly, she had believed in Him as a child but that had been long ago. Over the years, after all the depravity she had seen, she simply had come to the conclusion that He didn't care.

And so she didn't care in return…until that fetid night. Something finally snapped inside and her approach had been anything but meek. She raised her voice and lashed out as both prosecutor and judge. God was on trial for his neglect of her trial.

"Are you enjoying this? Are you having a good time? Or are you even watching?" Her anger felt like a lash whipping out.

"A God of love? Hah! You don't love me. A loving father wouldn't leave his daughter alone like this… in this rotten, stinking cell."

Her volume rose. "It's been months now! What have you got planned? A year? Two years?"

Tears of self-pity filled her eyes but she swiped them away, continuing her harangue against Heaven.

"If you're so all powerful why don't you get me out of here? Huh? I'll tell you why."

She had then screamed at the top of her lungs. "YOU CAN'T!"

Even now, two months later, the accusations of that night seared her conscience. They had cleaned out her toilet and cell the next day, but nothing could clean out her soul. She had chosen blasphemy instead of prayer.

Why couldn't she pray? Perhaps, if she started, the words would form. Maybe the promises of her child-hood Sunday School classes would prove true. It might make some small difference.

Theresa returned to her mattress to hide the book. Then she bowed her head. Her voice began in a whisper of shame.

"Dear God, I don't have any right to ask you for any-thing. I forgot you all these years. I even turned my back on you. Here in prison I blamed you, and yelled at you. But please, don't leave me here. Let me see my family again. You gave me a friend in Tariq. Please give me back my family. At least, help my mother know I'm alive. Help her not to give up hope. Help me not to give up hope. It's too hard spending day after day looking at these walls…"

Her lower lip began trembling, but she shook it off and went on, wiping the tears from her eyes.

"Help me see beyond these walls. I can't be free, but help me remember what it's like to be…"

At this point, she broke into sobbing. Why should God even listen to her? She had turned from Him. And how could He possibly love her now? She had no faith.

If He truly loved her, why did He let her lie here alone and forgotten by all but a Muslim Iraqi who pitied her?

She sobbed for a long time, in despair and loneliness. Even if she were released, what would she go back to? A life of solitude and searching? Of course she wanted to see her family. But what would she say to them? They had not turned away from their faith. Could they ever understand her cynicism, accept her despite her questioning?

It dawned on Theresa that she had found more intimacy with Tariq, her jailer, over the past six months than with anyone she had known in almost forty years of freedom. The irony struck her with such force that the sobbing turned to a self-deprecating laughter. Slow and airy at first, it built until she doubled over.

After a minute the laughter transformed to weeping again. For several minutes, she alternated between sobs of anguish and mirth until, worn out, she put the book back under her mattress and lay down, staring vacantly at the ceiling.

Tariq found her two hours later, still lying there, staring at nothing. She didn't move when he unlocked the door and walked in. She didn't even turn to look at him. He closed the door and knelt beside her.

"Theresa?" He set down an Arabic magazine he had under his arm.

She blinked, but still gazed upward, saying nothing.

"Are you having an episode?"

Her lips barely moved. "No."

"What's the matter?"

She turned to look in his eyes. "Do you believe in God?"

Her question surprised him. "Yes."

She sat up and spoke earnestly. "So you believe there's someone up there in charge of all this?"

He lowered his voice. "If you mean this prison and this chaos of inhumanity, I would have to answer no. He is not responsible for this. But if you mean this world, then yes, I do believe Allah is all-powerful. Don't you?"

"I used to. I wish I could. It would be comforting to have someone else to talk to when you're not here."

"Your prayers give you no comfort?"

She looked away. Tariq saw a tear lining her right eyelid as she turned her head. She said nothing.

He attempted to lighten the moment. "What happened? Did a cockroach interrupt?"

Theresa smiled and wiped her eyes. "No. But tell me, if there is a God, why did He make cockroaches?"

"That's easy. To eat the ants."

She chuckled. "And…"

"And he made ants to teach us patience."

She grew serious again. "And why did he make tyrants?"

His smile faded, and he almost whispered his response. "To make us pray."

She nodded and began speaking slowly. "My father taught me how to pray. Mom showed me, too, but what Dad said stuck with me. He told me you have to imagine

He's sitting right there on your bed listening. And even though He's God, He's your Father so He wants you to tell him everything that's making you happy and everything that's making you sad."

"It sounds like you had a good father. Have you prayed like that in here?"

"I tried. Until I realized I didn't deserve His attention."

"Why do you say that? A father loves even a wicked child."

She looked at him. "I'll bet you have a good father. Tell me about him. What is he like?"

His face reddened and he looked down. "Well, maybe not every father loves every child. Mine didn't even stay long enough to find out what I was like."

She wanted to reach out, but restrained herself. "That was his loss. You never tried to find him?"

Tariq sneered. "I have no desire to know the man who would leave my mother. Besides having no heart, he had no intelligence."

"When you pray to your God, Allah, do you think of Him as a father?"

He shook his head firmly. "No. I wouldn't presume to think of Him that way. He is too great, too distant…so different from man."

"But why should He care to hear our prayers, then?"

"He listens to our poor prayers because He is compassionate."

Theresa remained unconvinced. "Does he do anything about them?"

"What do you mean?"

"Do you believe He answers prayers?"

Tariq turned the question back. "Do you?"

"I did once. A long time ago. When I had more faith." She looked past him to nothing.

Tariq looked over at the toilet, glanced at his watch, and then sought her eyes. "Theresa." His voice was hushed.

She looked at him and wondered for the first time if the audio feed had been reconnected. She found it strange that he hadn't taken up his normal position to block the camera's view. Was the audio on and the video off?

Tariq moved closer. "I don't know what caused you to first question your faith. And I don't know if God answers all our prayers. But I know that in here…in a place like this, those who reach out for Him are made stronger. They last longer. They don't go mad as quickly."

She blinked. "So I should pray."

"Please."

"All right. It's the least I can do for you. You've done so much for me."

"You promise?"

She nodded. "I promise."

His whispering grew softer. "People are looking for you, and I promise I won't let you die in here. The war is coming."

"What people? Is the U.S. ready to attack?"

He ignored the first question. "Your country is preparing to invade Iraq. They are debating in the United Nations. We've had weapons inspectors here again. But whether they find any weapons of mass destruction or not, your president is determined to change this regime."

"Why didn't you tell me any of this before?"

"I almost said something last week. But I didn't want to get your hopes up. According to the news reports, much of the world doesn't want this war to happen. The French are against it...and the Germans. Right now only the British are standing with your president. I thought I should see how the debate proceeded."

"And...?"

"Let me just say that all of us, everyone in Baghdad, know it's coming...and coming soon."

"How soon?" She had leaned forward to within inches of his face because he was speaking in such low tones.

He shrugged. "No one knows for sure. They're guessing mid-March. The government has already begun emptying the warehouses, encouraging us to stock up on the essentials."

She looked past him in the distance. "One more month."

"Theresa, no one knows for sure. I'm telling you this so you won't lose hope. It may be more than a month. Or less. Keep praying and we'll get through this."

She smiled, grasped his hands, and kissed them. The gesture was so unexpected, they both looked shocked at what she had done. When she realized she still held his hands, she dropped them. Tariq picked up the magazine and stumbled to his feet, looking away from her.

With the magazine under his arm, he thrust his hands in his pockets. "I must be going."

She nodded, too abashed to look at him.

"I'll see you next week." He stepped to the door.

"Yes. Goodbye."

Theresa didn't look up until she heard the door lock. Her heart hammered. Why had she done it? Was it the prospect of being set free, or something more? And what did he think? Would he come back next week or stay away? The thought of never seeing him again made her sick.

TAPED PROOF

(Intelligence Headquarters—February 10, 2003)

Peter stood in Colonel Badr's office stunned. He couldn't deny it was Theresa, a good four inches of her true blonde hair showing now from the roots. But the incompatibility of the two hair colors hadn't jarred him nearly as much as what he had seen seconds ago. She had kissed the captain's hands. What hurt even more was the way Theresa looked at this Iraqi. And the man responded as any lover caught on tape—uncomfortable, embarrassed. As much as he wanted to disbelieve the television monitor, Peter had seen the officer enter Theresa's cell with the same magazine Badr had handed the captain moments ago. This was undoubtedly a live feed.

Badr clicked off the set behind his desk. "Have you seen enough? As you can tell, Miss Fuller is quite content."

Peter's cheeks flushed red. "She has lost a lot of weight."

"But she has not been sick, and manages to keep quite active. If we had the time I could show you tapes of other days. She can be quite entertaining with her songs."

"You have an audio monitor as well? Bring out some other tapes. I have a few minutes to spare." He wondered if the captain appeared in any of these, as well.

Badr's face hardened. "You may have time, but I don't. I have met my part of the agreement. You drove all this way from Jordan for proof that she is alive. I have proven it. Now give me the information you promised."

"Release her to me and I'll tell you what I know."

The colonel leaned back in his chair. "That was not the agreement, Mr. Cranston. Are you an honorable man or not?"

Peter glared at this man who had directed his torture five months ago. "How can you speak to me of honor?"

Before Badr could answer, Tariq came to the door. The colonel waved him off. "Leave the magazine on the table, Captain. You are dismissed for the night."

Tariq set the magazine down and turned to go.

"Oh, and Captain?"

Tariq looked back at Badr.

"On your way out, check to make sure the audio feed is in order. We had no sound here."

Tariq glanced curiously at Peter before leaving.

When the door shut, Peter turned back to the colonel. "What's his last name? He told us when we were arrested, but I can't remember."

"The captain? Why do you want to know? Are you jealous?"

Peter reddened. "Only curious."

"You do not need to know his name. The less you know, the better. Returning to the subject of your information…"

"And Theresa's release," Peter said.

Badr began twirling his pen between his fingers. "I am a reasonable man, Mr. Cranston. Should your information prove that neither Miss Fuller nor her father was ever engaged in espionage here in Iraq, I might consider releasing her. Tell me what you know."

Peter glanced at the television set again. "Let me talk to her first."

"Out of the question. You are trying my patience. Have you forgotten what we can do to those who do not cooperate?"

"Of course not. That's why a CNN crew is waiting back at the Rashid Hotel." Peter looked at his watch. "If I'm not back there in twenty-eight minutes, they go live with a report of another missing journalist. I don't think your president would be very happy with that kind of development right now, do you?"

Badr squeezed his lips together. "Give me the information. Then we will talk about a meeting with her."

Peter exhaled. "When I visited Mrs. Fuller in California, she told me that a good friend of theirs here in Baghdad, someone high up in the Ba'ath Party, assured her their government had realized Professor Fuller wasn't a spy. But to save face after arresting him, they convicted him anyway. This man promised her the professor would be released in a month or so. After Theresa's father was murdered…"

Badr leaned forward. "How do you know he was murdered?"

"Executed, murdered. What's the difference? She had his body flown to the United States. An autopsy proved he had been beaten and hung."

Badr's eyes hardened and he began writing in his note pad.

Peter continued. "Anyway, after he was killed, this Iraqi helped speed up the Fullers' arrangements to return to California. If you can find him…"

Without looking up, Badr asked, "Who was this Ba'ath Party official?"

"She said his name was Ibrahim Awali."

The colonel stopped writing. After a lengthy pause, he set his pen down, and stood up. "Thank you, Mr. Cranston. You have been most helpful. My guards will see that you are returned to the hotel immediately."

Peter sputtered. "Wai…Wait a minute. Don't you see? According to this man, the government knew the professor wasn't a spy. All you have to do is find this man to verify what I'm telling you."

"Yes, I am sure we will be talking to him." Badr moved out from behind his desk to open his door and call for a guard.

"What about letting me see Theresa? What harm will it do? I'm telling you she's not a spy."

"I do not think anything you have told me proves that. In any case, we must return you to the hotel in time. As you pointed out, we would not want CNN to broadcast your disappearance."

Peter continued to argue as the guard handcuffed him again and replaced his blindfold. "Just let me see her for a minute. Only a minute. I won't be late."

Badr didn't respond and he was led away. The guard pulled him along a hallway. They entered an elevator and descended. Ten seconds later they stopped and when the doors opened they walked a hundred paces or so until he felt cool air against his cheek. The Mukhabarat agents were returning him the same way they had brought him, after picking him up at the hotel. Or were they? He still didn't know where Theresa was being held. Perhaps he never would.

During the ride, Peter fingered Theresa's ring and reviewed what he had learned tonight. She was alive, at least for the moment. Thin, but alive. And she had grown attached to her Iraqi captor. Was it Stockholm Syndrome, or was she feigning affection for her advantage? He wanted to believe either scenario, but his gut told him otherwise. Theresa had looked at this officer in a way she had never regarded Peter. Had he made all these arrangements—the meeting with the Iraqi Embassy official in Amman to pass word he had important information, the drive across the desert from Jordan with a CNN crew to cover his story, the pickup by the Mukhabarat—only to have his heart crushed? Peter buried his covered face in his cuffed hands. What should he do now?

His thoughts returned to Theresa and all he had learned. She was in grave danger. Upon arrival at this unknown prison, even before the blindfold had been ripped from his eyes, Peter had heard the British accent and shuddered. Hearing that voice again dredged up the ripping pain in his arms and shoulders. This colonel was capable of anything. Peter hoped, for Theresa's sake, that the love and concern in the young captain's eyes had not been pretense.

The car slowed and stopped. He felt his cuffs being removed, followed by the blindfold. He was back at the Rashid. Peter felt a rush of relief as he got out of the car and, before he could turn around, it was gone. He walked into the lobby to search for his CNN colleagues and provide the promised interview. At least now her family would know for certain Theresa lived.

Later that night Peter lay in bed, unable to sleep. His life had revolved around Theresa these past several years. He realized now she would likely never love him in the way he wanted. To her, he would never be more than a friend. Peter held his hand up. Her ring glinted in the moonlight suffusing his hotel room. He took hold of it, intending to pull it off, but couldn't.

He wondered what Barham would say. The Kurd had always ribbed him about the ring, questioning its value as a good luck token. Peter thought back to their days in prison together, the camaraderie they had developed. He remembered the tragic story Barham told of his family's loss. It still had not been told to the world. The more he thought about it, the more he felt pulled to finish what Theresa had begun. That seemed to be the only thing left that he could do for her.

He decided then and there. He could not free Theresa from an Iraqi prison, but he could help Barham free his people from this regime, and tell their story. Unlike the rest of the world, the Kurds weren't waiting for Bush to attack. Fighting had already begun in the north, and Peter suddenly felt an urge to help. He was tired of standing by and simply taking pictures of victims.

ASIL

(Intelligence Headquarters—March 10, 2003)

Four Mondays had come and gone with no visit from Tariq. Theresa was desolate and near collapse. She had passed a month in seclusion and now there would be at least another week. As the light went off in her cell, she lay down. Tears soon dampened the small section of the filthy mattress under her head.

Had her touch scared him off? She couldn't believe that. Had his attention all been an act? Had Badr orchestrated all of this to break her? If so, she had to give him credit. Without Tariq's kind words and eyes, she was close to slipping out of the real world. And now her epilepsy was in full swing again. The pills had run out three weeks ago. She had suffered four episodes this past week alone.

Right now she didn't care if war came or not. She didn't care about being released. All she wanted was to see him again. Each Monday, she had scratched a line and waited. The first time he missed, she blamed herself. She shouldn't have kissed his hands that way. But he would be back. She told herself he needed some time away.

When he didn't come the following Monday, she began to worry. Had something happened to him? Had Badr found out about the book? Maybe he had been reassigned. She continued her routines of reciting history and poetry, interviewing celebrities, and humming classical music…but only half-heartedly. By the third Monday, she was frantic. Her routine evaporated. She began pacing her cell from morning to night each and every day, until today.

Today, she had opened her eyes with a feeling of dread. She scratched another line, starting a new row. It was March 10th, exactly a month since she had seen Tariq…or anyone, for that matter. She sat like a stone on her mattress, waiting. Breakfast came. She didn't move. The afternoon wore on. Her eyes grew vacant and glassy. At dinnertime, the person who retrieved her full breakfast plate said something in Arabic. She ignored the voice and the dinner he shoved through to her. Roaches attacked the untended food. She didn't care.

Now the lights were out, and she could not bring herself to pray. The first week she had done well. She kept her promise to Tariq. And it comforted her. After a few days of praying, she felt more at ease, more acceptable to God. But tonight, she was giving up. She had kept her part of the agreement. What about Tariq's? He had promised not to let her die in here. He said he would get her through. Where was he?

She lay for hours, sleepless and bereft of hope, until she heard faint footsteps in the middle of the night. They stopped outside her cell. Her door unlocked and swung open, and the beam of a flashlight blinded her eyes. Someone strode in, grabbed her, pulled her up roughly and tied a blindfold around her head. He dragged her out of the cell and forced her down a corridor. It wasn't Tariq, she knew that much. This man reeked of sweat and garlic.

Theresa didn't bother resisting. She imagined this was it. She said a final silent prayer asking God to help her be strong and help her family be stronger. She hoped Tariq would remember her fondly.

She was pulled up short after several turns, and shoved into a lighted room. She managed to keep her footing, but only barely. A door closed behind her and someone barked a command in Arabic. Was it Badr? The man with body odor forced her into a chair and jerked her blindfold down. Theresa blinked to focus.

She almost cried out in relief when she saw Tariq, but the look on his face froze her. He was seated behind a table to the right of Badr. His mouth stretched thin and tight. His black eyes, bloodshot and weighted with shadowy circles, begged her to be silent.

To Badr's left sat someone new, dressed in an expensive European-cut suit and silk tie, with gold cuff links at the wrists. The man looked like a younger version of Saddam Hussein. Badr paid him a great deal of deference as he whispered in the stranger's ear.

Theresa examined the man's face again and looked to Tariq for confirmation. When he gave the barest hint of a nod, she knew and sucked in a breath. She faced Saddam's younger son and heir apparent, Qusai. Her mind raced. Qusai Hussein directed all security in the state. Why was he here? Did this bode good or ill? Release or execution?

Badr cleared his throat before beginning. "I must say, Miss Fuller, you do not look very well. Of course, it has been some time since I saw you."

She didn't respond.

"We have brought you here tonight to ask you about your father. Have you remembered anything else since our last talk?"

She shook her head.

"That is a pity. It has taken time and a good bit of research as well as, shall we say, interviewing. But I believe I am in a position now to help jog your memory."

She still said nothing, but glanced at Tariq. Had he shared all their conversations with the colonel?

Badr noted her glance. "Captain al-Awali knows nothing of what I have uncovered. At least not yet. And I must apologize for keeping him so busy these past few weeks. He was unable to pay you his usual visit as a result. I hope you have not suffered Tariq's absence too much."

Inwardly, she rejoiced. Tariq hadn't avoided her. He had been forced to stay away. Outwardly, she gave Badr no more than a shake of the head.

The colonel smiled. "No? I am surprised. He has been known to have a much more lasting effect on most females."

Tariq's eyes belied the colonel's claim. Theresa relaxed again. She knew the captain's affection for her was true despite anything Badr might spin.

"I'm not like most females."

"Possibly not. But we shall see."

Badr opened a file that lay in front of him on the table, taking care to block Tariq's view of its contents. He took a moment to glance over the page lying on top before he looked up. "After a good deal of trouble I was able to locate your father's original case file. There were some very interesting aspects to his case."

Theresa's heartbeat quickened. Qusai leaned back in his chair, fixing her with his eyes. She shivered.

"For example, all of the witness reports against him are missing."

"What was he charged with?"

Badr snickered. "You still claim not to know?"

"Of course I don't know. I've already told you. I can't remember." Her voice carried more frustration than she wished to show, and she breathed in deeply to calm herself.

The colonel closed the file. "I want to help you re-member. But are you sure you don't recall anything about your father's case?"

She gritted her teeth. "I don't."

"Well, I believe I have located someone from your past who may help." He spoke in Arabic and a guard stepped out of the room.

When the door opened, she heard the high-pitched whimpering of a terrified woman being led in. Theresa wanted to turn and look, but she sat up straight, push-ing her back into the chair. Eventually, the woman was brought forward to stand in full view of Theresa.

Blindfolded and hands cuffed behind her, the wom-an's short, pudgy figure wobbled. Her hair held more gray than black. Theresa guessed her to be near sixty.

Badr barked something in Arabic and watched The-resa's face as the woman's blindfold was pulled down. The woman shrieked in surprise and then blinked at the lights, trying to get her bearings. Theresa squinted. There was something about her.

The woman scanned the men seated behind the table. At the sight of the man in the suit, dizziness over-came her and her knees buckled. One guard caught and held her while another pulled over a chair. Once she was seated, they slapped her face to bring her around again. This time her eyes swept in Theresa's direction and froze on her face.

She breathed in sharply and cried out. "Madame! Madame Fuller?"

As she spoke words Theresa had heard so often as a child, the woman revealed herself. It was Asil, their maid and childhood nanny. Theresa choked back tears. The woman looked at her in terror and confusion.

"Asil." Theresa pointed to herself. "*Inti* Theresa. Theresa, not Madame." As she said this, she noticed Tariq's face. A new fear filled his eyes. Was it for her or Asil?

Wonder spread across the old woman's face. "Ah, Theresa!" She started to babble in Arabic, commenting on how much Theresa had grown and how much she resembled her mother.

Badr cut in. "I see you recognize each other."

Asil's smile faded along with her Arabic. She now looked back and forth between the colonel and Theresa, searching for some clue as to why she had been hauled in here. What little English she had learned nearly forty years ago in the Fullers' employ had apparently been forgotten. The officer's use of English seemed to only add to her fear.

His voice oozed insincerity. "I am so touched to have brought you two together after all these years. It was not easy. Fortunately, these Assyrian Christians all seem to live in the same neighborhood, making my search a bit simpler. I am afraid, however, that time is short. You will have to exchange family news later."

The colonel gave his attention to Asil and began firing questions in Arabic. She nodded her head in assent and said, *"Naam"* to the first few. Theresa understood

Badr was establishing Asil's background as their maid years ago, but continued to act the innocent.

"Do you mind my asking what you're talking about?" she asked.

Badr gave her a cold look. "Yes, I do mind."

He turned back to Asil and resumed in Arabic. She began to look fearful, shaking her head and answering *"La"* to several questions. Theresa understood enough to know he had begun to hone in on her father's supposed clandestine activities. Despite a warning look from Tariq, she tried again.

"Are you asking her about my father? I thought I heard his name."

"You are becoming most tiresome, Miss Fuller." Badr's pitch heightened in irritation. "I cannot question one prisoner and translate for another at the same time. I will come to you presently."

Theresa argued. "But I'm sure I heard my father's name. I think you're asking her about my father."

"How astute of you."

"I have a right to know what you're asking."

The colonel and Qusai exchanged looks. Badr addressed her without smiling. "You have no rights. Remember? If you speak out of turn one more time I will have you choked and gagged."

Helpless, Theresa looked at Tariq. He avoided her eyes and her heart sank. Could he do nothing for her?

Asil's interrogation in Arabic resumed. The more the maid shook her head, the louder Badr yelled.

After five minutes of verbal haranguing, he gave an order and the two guards began to take turns beating the old woman about the face. Tears edged Theresa's eyes. She looked Tariq's way and felt relieved to see he was fighting his emotions, at least.

One of the guards picked up a metal rod and, aiming carefully, cracked it against Asil's jaw with one roundhouse swing. The old woman groaned, almost passing out. Theresa could no longer stay silent.

"Stop! Ask me these questions, not her."

Badr turned to her. "Very well."

"Let her go. Please."

"She stays. For every unsatisfactory answer you give, she will be struck. Was your father a spy?"

Theresa's mind raced. How should she respond? If she said no, they'd hurt Asil. If she said yes, maybe they wouldn't hurt her, but it wouldn't be true and it might be a trap for Theresa.

"Well?" Badr drummed his fingers on top of the file.

"I...don't think so."

"That is not good enough." He gave a quick nod to the guards and the one with the rod lashed out again. Asil's face began to swell.

"Stop it," Theresa begged.

"We can stop all of this as soon as you tell us about your father's assignment here in Baghdad. We know he was CIA. Who was his contact?"

She groaned and looked to Asil for forgiveness. "I don't know."

Badr started to give the guard the signal to strike but stopped, holding up his hand. He turned to Tariq. "Captain. Take over for the guards. Hit her."

The young man looked stunned. Theresa's heart pumped harder. Surely, Tariq wouldn't strike this old woman. She had told him so many funny, touching stories about Asil.

"Now." Badr sat back, waiting. In that moment Qusai leaned forward to regard the younger Mukhabarat officer. His look propelled Tariq to his feet. Wooden, he walked from behind the desk to face the figure of this battered old woman.

The colonel yelled, "Hit her!" Tariq flinched, closed his eyes, and swung hard. His blow caught her flush on the side of the face and sent her sprawling onto the floor. He stooped to help her up and seated her back down, whispering something in Arabic.

Badr noticed. "What did you say to her?"

Tariq turned with his head down. "I only told her she should have told the truth." He wouldn't look at Theresa as he sat back down by the colonel.

Her stomach churned. She realized Tariq had no choice. If he wanted to stay alive, he had to do Badr's bidding, and do it convincingly.

Badr whispered something to Saddam's son, who nodded. The colonel turned back to Theresa. "Perhaps now you will tell us about your father." He paused. "If not, we could have your maid raped. Would you like that? In this case we could have the captain here do the honors."

Was there no end to the evil in this man? Theresa looked at the panic in Tariq's eyes and gave up. She would lie, say whatever they wanted to hear, for better or worse. Anything to end this torment.

"That won't be necessary," said Theresa. "I'll tell you about my father."

Badr smiled and leaned forward. "He was a spy, yes?"

"Yes." The lie curdled her stomach.

"I knew you would remember. CIA?"

"Yes."

"How did you find out?"

Her mind raced. She decided her only recourse was to recount every little suspicious thing she had ever seen him do.

Badr repeated himself. "How did you know he was a spy?"

"It dawned on me gradually. You have to remember, I was only nine. We saw a James Bond film that year. I don't remember which one. Maybe it was 'Goldfinger.' We saw it on the outdoor screen at the Alwiya Club. And something about his character made me think of my father. He always had secret hiding places to conceal weapons and notes and things."

"Your father?"

"No, Bond. But one day I discovered my father had a secret place too."

"What kind of a secret place?"

"In his bookshelf in the study. I walked in one day when he was putting a piece of paper in a hidden compartment."

"Where in the bookshelf?"

"At the bottom. I tried to open it later."

Badr started scribbling notes. "Did you succeed?"

"Yes, but it was empty."

"What color was this bookshelf? What kind of wood?"

She closed her eyes to visualize it. "A light colored wood. I don't know what kind."

The colonel looked at Asil and asked her about the bookshelf in Arabic. Her reply seemed to satisfy him. He turned to Theresa. "Go on. What else made you suspect him?"

She searched for something else to say. "He and Mom were always going to parties, meeting lots of different people…just like Bond."

Badr dismissed this with a wave. "Did your father meet or contact anyone in particular in a secretive way?"

The tension in the room had diminished. Theresa decided to take advantage. Perhaps Badr would let Asil go.

She made an attempt. "There was someone. I'll tell you, but there's no sense in keeping Asil here. All his meetings with this person were at the Alwiya Club. She never saw this person. Let her go now and I'll tell you more."

Badr considered, and looked at Qusai, who leaned over and said something. The colonel nodded.

"Very well. I'll send her back to the holding cell. She can always be called again should you become less co-operative."

Theresa nodded and Badr gave the order. She watched sadly as the maid was blindfolded again and taken from the room. She prayed that Asil was being sent to a cell, and not an execution.

The door closed and Badr resumed. "Now, tell me about this contact. How old was he?"

"The contact was a woman, not a man."

Badr and Qusai exchanged surprised looks. They reviewed something in the file and whispered back and forth for a moment. Saddam's younger son looked at his watch. He pushed his chair back and stood up. Everyone in the room stood and came to attention—everyone but Theresa. Qusai swept out of the room without so much as a glance in her direction.

Once Saddam's son was gone, the collective sigh in the room almost brought a smile to Theresa's face.

But Badr gave her little time to relax. "All right. You said a woman. How old?"

"She looked like she was in her early twenties."

"Iraqi?"

"Yes."

"How can you be sure?"

"She and her mother were introduced to us one day at the club. And I remember Mom saying that the father was an important member of the Ba'ath Party."

Theresa wasn't lying. She had met this woman under those circumstances. She only thought to use her because she had seen this Iraqi with her father and they had acted in a sneaky kind of way. Fortunately, Theresa couldn't remember her name, so she wouldn't cause trouble for her as she had for Asil.

Badr was skeptical. "How can you be sure you are remembering this correctly? What nine-year-old would know what the Ba'ath Party meant?"

"That's just it. I didn't. I embarrassed myself and my parents by asking how many baths you had to take to be invited to a bath party." She smiled weakly. Tariq coughed. Badr frowned.

Theresa continued. "That's why I remember that day. My brother called me stupid. He yelled at me in front of this woman and her mother. But the woman smiled and patted me on the head. She seemed nice."

"Describe her."

Theresa looked down a moment and shook her head. "I remember she had shoulder-length black hair and she was very pretty. That's all."

Badr sat poised with his pen. "What was her name?"

"I don't know."

Frustration tightened his mouth. "What do you mean you don't know. You say you remember that day, being introduced to her. Surely you can remember her name."

Theresa shook her head. "I remember the incident. I don't remember the names. Mom and Dad were always introducing us to their friends. They had so many. All those Arabic names confused me."

"But you gave me some names back in the other prison."

"Yes," Theresa agreed. "I gave you a few names, ones that I'd heard several times, but I wouldn't be able to match them with faces."

The colonel rolled his pen between his fingers. "You can't remember either her first name or her family name?"

"No." She hoped he would give up.

"How many times did you see her with your father?"

"Three or four."

He began taking notes again. "And they met alone or in a group?"

Theresa thought for a moment. "Other than the time I was introduced, they met alone."

"Where? And how did you see them?"

"At the club. They usually met by the snack bar. Once, I saw him pass a note to her there."

Badr stopped writing and looked at her. "How can you be sure it was a note? How close were you?"

"I was up on the high diving platform…only about ten feet away. They didn't know I was watching."

He put his pen down. "So you were doing a bit of spying yourself? What was in the note?"

"I don't know."

"What did she do with it?"

Theresa hesitated. "I think she put it in her bag. Then she left."

"Did your mother know about these meetings?"

"I don't think so."

Badr regarded her strangely. "Your mother didn't know about these meetings? You didn't tell her or anyone else?"

Theresa paused. "No."

"Why not?"

Why hadn't she told her brother or her Mom about what she had observed? She thought for a moment. "I don't think I told because it felt good to help keep his secret."

Badr's smile looked dangerous. "Maybe it still feels good."

"What do you mean? I'm telling you everything now."

"Are you?" He picked up the top page from the file, stood and came around the table in front of her. "I think there is a lot you are not telling me. Why is your name one of the few on this witness list that is circled? All the names are checked off, including those of your mother and brother. Apparently the three of you were questioned. But yours is the only family name circled. Can you explain that?"

A chill ran up her spine to the back of her neck. "I was questioned about my father?"

Badr nodded. "You don't recall that?"

Stunned, Theresa shook her head.

Badr put the paper on the table behind him, face down, and turned back to face the American. "You have one last chance to give me the name of your father's contact."

She couldn't stop thinking about her name being circled. "I've already told you. I don't remember."

"Either the first name or the family name."

"But I don't…"

Her reply was cut off by a vicious backhand to her left cheek, knocking her head to the side. Tariq jumped up from his seat to come to her aid. At the sound of his chair scraping the floor, the colonel turned and stopped the young man in his tracks.

"Do you object, Captain? Or perhaps you would like to take over for me?" Badr massaged the back of his left hand.

Tariq sat again, unable to look Theresa in the eyes.

The colonel turned back to his prisoner. "We have been very patient with you, Miss Fuller. I think that up until now you would have to agree you have been rather well treated. Have you not?"

Her cheek still smarted from the blow, but she now knew better than to cross this man.

"Have you not been treated well?"

She mumbled in the affirmative.

"Yes, you have. I allowed the captain here to conduct most of your interviews in the belief that a less confrontational style might elicit the information we need. You may find this hard to believe after all that you have witnessed, but I am not generally given to violence. In fact, I try to avoid it. But I believe now we have taken an altogether too kind approach with you. We have threatened, yes, and we have even hurt some of your friends and acquaintances. We could continue on that track but I think it would take too long. Times are urgent. We must know all our enemies now. Both those outside our boundaries and particularly those within."

"But I don't see how I can help…"

He slapped her hard on the right side of her face, stinging her other cheek. "You said this woman was the daughter of a high Ba'ath official. Someone who has cooperated with CIA before may choose to do so again. Give me a name."

Afraid, she looked to Tariq for assistance. As she did, the tingling began in her throat. She stared past him, welcoming the episode, losing herself in the waves of sensation she felt lapping in her head.

"Answer me!" Badr yelled.

She heard his yell but could not muster the will to respond. Every part of her focused inward, away from Badr and Tariq, away from all of this. She barely sensed the colonel grabbing the metal rod from the guard and swinging, catching her with its sharp end. The blow nearly knocked her off the chair and opened a cut on her cheek. Rather than interrupt the episode, the pain served to increase the intense feelings in her head. The pulsing became a roar.

SEIZURE

(Intelligence Headquarters—March 10, 2003)

Enraged by Theresa's continued unresponsiveness, Badr handed the rod back and ordered the guard to continue beating her with it. But before the guard could take up a position to strike, Tariq stepped forward. He had seen the distant look in her eyes and understood.

"Wait, Colonel. I think you should know this woman suffers from epilepsy."

Badr spun around. "What?"

"I only learned recently that Miss Fuller has epilepsy and she has run out of her medication. She's not responding because she's having a seizure."

Badr scoffed. "Ridiculous. No doubt she made that story up to manipulate you. She is not responding because she is being obstinate." He turned back to the guard and barked, *"Yalla."*

Tariq caught the rod before it could touch Theresa's face. "Colonel, it's true. I've seen these spells before. You must wait, at least, until she comes out of it."

Badr sneered. "This is no seizure. Need I remind you what a seizure looks like, Captain?" The colonel called for a machine in the corner of the room to be brought forward and placed on the table. He gave instructions in Arabic. A guard tied Theresa to the chair, clamped electrical wires to her ear lobes, and waited for the order.

The colonel looked at Tariq, whose eyes had grown wide with fear. "You have a choice, Captain. You may flip the switch, yourself, or face the same fate later. Only with you I will not be so considerate as to where the electrical clamps are placed. I am having serious doubts about your loyalty to me and our president."

Tariq bit his lip, drew himself up and saluted. "There is nothing to doubt, sir." He walked to the machine, located the appropriate switch and, looking into Theresa's staring eyes, pushed it forward.

Her whole body immediately seized as an excruciating current of electricity coursed through her head, wiping out the episode's waves. She strained against the ropes, agonizing for five seconds until he flipped the switch back.

Badr's lip curled at the sight. "Now that is what I call a seizure. But you didn't do it long enough. Hit it again."

THE RECKONING

Tariq paused before complying. In that moment of hesitation he saw Theresa slump in her chair. The muscles in her arms stiffened. For a moment she looked frozen. Then she began to convulse violently, tipping the chair over and, in the process, dislodging both electrical clamps.

She lay on the floor, still tied to the chair, shaking and jerking for a minute before Tariq realized what was happening. He rushed to her side and started to untie her, but then changed his mind. Realizing the chair and ropes kept her limbs safely restrained, Tariq concentrated on trying to hold her head still without getting hurt or bit.

Confused by the sight of drool around her mouth, Badr tried to regain control. "What game is she playing?"

Tariq looked up while holding her. "It's not a game. I told you, she's an epileptic. The electric shock must have brought on a grand mal seizure."

The colonel watched, for the first time unsure, as the spasms eased gradually. The thrashing stopped. When Theresa lay still, Tariq loosened her cords and stood to face his superior.

He spoke quietly, but firmly. "She's of no use to you now, sir. She'll probably sleep for several hours. And when she wakes up, she won't be able to think clearly for some time."

"How long?" Badr seemed anxious, even afraid.

Tariq took advantage of his discomfort. "She'll have to have at least a week to recover and two weeks of no stress if she is to be in shape for further questioning."

"Two weeks? But the Americans may attack any day now."

Tariq held firm. "Two weeks. You can't press her any more until she's rested. It would be useless."

Badr argued. "How can I be sure you know what you are talking about? I could call for a specialist."

The captain shrugged. "Go ahead. He'll tell you the same. My grandmother showed me many cases like this. Stress makes the seizures worse."

Badr bent down to take a closer look at Theresa. He slapped her face hard. No reaction. She slept on. The seizure had caused her to wet her pants. He straightened up in disgust at the sight and smell.

Tariq pressed the advantage further. "She should also have a bath and a change of clothes."

The colonel waved his arm, wanting to be rid of her and the stink. "Very well. See to it…once she's awake."

Far from pleased, Badr snapped at the guards in Arabic. They reached down, picked up Theresa's limp body by the arms and legs, and carried her out of the room back to her cell.

The colonel picked up the file on the table and turned to leave. On his way out, he paused in front of Tariq. "Check on her again in a week, Captain. Not before. If she seems rested, you will let me know immediately."

Tariq waited until Badr left before righting the chair. He looked again at the machine on the table, closed his eyes for a moment, then hastened to Theresa's cell to keep watch.

THE WOMAN

(Intelligence Headquarters—March 10, 2003)

The door clanged shut and Theresa stood, unable to move, hardly able to think. Her body ached all over and her head pulsated with pain. Had the bath been real? She had felt the warm water soothing her tender scalp as an unknown woman washed her hair, and then heard the snips as her dyed brown locks fell around her, but perhaps the experience had been a dream or an episode. She lifted her arm and smelled. Roses and soap. She ran her fingers through newly trimmed hair. Was she fully blonde again?

The hatch opened behind her. She turned to see stew and bread pushed in. It slammed shut again. Dinner? But she had already had dinner…before the midnight session. Had she slept all day? Her brain tried to calculate but a fog blurred the numbers. She ignored the food and looked back at her mattress.

Theresa yearned to collapse into sleep again, but she couldn't will her legs to lead her. So she stood, rooted to the floor of her cell. An hour later, the light flicked off. Still, she stood.

Eventually, her mind began to focus, recalling Badr's words about her name and the witness list. They sounded strange at first, as if played on a machine at the wrong speed. By the fourth repetition the speed was right and the words were as clear as their implication: she had somehow helped put her father in prison.

A high-pitched scream reached her ears from far down the hall. She closed her eyes and brought her hands to the sides of her head, trying to block the sound. What were they doing to that poor woman? Or was it a man? Theresa began to shake involuntarily. She rocked back and forth to control the shaking until the screaming stopped.

In the ensuing silence, her thoughts returned to her father. Could it be true? Or was the colonel playing games with her? She couldn't recall ever being questioned as a child by any Iraqi official. If they had indeed suspected her father of spying, would they really have hauled in his family for interrogation? She could understand their questioning her mother...but the children?

Theresa staggered forward and sank down to her mattress. She sat with her back against the wall, careful of her bruises and determined to reason her way through this puzzle despite her overwhelming fatigue.

Under Saddam Hussein, children had been taken into custody and questioned. She had even read accounts of some being beaten and raped in front of their parents to loosen a mother or father's tongue. But her father's arrest occurred almost forty years ago…before the Baghdad Butcher came into power.

Theresa closed her eyes. Had she ever felt threatened by others as a child? They lived through the two 1963 revolutions—the one in February bringing the Ba'ath Party to power, and the second in November when the party was exiled again. But she had seen these through a child's eyes, noticing the excitement, not the danger.

The anti-aircraft fire and bombing of the Ministry of Defense near the city center, seen from such a distance, were like colorful fireworks displays. Cooped up in the house and kept from school during two-week curfews, she and Jimmy and Angela had run for the nearest roof at the first sound of gunfire or explosions. The whole family gathered to watch. Their large two-story home had two separate roofs, providing prime views of any military firepower. All of it seemed more exciting than dangerous.

But, gradually, Theresa remembered something else. Her mother told them later that they had been fortunate the Ba'ath beat the Communists to the punch in 1963.

"The Communists were also trying to get rid of Qasim?" she had asked her mother.

"Yes." Her mother's eyes had grown solemn. "Shortly before that day in February, we found our black metal gate marked in chalk. A friend later told us that, had the Communists revolted successfully, we had been marked for removal."

The memory of her mother's reply had a more chilling effect on Theresa now. Perhaps her father had been a spy, after all, or, at least, suspected of being one. Why else would their whole family have been targeted? Perhaps children, regardless of nationality, have never been safe in Iraq. Maybe they were always blamed for the sins of their fathers. She decided it was conceivable, after all, that she had been questioned about her father.

But why couldn't she remember it? What could she possibly have said to get her name circled? She shook her head in frustration. Try as she might, that last summer of 1965 remained a blank in her mind.

Perhaps she was going about it in the wrong way. Rather than trying to recall events and facts, maybe she should examine the change in her feelings and attitudes.

For a long time now, Theresa had acknowledged very mixed feelings for her father, feelings she had been unwilling to probe. She could no longer afford to avoid it.

As she had grown, few men came close to equaling Nathan Fuller in her eyes. Tall and assured, with the contemplative gaze of a thinker, he had been her hero…able to answer any question and solve any problem. As much as she loved her mother, she had aspired to be like her father. Until…until what? Something had happened that summer. Something came between them.

She had been his favorite. At least, she always felt that way. And they had often enjoyed long talks together. She believed everything he ever told her about people, about the world, even about God. She believed in God because he did. He was never wrong about anything.

The crowning moments sealing them together, in her memory, had occurred Easter weekend of 1964. On Saturday, the day before her scheduled baptism, they climbed the ziggurat at Samara together. They lingered at the top and talked of the importance of the step she would be taking the next morning. A lay minister, he shared his own feelings about Jesus and she shivered in the calm and powerful spirit around them as he talked. The next morning, at six o'clock, he helped her down into the pool waters before the Alwiya Club opened to the public; he was the last one she saw as she was dipped under the water and the first when she was brought back up again.

She recalled the look of pride in his eyes that morning and the memory now brought a wave of guilt. She had stayed true to her faith for little more than a year… until he had been arrested and imprisoned. Had she prayed for his release? She couldn't remember. After his death, her prayers became hollow utterings, voiced to show her mother she still believed. But she didn't.

Indeed, she began to doubt everything about God and organized religion. She kept it concealed for a time, continuing to give all the expected answers in Sunday School. But by the time she turned fourteen, Theresa no longer cared about appearances. God was irrelevant, His church a sham. She loved her mother, so she took care not to engage in emotional scenes about religion, but her determined, matter-of-fact rejection hurt her family nonetheless. Eventually, they learned to accommodate each other by avoiding any discussion of church or God.

Theresa had always thought her loss of faith was due to her father's imprisonment. How could a compassionate God allow such a man to die in prison? She suspected now, however, that there was more to it. His imprisonment, by itself, was not a sufficient reason. After all, Jimmy had remained true to his faith…as had Mother. But what other reason could there be?

The headache lingered in the recessed areas above her ears. Theresa brought her hands up to rub her temples, but flinched at the pain from Badr's bruising. She touched her earlobes and recalled the pleading look in Tariq's eyes as he had flipped the switch.

She tried to imagine him doing it again and, instead of feeling the high voltage shock, she sensed the subtle tingling beginning in her neck. Another episode. Would it be difficult or pleasant?

With the aura came a vision.

She was walking out the gates of their Baghdad home with Asil and her sister, Angela. Theresa looked as she had at seven. Angela, with her five-year-old legs, took twice as many steps to keep up. The young maid walked between them, holding fast to their hands. Beyond the gates, they turned left and headed toward the grassy circle near their house in Saadun Park. They had walked that way many times. But today Theresa wanted to explore something new. She urged Asil to keep turning left. She wanted to walk past the small sarifa village across the street on that side of their walled home, and climb the hill behind.

Asil tried to argue. "No. We go circle. Circle nice for sitting. Meet my friend there."

One of their maid's best friends worked for the Indian consul's family across the way and they often met in the grassy area to gossip while their charges played together.

Theresa insisted on altering the plan today. Supported by Angela, she convinced the maid to give in and lead them up the hill first. It looked like a mountain to their young eyes, and Theresa had often wondered what lay on the other side. They lived in a newer, well-to-do area of the dusty city and she imagined palaces and other wonders beyond that hill.

The climb was arduous but several minutes later they crested the top. The smell struck Theresa before she could take in the view. At that elevation, a strong breeze carried the awful stench of the poverty laid out before them. Both Theresa and her sister covered their noses to keep from gagging. A mud brick sarifa city stretched for miles, populated by peasant families. Farmers worked their water buffalo and women baked bread in

*outdoor ovens or hung laundry to dry in the sun. Everywhere
they looked children, mostly naked, ran and played in the dirt,
mud, and open sewers.*

*Theresa pulled on Asil's hand. She had seen enough. She
wanted to go back to her home and breathe again. Descending
the hill, she asked the maid why those people lived like that. Asil
only said something in Arabic and shook her head.*

The vision ended. Theresa was back in her black-
ened cell, struck again by what she had seen that day
through younger eyes. The adventure had provided her
first clue in life that things are not always what you imagine. She realized again, sitting on her prison mattress,
that most of her world was a self-contained thing, having little in common with much beyond her walls.

Exhausted from the interrogation, the seizure, the
puzzle of her father, and now this, Theresa lay down
and closed her eyes. As she did, the far-off screaming
resumed, accompanied by yells and shrieks from other
corners of the prison. Had she screamed like that? She
clenched her teeth and curled into a fetal position, waiting for sleep to rescue her.

It didn't. Instead, the tingling began again, creeping up her throat. She swallowed as the pulsing inside her head returned. Another so soon? She needed
more medicine. Unable to fight the episode's inexo-
rable pull, Theresa opened her eyes. Instead of seeing
the darkness of her cell, another vision opened to her
mind.

She lay in bed, sick with the flu. A fourth grader, she had stayed home from school under the care of Asil. But she heard her father come home early and send the maid out for some groceries. She wanted to call out for him, but felt too weak. Her eyes gave in to sleep but other noises soon woke her. Hot and thirsty, she heard a woman's giggle coming from her parents' bedroom. Was Mother back already from her Wednesday Kaboul—the weekly coffee party?

She slid out of bed, opened her door, and walked barefoot toward the Master Bedroom at the end of the hall. Mother could get her something to drink. She turned the doorknob and pushed. But the giggling made her stop at the doorway. Bodies moved under the sheets of the king-size bed. Theresa's mouth fell open when the cover sheet slipped. She saw her father, undressed, lying on top of her mother, caressing and kissing her in a way the young girl had never seen before.

Theresa's cheeks burned hot and she turned to run. In her hurry, she bumped against the door. Her mother looked toward the noise and the nine-year-old child gasped. The face was not her mother's. The eyes of the young Iraqi woman—the one she had seen at the pool—locked on hers, freezing her.

Her father's voice broke the spell when he addressed the woman. "What is it, Tahira?"

Theresa fled back to her bedroom, shut the door and buried her head under her covers, sobbing into her pillow.

She came out of the vision still sobbing as the tingling ceased.

REUNION

(Sulaimaniya—March 16, 2003)

Black flags flew everywhere. Peter had arrived in Sulai-maniya, in Kurdish Northern Iraq, late the night before, so he hadn't noticed them in the darkness as the taxi took him to his hotel. This morning, they fluttered from buildings and car antennas all over this city of six hundred thousand.

He left the Suleimani Palace Hotel at eleven o'clock, passing through a ring of armed pesh merga for the Patriotic Union of Kurdistan. The PUK, one of the two main Iraqi Kurdish parties, had established its head-quarters here only thirty miles from the Iraqi-controlled front lines, where Saddam's army patrolled. From Su-laimaniya, the PUK controlled the eastern portion of Iraqi Kurdistan, leaving the western part to its rival, the Kurdish Democratic Party, or KDP. Together, under the protection of America's northern no-fly zone, they had run an autonomous, self-styled government free from the dictates of Baghdad for several years now.

Since the end of January, the PUK had been on heightened alert, however. With war on the horizon, threats from the Iraqi regime had recently been made against Americans in Northern Iraq. Journalists, in particular, had been warned they might be targeted for assassination.

At the hotel Peter had been offered a bodyguard, but he declined, not having used one the previous August when he and Theresa passed through. But tension filled the city now that war loomed. He would breathe easier once he found Barham.

Peter shook off his unease and hailed a taxi. "Take me to PUK headquarters."

The driver gave him a funny look, shrugged, and put his car into gear, merging into traffic.

Peter settled back in the seat and mapped out his plans for the day. He hoped to begin with an interview of the Kurdish party leader, Jalal Talabani.

After leaving Baghdad a month ago, he had driven by car back to Amman, Jordan, obtained his press permit from the American Embassy, then set out for Turkey with his CNN crew. The bureaucracy was a lot less organized in the north. Peter was counting on the chaos to provide an opportunity to slip back over the border into Kurdish-controlled territory in order to locate his old Kurdish friend.

Fortunately, a conference of Iraqi opposition groups was scheduled to start sometime later in February in the Kurdish-run enclave. Rumors spread that the Turks would soon open their border, allowing journalists into Iraq to cover the conference. Peter had fingered his good luck ring over and over and, sure enough, days later he had joined a convoy of over one hundred reporters heading for Arbil, the undeclared capitol of Iraqi Kurdistan.

The weather had been cold and rainy the day the group crossed the border from Turkey...far different from the Iraqi climate he had left in November. Regardless of the chill, Peter was back and determined this time to do more than take pictures. He spent an obligatory two weeks reporting on the conference and the status of Kurdish preparations for war. Then he parted company with the CNN crew and headed east to Sulaimaniya.

First, he would talk with Talabani and seek official permission to accompany Barham and his group wherever they patrolled. Next, with or without the leader's sanction, Peter would seek his old friend out at the café Barham had mentioned more than once as his favorite hangout in the city.

Peter still thought of Theresa, but her release had now become, by necessity, a secondary goal. Since the Turks had chosen not to cooperate fully with U.S. war efforts, he couldn't head south toward Baghdad until Saddam's troops in the north had been beaten and scattered. If he was lucky, he might join up with a Special

Forces group assigned a mission in that direction. Until then, he would cover the Kurds' war and hopefully play a part.

The taxi slowed to a stop. When it didn't move after a minute, Peter looked up. It had come to a standstill in the middle of the street without even pulling over. Every other vehicle had also braked. Peter looked out the window and noticed everyone on the sidewalks frozen with heads bowed.

He questioned the driver. "What's going on? Why is everyone stopped?"

The Kurd raised his head, glared at Peter in his rear view mirror, and brought his finger to his mouth. "Ssshh. March 16. Halabja." He bent his head again.

After several seconds, cars started forward again, people resumed their normal routines, and Peter's taxi driver looked up and continued down the street.

The Canadian's eyes squinted in confusion. "I don't understand. What happened back there?"

The driver turned his head, incredulous. He spoke in broken English. "Fifteen year ago, this day, Halabja attacked with chemical weapons. Every year, 11:20 a.m., we remember. Five thousand dead. We do not forget. Ever."

It finally dawned on him. "That's why you have black flags everywhere."

The driver nodded vigorously. "Stores close today. Why you go PUK? No one there."

"No one?"

The Kurd shook his head. "Talabani and others not there. Maybe they go to meetings to remember Halabja."

Peter looked at his watch, wondering if he should ask to be taken to one of the memorial services. After all, if he was going to join their cause, he ought to seek more clarification of what drove them. But it was almost lunchtime and he didn't want to miss Barham. Besides, he was ravenous. Since prison, he had eaten twice his normal portions, partly to regain the weight he had lost, but also because he was always hungry. Perhaps Barham would escort him to a memorial after lunch. If he found him.

He tapped the driver's shoulder. "Do you know Bosch Cafe? For eating?"

"You want eat? Kurdish food, yes? Bosch very good."

Peter nodded, nervous about trusting his still queasy stomach to genuine local fare. Perhaps he should try and convince Barham to join him back at the hotel where the cuisine was safer.

The driver turned down a narrow street. "Pesh merga eat this place. Talabani love food this place."

"Good." Maybe he would run into the PUK leader here, as well as his old friend.

They pulled up outside a narrow doorway with a sign in Kurdish he couldn't read, guarded by two Kurdish fighters. As the journalist leaned forward to pay the fare, he saw the door open. Four more pesh merga emerged, guns slung over their shoulders. They paused to light up cigarettes. Bidding farewell to the guards, they headed across the street to a battered car.

The taxi driver accompanied Peter to the door, and explained that the Westerner was a journalist looking for good food. Smiling, the guards stood aside to let him enter. Peter made arrangements for the taxi to return in an hour, in case he wasn't able to find Barham, and walked into the dim, smoke-filled room.

In the time it took his eyes to adjust, the talking and singing ceased. More than twenty heads turned his way. One rose above the others.

"Peter? Peter, you came back!" The unmistakable figure of Barham bounded toward him, wrapping him in a bear hug that sent waves of pain up through his shoulders. The Kurd let go only to grab the Canadian by the arms and kiss him on both cheeks.

Groaning, but pleased, Peter looked his old friend over. "Well, check it out. In a uniform, no less."

Barham puffed his chest out and turned around. "You like it? I command a PUK brigade now. Many of these are my men."

Peter scanned the room and nodded approvingly.

The Kurd poked him in the chest. "But how did you find this place?"

"Bosch? How could I forget the name? You must have told me about the food here a hundred times back at Abu Ghraib. A taxi driver brought me here."

"Come, sit and eat." Barham took his friend by the arm and led him back to his table. After introducing

Peter to his comrades, he arranged for them to sit at another table so he could talk with his old prison mate alone.

As soon as Peter sat down, a waiter approached with two bottles of beer, compliments of the house. Barham ordered for both of them. It seemed strange to hear him speaking in Kurdish rather than the Arabic he had used with Pants.

The waiter left with their order, and Barham faced his old friend. "Did you ever find Theresa?"

Peter nodded. "It took me a while."

"Where was she?"

"Some prison in or around Baghdad. I still don't know which one."

Barham squinted. "What do you mean? I thought you said you found her."

"I put the word out that I had information on her father, and the Mukhabarat came knocking. They blind-folded me, pushed me into a car, and guess whose office I ended up in?"

Barham shrugged.

"That colonel. The one who tortured us."

"I do not remember him clearly."

Peter took a sip of his beer. "Well I do. He's inhabited half of my nightmares for the past six months."

"And he let you see Theresa?"

"Not directly. She's being kept in isolation in a cell with a hidden camera. He turned on the TV monitor to prove she was still alive."

"Maybe it was a tape."

Peter shook his head. "He had that captain, the same one who arrested us, take a current magazine into the cell while we watched. Do you remember that guy's name, by the way?"

Barham thought for a minute. "Tariq something. I am sorry, I cannot remember his last name. Why?"

"Yeah, I couldn't remember his last name either, and the colonel wouldn't tell me. Never mind. She looked okay except she'd lost a lot of weight."

"What information did you have to trade?"

Peter told him about his Thanksgiving visit with Theresa's family and his conversation with her mother.

Barham interrupted. "So Theresa had lived in Iraq as a child. The colonel was not lying."

Peter nodded. "Her father was a professor at Baghdad University. I saw pictures of him with his fellow professors."

"Was he CIA?"

"Her mother said no. But he was arrested and charged as a spy. And get this. He died in prison." Peter leaned back in his chair.

Barham was shocked. "They executed an American?"

"The Iraqis claimed he killed himself. Mrs. Fuller couldn't accept that. When his body was returned to the U.S., there were a lot of bruises on it and she had it autopsied. He died by hanging, but she refuses to believe he did it to himself."

"Why?"

Peter shrugged. "She said he wasn't that kind of man. I guess his grandfather committed suicide and he had a hard time getting over it. She couldn't imagine anything would lead him to do the same."

Barham poured beer for both of them. "Still, you and I both know that prison and torture can change a man. In any case, this cannot be good for Theresa. Saddam is paranoid. A whisper of treachery or disloyalty by one person can mean death for the whole family. If he thinks her father was a spy…"

"I know. I gave them the name of a high Ba'ath official involved in the case. A friend of the Fullers. Hopefully, he's still around and the authorities will look him up. If only I could figure out what building she was in."

"What about the U.S. government?"

Peter rolled his eyes. "They won't do anything. They're gearing up for war. This just gives them one more reason to invade. The State Department believes me, of course. But there's no paper trail. There's nothing to prove she ever entered Iraq, other than my word. Not even pictures, since the Mukhabarat confiscated all my cameras."

Barham put his glass down. "Perhaps I can help."

Peter's heart skipped a beat.

"My brother and father were at the same place as she. They saw her. A date farm outside Baghdad."

"You don't mean Radwaniyah? I had that place checked out."

Barham shook his head. "No, this was a small farm, small prison, quite isolated from what they could tell."

"What were the cells like?"

"Old, dirt floor. They had windows."

Peter shook his head. "They must have moved her since then. This was a newer cell. And I think the building has an elevator. I'm pretty certain it's in Baghdad. I'll just have to wait until the war starts and the American forces occupy the capitol."

Barham poured more beer. "Not to worry. Theresa is strong. She will be okay."

Peter thought of her with the captain, and changed the subject. "How did you find your father and brother? Did they get released the same day we did?"

Barham smiled. "Long before that. Back in August. I spent one week in Baghdad looking, gave up, and came home. I opened the door to our house and there they sat."

Peter was happy for his friend. "That's wonderful. Are they part of your brigade?"

Barham looked down. "No. They had been tortured."

"Worse than us?"

"They cut off my brother's right hand. He can never fight again."

Peter gasped. "Why? Why did they cut it off?"

"To get Theresa to talk."

"I'm sorry…"

Barham held up his hand. "This is what happens here. At least she began to cooperate and he didn't have to lose the other one too."

Peter put his hand on Barham's shoulder. "And your father?"

The Kurd shrugged. "He was only beaten. You can still see some of the bruising, and his left eye droops. But he has mostly recovered. Massoud depends on him, though. So I am the only fighter left in the family."

"Well, as far as I'm concerned, one of you is worth ten Iraqis."

Barham smiled. "So what brings you here? Are you here to cover the war?"

"Well, maybe a little...but, mainly, I came to find you."

The waiter brought their food, beginning with *dowjic*, a chicken and yogurt soup. Moments later he set steaming plates of bulgur pilaf down before them. Skewers of juicy lamb kebabs, with chunks of green peppers, tomatoes, and onions, bordered the pilaf. Despite the intoxicating smell of spicy lamb and the nutty flavor of the bulgur wheat, Peter ate with diminished appetite. His thoughts kept returning to Theresa.

As they finished, and sipped from small glasses of sweet Kurdish tea, their conversation turned to the coming war. Peter asked what role the Kurdish fighters could play since American troops wouldn't be on the ground in the north in the numbers previously envisioned.

Turkey had refused to allow their bases to be used as staging grounds, making the original battle plans in the north unfeasible.

"Even with small groups we can make a difference," Barham replied. "Besides, we are working with some Special Forces already."

"Doing what?"

Barham smiled. "Preparing to root out the rats in the mountains."

Peter leaned forward. "You mean Ansar al-Islam?"

The Kurd nodded. "We think the Ansari are the ones behind the recent threat against Americans here. There are plans being drawn up by the Special Forces to attack them in a big way, soon. In the meantime, we are helping to scout out their locations."

"Can I come along?"

"Are you after a story?"

Peter nodded. "I want to finish the story we set out to do...and more."

Barham raised an eyebrow. "More?"

"I want to tell the world about your fight for independence. And help in the fight, if I can."

The Kurd looked down for a minute. "I suppose all of your equipment is back at the hotel?"

Peter nodded. "Only two 35 millimeter cameras. I'm freelancing for the Los Angeles Times. Since Abu Ghraib I can't lug around anything much heavier."

"Are you sure you want to do this, Peter? Remember that these men are ideologues. Extremely dangerous. As we well know."

Peter cleared his throat and stood up from the table. "I'd like to think that if I lived through Abu Ghraib, luck is on my side." He pulled his ring back up past the knuckle of his middle finger as he spoke. He had lost so much weight in prison that he had moved it from his ring finger. It continued to slip off too easily.

"You've still got that lucky ring?" Barham slapped him on the back. "Good. We'll need it."

BREAKING POINT

(Intelligence Headquarters—March 17, 2003)

Theresa's cheekbones stuck out and she had to hold up her pants the few times she stood to use the toilet. Racked with guilt and tormented by the memory of her father's betrayal, she had languished prostrate for seven days and nights on the mattress in her cell. Food had been delivered and removed for a week now without being touched, except by the roaches. She hardly noticed the lights coming on in the day, flicking off at night. Between long crying spells, she stared at the wall trying vainly to make some sense of it all.

Theresa had thought her life had purpose in her single-minded search for justice. Now that she was the victim, why could she not rally, strike out? She had tried to keep fighting through physical and mental exercise. Somehow, the effort seemed meaningless and empty now. Theresa knew "they" were watching. But was Tariq? They meant nothing. He meant everything.

She sucked in a breath, realizing for the first time that to live without love, as she had done for years, was to slowly suffocate. She longed to breathe again. Despite her anguish, she continued to mark each new day. It was Monday. Would Tariq come today? Or would Badr keep him away? She knew if he didn't come, she would give up.

The day wore on. Theresa's head drooped lower. Dinner arrived and Tariq had still not appeared. She threw her head back in despair hitting the wall. The sensation was somehow comforting. The pain told her she was alive. So she did it again. And again.

By the time Tariq opened her cell door, blood matted her hair and marked the wall. He rushed to her side and pulled her away from the wall.

"Theresa, what are you doing? You're bleeding."

She looked up vacantly, unsure who had spoken.

He examined the back of her head and yelled an order in Arabic to the guard at the door. The guard left.

Tariq knelt in front of her, his back to the hidden camera, and lifted her face to look directly in her eyes. "Theresa, it's me. Tariq. We can talk freely. I've disconnected the audio feed."

A light of recognition shined its way from deep inside her brain to her eyes. She started to cry. "Where were you? What happened to me?"

He pulled her into his chest, enfolding her sobbing body in his arms. "Shhh. It's going to be okay, now. You'll be all right. I've sent for water and disinfectant. And something to bandage your wound."

Theresa spoke between sobs. "My…wound? What do you mean?"

He chose his words with care. "You've hurt your head. Here in the cell." He gently probed the bloody area at the back of her skull. She didn't flinch.

"How?"

"Never mind. It will be all right."

Tariq continued to hold her as he talked. He told her how she had seized, passed out, and been returned to the cell a week ago. He explained that he waited and watched her until she woke up in the late afternoon on Tuesday. Once assured she was well enough to be moved, he arranged for one of the female housekeepers to give her a bath and haircut, as well as change her clothes. He had tried to visit again on Thursday, but the guard on the floor denied him access. When he pressed, the guard phoned upstairs to the colonel's office. Badr would not relent, reminding Tariq of his stipulation that she not be disturbed for a week. The young man rocked her gently as he talked.

Her sobbing gradually eased. There in his arms she was safe. There nothing could hurt her. He hadn't forgotten her. He came back. As always, he smelled of sandalwood and cardamom. Theresa inhaled deeply and gave a low sigh with each breath she exhaled. She began to time her breathing with his so their chests rose and fell together. He held her all the tighter in response.

Tariq pulled back when the guard's footsteps announced his approach. Theresa kept her eyes down as the captain stood to take the bandage, cloth, and disinfectant. He instructed the guard to leave the plastic bowl of water and sponge near the mattress. The guard closed the cell door on his way out.

Tariq waited until the footsteps retreated down the hallway before kneeling by Theresa again, once more with his back to the camera. "Turn that way so I can see the back of your head."

She turned to the wall and bowed her head. Tariq examined the wound. A small area of scalp beneath her hair resembled raw meat filled with gristle. He dipped the sponge in the bowl, squeezed it out, and gently began dabbing at the blood. The water grew pinker each time he squeezed out the sponge.

He whispered in her ear. "I'm sorry if this hurts."

His warm breath raised bumps on her flesh. "It doesn't matter. I don't know what came over me. I don't..."

"Never mind, Theresa. I'm surprised you didn't do this long ago. There is always a breaking point."

She turned her head to look at him. "Do you think I'm at that point?" She read his answer in his eyes before he spoke.

"Yes."

He daubed the wound with disinfectant. It stung and Theresa's neck and shoulders tightened. Tariq placed a gauze bandage over the wound and asked her to hold it there. Then he took a cloth normally used for blind-folding and tied it around her head above her eyes, se-curing the bandage in place. As Tariq knotted the cloth, he voiced another concern.

"They tell me you haven't eaten all week. Is it be-cause of me?"

She looked down and whispered. "No."

He finished his work and turned her around to face him. "Theresa. I did not want to hurt Asil. And the last thing I wanted to do was hurt you. I'm so…" His words trailed off.

She had looked from his eyes to his lips, back to his eyes. Did he want her as much as she wanted him? As he drew closer, her head lifted once, twice…and his mouth found hers. His smooth, full lips, at first tentative, barely brushed against hers and she felt a deep glow spread up from the bottom of her neck. The blushing warmth turned hot as she responded to his lingering kiss. She leaned into him, careful to place her hands on his chest for balance. His breath smelled of lemon and mint, and she tasted the tartness. A sour sweet combination that set her heart beating faster. Her eyes closed and there was no more prison, no more pain. No episode could match the wealth of sensations swirling inside her head. A different kind of tingling raced throughout her body.

Prison sounds stilled and in their place pulsed a throbbing like a drum.

Almost as soon as it began, it ended. Tariq drew back, took her hands in his, and squeezed them as he looked in her eyes. He bent his head and whispered. "We have to move soon. I'm concerned about Qusai."

"That was him?"

Tariq nodded. "Either he regards you as a potential shield, or there is something in your past that worries him. I believe it's your past. I overheard Badr mention a report of an American paying a Ba'athist to kill Saddam in the early years."

Theresa drew back. "He thinks it was my father?"

"Possibly. Qusai is specifically responsible for the safety of Saddam Hussein. If he thinks there's any chance of a Ba'athist in their circle with past CIA connections, he will have him killed immediately, particularly with the war this close."

"Has the fighting begun already? Have we attacked?"

"No. But the invasion should come any day now. Be ready."

"What can I do?"

"Resume your routines. Eat your meals, analyze poetry, sing your strange songs." He smiled. "The important thing is to make Badr believe nothing has changed. I need you to be strong in body and spirit. If you aren't, we'll both be lost. And my family too."

"Your family?"

He nodded. "They're already in danger. The Mukhabarat's had our house under surveillance every day this past week. And we've been bugged for months."

She drew back, alarmed. "But that means…"

"It means we have to act before they do. Trust me and be ready."

He kissed her hands, stood up, and left.

ARRANGEMENTS

(Mansour—March 18, 2003)

Tariq sipped the strong black tea slowly, savoring again the brief moments with Theresa the night before. He had lain awake half the night remembering, and planning. His mother and Ghassan were going out to scour the city for a few staples. They would spend the rest of the day waiting in line for petrol. Anxious, he looked at his watch. He had a mere three hours to make the necessary preparations, but first, he had to speak with his grandfather. And he couldn't do that until they left.

His mother entered the kitchen, purse in hand. "Aren't you late for work? I thought you said Badr requested a report on Theresa."

Tariq made a show of continuing to pick at his breakfast. "He did, but I have until the end of the day to provide it. I'll be leaving here in a few minutes."

She looked at her watch. "Do you mind waiting here until Amina comes to clean? The earlier I can begin this shopping, the better. But I don't wish to leave your grandfather unattended."

Tariq tried to sound more accommodating than anxious. "If you think she'll be here soon, I suppose the colonel can wait a while longer."

"Thank you." His mother bent to kiss him on the cheek, before turning for the door leading to the garage.

Tariq called after her. "When is Amina due to come?"

She answered on her way out. "She promised she would be here by nine. She will stay all day, so you do not have to worry about your grandfather."

He nodded. "Good luck. Oh, and Mother?"

She stopped. "Yes?"

"Tell Ghassan to get twice as much petrol."

She cocked her head to one side. "Why? I thought we decided to stay through the bombing. Your grandfather could not stand the trip, even if he wanted to leave."

Tariq reassured her. "I know, I know. I just want to be prepared. It can't hurt. After all, who knows how long this war will last?"

She shrugged. "*Tayyib*. Very well. We will see you tonight."

The door closed. Tariq waited to hear the car doors slam shut before taking his last sip of tea. As he took his dishes to the sink, he heard the car backing out of the driveway. He scraped off the plates and stacked them while waiting for their maid. She usually came once a week, but they had requested her more often these past few months as his grandfather's condition continued to worsen.

Amina, a trained nurse, had worked under Tariq's grandmother for several years until the doctor passed away. With Dr. Awali no longer there to protect her position, she had been let go by hospital officials to make room for a head nurse with Ba'athist credentials. Taking pity on her, the Awali family had offered her work in the house. She had gratefully accepted in an economy where jobs were increasingly difficult to secure. Tariq hoped she would be willing to cooperate in the plan he had evolved.

He heard the front door open. A minute later, Amina appeared in the kitchen doorway.

"Tariq, are you going to wash the dishes? I will do them."

"I just organized them for you. It gave me something to do until you came."

"Has Madame gone? Were you waiting for me to watch your grandfather?"

"Yes and no. Mother has gone with Ghassan. They'll be away all day. You knew that, right?"

She nodded.

"I waited for you so you wouldn't worry about my grandfather. He's been wanting to get out in the garden for some fresh air."

"That is good. He should get out more."

"Well, I didn't want you walking in, finding no one in the house, and becoming alarmed or something. So now that you're here, I'll go get him and take him out."

"Of course. That will give me an opportunity to clean out his room. I will start there and do these dishes after. Take all the time you want. But make sure he doesn't get too tired."

Tariq smiled at the fifty-year-old woman. "Yes, nurse." He walked down the hallway toward his grandfather's room.

Once he had helped his grandfather down into one of the wicker chairs outside, Tariq began pacing back and forth, unsure how to begin. He had no time to lose. His mother had cut shopping trips short before, out of concern for the old man. She had made arrangements to be gone all day, but that didn't necessarily mean she would be.

Ibrahim al-Awali's lips curved in a smile. "All right. What is the matter? I know you did not bring me out here to smell the roses. No doubt you must speak of something confidential?"

Tariq turned to look at his grandfather, and decided to come right to the point. "Grandfather, back in the 1960's did you know a Professor Nathan Fuller?"

The old man gulped and started coughing. Alarmed, Tariq bent over to help steady his grandfather. Perhaps his mother had been right. Was it a mistake to bring up the past?

"I'm sorry, Grandfather. Is this something you can't talk about?"

The elder Awali cleared his throat with one final cough and sat up again. "Where did you hear that name?"

"Fuller?"

The old man nodded. "Where did you come across that name?"

Tariq straightened. "We have his daughter in custody over at Intelligence Headquarters."

The old man's eyes narrowed. "His daughter? Which one?"

"Why? Do you know them?"

"Just tell me which one."

Tariq paused. Who was doing the questioning here? "Theresa. She's a journalist. She entered Iraq illegally last August to do a story."

His grandfather's jaw tightened. "Last August? She has been detained all this time?"

Tariq nodded. Old Awali's eyes closed and he didn't speak for a minute. When he looked up at his grandson again, wariness guarded his countenance. "Tell me what you know first, and I will tell you what I can."

Tariq filled him in on Theresa's capture, how they came to know about her father, and the original file his superior had tracked down on the professor's arrest.

His grandfather gave him a sharp look when he mentioned the file. "The file. Did you see its contents?"

"The colonel did his best to block my view. There only seemed to be two pages. He said much had been removed. But one of the remaining pages must have been a witness list because he insisted that Theresa's name was on it. It was checked off like all the others. But, unlike most of the others, it was also circled."

His grandfather asked, "Has he shared that information with Theresa?"

Tariq nodded.

Awali pursed his lips. "Did it mean anything to her?"

"No. She seemed shocked."

The old man's face and shoulders relaxed.

Tariq persisted. "Should it have meant something to her? What do you know of this, Grandfather? If you know anything, tell me. She won't be released until it's cleared up."

Awali tensed again and bowed his head. Several minutes passed and Tariq reached out to make certain he was all right. But before he could touch his shoulder, the old man looked up. Tears and pain etched the grief on his face.

"Grandfather, what is the matter?"

The old man waved his hand to the other chair. "Come. Sit down. This is a long and difficult story. One I had hoped I would never have to tell."

Tariq sat, uneasy, dreading whatever he was about to learn.

The old man took a labored breath and began. "We met the Fullers shortly after they moved to Baghdad. Delightful people. And beautiful children. His wife..." He searched through his memory.

"Ruth," Tariq prompted.

His grandfather nodded, remembering. "Yes, Ruth. She had a smile that would win the whole room over. And she talked to you in a way that made you feel you were the most important person in her life. Everyone loved her. And Nathan..." He paused for a moment. "Nathan Fuller was intelligent, besides being good-looking. We had so many interesting conversations about politics, religion, philosophy, literature, even music."

"You knew him well, then?"

He nodded. "Perhaps too well. He was a very good professor, a good friend, a very devoted father, but..."

Tariq pressed. "But what?"

"Well, his devotion to his wife proved less than true."

Tariq was confused. "But what does this have to do with his arrest?"

"Be patient. I am coming to it. Your mother took a course from Nathan Fuller in the spring term of 1965."

Tariq nodded. He knew this.

Awali looked away now. "During that course she fell in love with him and they began to meet secretly." The old man rubbed the back of one hand with the other. "And she got pregnant."

Tariq's mouth fell open. "What?"

His grandfather held up a shaky hand. "Let me say it all now before you ask any more questions. Your grandmother, as a doctor, was able to confirm the pregnancy privately. That was most important. We had to keep this a secret to preserve your mother's life, as well as her reputation. So we sent her to AUB to finish her studies. Your grandmother was able to arrange a sabbatical for herself there at the hospital in Beirut. That way she could accompany your mother, assist in your delivery…"

Tariq began to feel lightheaded.

"…and help care for both of you. Before that, of course, we had to arrange a marriage. I contacted a young cousin from Syria who was studying at AUB. I offered a very generous dowry and he agreed to marry your mother in name only. He understood you were not his son, but he promised to keep quiet about it."

Tariq couldn't keep the edge out of his voice. "Why would he do that?"

"Besides the money, I was very high up in the Ba'ath here in Iraq. Marriage to my daughter assured him a more rapid rise among the Ba'ath in Syria. That is why he returned there."

The old man paused here and leaned over to put his hand on his grandson's shoulder. "Tariq, you were not abandoned by your true father. If you must blame anyone for this, blame me. I was responsible for Nathan's arrest."

Tariq buried his head in his hands. Theresa's father was his father. That meant Theresa was…the thought made his head reel. He recalled the way they had touched and kissed just hours before. His stomach turned.

"Grandson, I know this is a shock. Believe me, I am sorry."

He looked his grandfather in the eye. "Was he a spy?"

"What?"

"Theresa's father. You said you were responsible for his arrest. Was he with CIA? The colonel mentioned a report that an American was trying to get a Ba'athist to kill Saddam during that time. Was Professor Fuller using Mother to get to you?"

Awali shook his head. "Nathan was not CIA. But I helped incriminate him as a spy, nonetheless, without dragging your mother into it. I wanted him punished for what he did to her. He was lucky I didn't kill him."

Tariq's eyes blazed. "Well, you did, didn't you?"

His grandfather recoiled. "Is that what you think? Oh no, my son. I only wanted to scare him. I knew putting him in a Baghdad prison would do that. But I thought he would be safe. After all, he was an American. I was sure he would be released without much delay and asked to leave the country."

Tariq stood. He began to pace again. "So why was he killed? Who killed him?"

His grandfather breathed in deeply. "Radicals in the Ba'ath. They refused to believe he wasn't CIA. They wanted to make an example. Some were serving time in that prison and they took the law into their own hands."

Tariq turned to face his grandfather. "How did they kill him?"

"They hanged him. They tried to make it look like suicide. But I knew better. Even as distraught as he was, Nathan would never have killed himself."

Tariq sat down again, his mind swarming with questions. "But why is Badr so desperate to know…"

His grandfather interrupted. "Badr?"

"My superior, Colonel Badr."

Awali sat back in the chair. "One of the two men who killed Nathan was named Badr. How old is this colonel?"

Tariq shrugged. "I would guess Mother's age."

The old man leaned toward his grandson. "Is this the same man who requested you to work with him in the Mukhabarat?"

"Yes."

His grandfather's eyebrows lifted. "He must be a relative. Does he know you are my grandson?"

Tariq nodded. "He knew from the beginning. He always spoke of you with admiration."

Alarm spread across his grandfather's face. "Once he knows my part in this, he will be looking for revenge. It may be too late already."

"Revenge? Why? What happened to the men who killed…Professor Fuller?" Tariq couldn't bring himself to say "my father."

"They were executed for murder…at my urging."

Now Tariq understood. "So that's why he wants to talk to you. Grandfather, this is becoming dangerous for all of us."

The old man edged forward in his chair. "You must take your mother and get out of Iraq before this Badr acts against us."

Tariq nodded. "I know, but I have to get Theresa out too."

"Is he torturing her?"

He looked down. "It's come to that. She's ready to break. Even if he didn't lay another finger on her…"

His grandfather grabbed his hand and squeezed hard. "You must get her out. Do whatever is necessary. I will not have the deaths of Nathan and his daughter on my conscience."

Tariq leaned forward. "Is it true what Badr says. That she testified against her father? She said he was a spy?"

Awali drew his hand away. "It is easy to get a nine-year-old to say what you want them to say. I am not proud of it."

"You took her statement?"

"Tariq, believe me. He was only supposed to be in prison for a short while. Had I known it would lead to all of this…" He lowered his eyes, shaking his head. When he looked at his grandson again, he spoke evenly. "Do what you have to, but get her out of that hell. Take your mother, Theresa, and Ghassan, and leave Iraq. Who knows how long this war will be? It is not worth the risk."

Tariq stood. "What about you?"

The old man waved off the question. "Do not worry about me. I am dying. Either I will die from the cancer or the bombing. No matter how you look at it, I will die."

"But you don't have to die alone," Tariq argued. "You can come with us and die with your family around you."

He shook his head. "The trip would only kill me sooner. I was born in Iraq. I will die in Iraq."

"At least, keep Ghassan with you to help care for you."

Awali laughed. "Ghassan? As soon as I start vomiting, he leaves the room. He will be of more use to you. Two men with two women will be better."

"But who will care for you?"

"Amina will take care of me. Now, help me back into the house. I am tired and you have things to do."

Carefully, Tariq hoisted his grandfather to his feet. He walked the old man back to his bedroom. The room had been cleaned, his bed freshly made. He pulled the covers back, eased his grandfather down, and tucked him in. As he turned to go, the old man called his name.

"Tariq. I will tell your mother about our talk. I know she doesn't want to leave me, but I will convince her to go."

The young man nodded. He didn't know how he could look his mother in the eyes again, knowing the secret she had kept from him all these years. And how could he ever look at Theresa the same way? What could he say to her?

TAKEN IN THE NIGHT

(Intelligence Headquarters—March 20, 2003)

She stood in the prison courtyard peering up at her father. He was trying to tell her something. But the sunlight behind his head glared in her eyes. She couldn't see the words his cracked lips formed. Theresa strained harder. She was ready to give up when a cloud rolled in front, blocking the light. Her eyes refocused as his lips started to move again. The sound of his voice began to come through. He was saying...

The dream shifted violently as Theresa felt a man's hand over her mouth. A gag quickly replaced the hand to muffle her screams, and she was yanked up to a sitting position. Her eyes opened, taking in the darkness of her cell and a man's figure beside her. Before her pupils could dilate sufficiently, he drew a cloth around her eyes and nose and tied it tightly. She winced. Still tender, her head wound throbbed.

Theresa reached up to loosen the blindfold. But the man grabbed her right wrist in the air and snapped a handcuff around it. He pulled her hands down behind and finished cuffing her. Who was this? In seconds he had shoved her feet into shoes, which he laced and tied before pulling her up and thrusting her forward.

Theresa heard the cell door creak open. She tensed as hands pressed against her back. He pushed her ahead and closed the door behind them. In his hurry, the man half pulled her down the hallway in the direction of the elevator. Theresa's heart pounded. Where was Tariq?

On the way, she heard the stranger speak in hoarse Arabic to a guard who snickered. Something about "the women's facility." Were they moving her? Did Tariq know? She balked, refusing to go any further, but he dragged her on. Soon the man stopped her and turned her around. She heard elevator doors close. All sounds were shut out except the quickened beat of her heart. As they rose, she began to count under her breath. One one-thousand. Two one-thousand. An unexpected groping of her breasts broke her concentration. Theresa jumped and tried to turn away, but her captor only laughed as he cornered her with her back to the elevator's wall. With her hands cuffed behind her, she could do nothing to stop the man's pawing and fondling. But once the elevator stopped and the doors opened, the groping ceased. Her captor pushed her out roughly, turned her toward the left and urged her on, poking her in the back. Her shoes squeaked on the smooth floor.

She recalled the sounds from months ago. Theresa was leaving this place the same way she had come in.

Someone ahead to the left called out a greeting in Arabic. He used a strange dialect, but the voice seemed familiar. The man holding onto Theresa pushed her in that direction, responding as they walked. His speech was rushed, but she caught Badr's name in the conversation. Was she being moved on the colonel's orders?

The other voice said something she couldn't make out, raising his tone in a question. The men began to argue. Then shouting. Something about a body. The man was no longer behind her. She heard the push of buttons on a desk phone. Five buttons had been pushed before she jumped at the airy popping sound of two silencer rounds, in quick succession. Something heavy thumped against wood. Theresa heard the phone placed back on the receiver. She gulped mouthfuls of air when warm metal rubbed against her back. Who had been killed?

Theresa's heart double pumped, as a man with a gun propelled her on. This was a different man. He took longer strides and had a different smell about him. He moved ahead of her to open a door and she felt cool air on her face. She stumbled a bit down some steps, but he pulled her up and dragged her forward. In that instant, when he stooped beside her, she thought she breathed in sandalwood. Tariq?

After some twenty paces, they stopped. She heard a car door open. She was pushed down and in. Theresa almost fell on her face on the floor of the car. With difficulty, she scrambled to an uncomfortable sitting position. She had to lean with her side against the seat to avoid pushing against the cuffs behind her. The door slammed shut and she heard feet running around to the driver's side. She assumed it was the same man. He got in, started up the engine, and pulled ahead.

His silence scared her. If this were Tariq, he would say something now to reassure her. But the man said nothing.

The car slowed to a stop and Theresa strained to hear while the man spoke briefly. She hoped to recognize his voice, catch a place name for some clue to their destination. But he continued to use a strange guttural dialect and none of his Arabic was familiar. Another voice answered. She sensed a light shining on her face. A moment later it was gone. She heard the other voice say something else and her driver responded. The car moved forward, slowed for a turn, and merged onto a street, picking up speed. Would she ever see Tariq again?

THE SCAR

(Mansour—March 20, 2003)

The car slowed to a stop and Theresa's heart clenched. The driver's door opened and closed. Someone got into the back seat next to her and unlocked her handcuffs. Her gag came off. As hands worked to unfasten the blindfold, she heard a welcome voice in English.

"Theresa. You're safe now."

The blindfold dropped and she turned around to see Tariq's eyes shining like obsidian. She threw her arms around him and began to sob.

He didn't return her embrace, but spoke in soothing tones, stroking her hair. "It's all right. I'm sorry you had to go through that, but there was no other way. Once I heard Badr was going to move you, I changed plans so that I could intercept your guard near the entrance. It's going to be all right. You're safe now."

Theresa squeezed him for several seconds, letting go only to wipe her eyes. "That was you back there with the gun? You took me out of the building?"

He nodded. "I had to make it look real."

She looked back through the car window. "Where are we?"

"In Mansour. We're going to my house. Stay back here and put on this abaya. Try to cover up as much as possible." He handed her a black silk robe, opened his door, and got in front behind the wheel of the Land Rover again.

She spoke as he started the engine. "But you said they're watching your house."

"They were. But I took care of them."

Theresa leaned forward. "You killed them?"

He nodded as he pulled ahead.

"Did you also kill the man who had me? I thought I heard popping sounds back there."

He looked at her in the rearview mirror. "I did what I had to do. I killed the desk clerk, took his place, and waited for you and your guard. When he saw the clerk's body, he tried to call Badr. I stopped him in time."

"But they'll find the bodies."

"We'll be long gone. Please, put the abaya on. In case we're seen."

Tariq pulled out a cell phone and punched in a number. After a brief pause, he said something in Arabic. Without waiting for a response, he ended the call and put the phone back in his uniform pocket.

She maneuvered awkwardly into the silky black robe, tugging and pulling until the top part stayed on her head. Once covered, Theresa took a deep breath and let it out slowly.

"What time is it, Tariq?"

He checked the clock in the car. "Shortly after four. We must be gone before dawn."

"Are we close to your house?"

"Just a few minutes now."

"We're in Baghdad, right? You said this is Mansour."

He nodded.

She peered out the windows at the darkened shapes of stores, restaurants, and houses. "It's so changed from what I remember. Much more built up."

He looked at her in the mirror. "You remember Mansour?"

"One of Jimmy's good friends lived out here. And Mom used to teach folk dancing at the Mansour School for Girls. There was a lot more open space back then."

Tariq smiled. "I remember that school as a child. It's long gone. Who knows what this neighborhood will look like after the Americans start bombing?"

"You think they'll bomb residential areas?"

"If they have good intelligence they will. There's more to this area than meets the eye." He shifted in his seat. "We're coming up to my house now. Cover up. I'm going to pass it and circle around to make sure no one's watching."

Theresa pulled the robe tighter around her face so only her eyes showed. As she did, the tingling started. She thought about saying something to Tariq, but the picture in her mind distracted her.

The old shoeshine man sat hunched before his brass inlaid wooden kit in the portico of their Baghdad home. She watched in fascination as the white-haired tradesman chose between his various cloths and small bottles of polish. The smells of leather and polish intoxicated her. Theresa could not pull her six-year-old eyes away from the large mottled scar on the left side of his face. She went back into the kitchen to ask Asil about it.

The maid glanced briefly through the screen door. "Scar from boil. Baghdad boil."

The vision began to fade. Theresa shook off the end of the episode and looked down at the small scab on her left arm. Would it leave a scar like that? She remembered now how many of these scars she had seen in Baghdad as a child. By the time they had arrived there in the 60's, an inoculation had been developed. If administered soon after being bitten, the boil could be prevented.

"Theresa?"

They had arrived. Tariq extended a hand to help her out of the Land Rover. She took it, and held the abaya close as she stepped out onto his driveway.

"This way."

Tariq led her through the garage and opened a door into their kitchen. An attractive woman in her fifties, dressed sharply in a lavender suit and black pumps, jumped up from her seat at the table. An older man also stood, eyes fixed on Theresa. She saw empty tea glasses before them on the table and a plate of biscuit-style cookies. Few had been eaten. A third glass of tea had hardly been touched. It stood in front of an empty chair.

Before Tariq's mother could speak, he put a finger to his lips and pointed toward the next room. She looked uneasily at Theresa, and led them back through a study and out into a garden. Theresa saw something familiar in the woman's face, particularly her eyes. But Tariq was rushing introductions.

"Theresa, this is my mother and our long-time servant, Ghassan. The house is still bugged. But out here we can talk safely."

Theresa shook Ghassan's hand and turned to Tariq's mother. "I'm sorry, I don't remember Tariq's last name. What should I call you?"

His mother cleared her throat before answering. "You may call me Mrs. Awali. Never mind the 'al.' It will trip your tongue." She smiled, embarrassed.

The smile was so familiar. She tried to remember where she had seen it before.

Tariq took Theresa's arm to get her attention. "Here, let me take your robe. It can be awkward."

"Thank you." Theresa removed the long black abaya and handed it to him.

He draped it over his arm. "And now I would like to introduce you to my grandfather, Ibrahim al-Awali, and his nurse, Amina." He gestured toward an old man sitting in a wicker chair. He had been wrapped in a blanket against the chill morning air. The nurse stood behind him.

Theresa sensed a tension as she stepped forward. Everyone seemed to be waiting. For what? She clasped the old man's frail outstretched hand. "It's a pleasure to meet you, sir."

He turned his face in the early dawn light and Theresa gasped. The scar. On his left cheek. The outline of his nose differed from that of the shoeshine man. But the scar was the same.

"Forgive me for not standing," he said, eyes down. "I am afraid I am too feeble. You are welcome in our house, Miss Fuller. Tariq has told me much about you."

She couldn't let go of his hand, and she couldn't stop staring. The cultured voice and the scar, together, held her frozen. When the grandfather looked directly at her, she finally dropped his hand.

His face, his eyes brought a rush of memories. This was not the shoeshine man. This was the man who had questioned her as a child. This was the man who helped her put her father in prison. He had plied her with sweets and soda as they talked. She recalled the small round tube of candy-coated chocolates he pressed into her hands that day.

Theresa's cheeks grew hot as she remembered the statement she gave that day. She had been angry with her father for his betrayal. So she let this man lead her to say things that were only half-true. But Theresa did it willingly. She preferred thinking of her father as a spy than as a man who did things behind her mother's back. Things that embarrassed her. Things that were wrong.

Now, the old man reached for her hand again. "I am so sorry for everything you have suffered. Everything." He blinked tears as he spoke.

He knew. He could tell she remembered. She saw it in his eyes. And now he was looking for forgiveness. But memories were washing over her, drowning her. Waves of questions followed. Did Tariq know about his grandfather? If he did, when did he find out? Had he known all along? Did they all know about this? She glanced back at Tariq, but he was looking down at his watch.

Theresa turned again to the old man. She opened her mouth to speak and, in that instant, felt smacked by a huge pulse of air. Oxygen was sucked from her lungs. The thudding only reverberated in her ears after she had landed on the ground.

Everyone was lifted up and thrown back in the initial explosion. More concussions followed. Tariq crawled to shield her as she lay on the grass, clawing for breath.

"Stay down," he gasped.

ESCAPE

(From Baghdad North—March 20, 2003)

Theresa watched, dazed, as Tariq lifted his grandfather off the ground and steadied him. Explosions no longer punctuated the air. They had been replaced by the wail of sirens and an acrid burning smell.

She rose awkwardly to her feet. Tariq and the nurse led the old man into the house away from his daughter's embrace. Ghassan had pulled a handkerchief from his pocket. He tried to stem the flow of blood from Mrs. Awali's nose.

"Put your head back," he instructed. "Hold this under and squeeze up here. The bleeding will stop."

Tariq's mother looked past the servant to address her son, re-emerging from the house. "Is he all right?"

"Grandfather says not to worry. Amina's staying with him."

Still holding the handkerchief to her nose, she started toward the house. "We cannot leave him to this kind of bombing."

Tariq took hold of his mother's arm. He spoke as an army commander, without emotion. "We must. Intelligence Headquarters has probably been hit. It's a chance to get out of the city, during all this confusion."

He turned to Ghassan. "Is the car ready?"

Eyes blanketed in shock from the attack, the older man nodded without speaking.

"Good. Let's hurry. We'll go across the Jumhuriyah Bridge, and head north on the Dawrah Expressway."

Tariq's mother began to cry. "I may not ever see him again. I cannot leave."

He held her in his arms. "You have no choice, you must. For all of our sakes. We must look like a family fleeing. Grandfather bid us God speed. We will see him in Paradise, if not before."

They got into the Land Rover left by the dead surveillance team. Theresa sat in the back on the passenger side. She stiffened when she saw the blood stains on the headrests. Tariq and Ghassan worked together to hide the spots beneath seat and headrest covers pulled from Tariq's Toyota.

Ten minutes after the sirens first sounded, the Land Rover was on its way. Tariq drove through the empty streets of the city, using his Mukhabarat credentials to breeze past the various checkpoints. With both women dressed in abayas, and supplies loaded in the rear and on top, Republican Guard soldiers assumed they were fleeing the bombardment.

Rounding Liberation Square, Theresa vaguely remembered the huge rectangular marble memorial decorated with black figures. But buildings loomed obscurely on the roads leading to the expressway and she was too stunned to focus on the city of her childhood.

Two hours later they were well beyond the capitol's limits, passing through Ba'qubah and Miqdadiyyah on an angle away from the Tigris River.

By now the shock had worn off. Theresa's mouth was set and closed. Fear eased its grip. But an uncomfortable anguish now enveloped Theresa's heart. In the face of this last revelation about Tariq's grandfather, she no longer cared if she was dead or alive, much less free. She had essentially put her own father behind bars. He had died there. How could she live with it? She bowed her head as tears welled.

If only Tariq could hold her, comfort her. He had barely touched her since their escape. She knew he had to focus on their escape. Still, a kind word or look would help. It was almost as if he was avoiding her. Had he known about his grandfather?

Tariq's mother reached over and patted Theresa's hand. "It will be all right. You have been through a great deal. But we will be safe soon."

Theresa nodded and gave her a weak smile.

Mrs. Awali turned her attention to her son behind the wheel. "Tariq, how did you know the target and when they would strike? You told us to be ready by four o'clock, and shortly after four it came. How did you know?"

Theresa recalled him looking at his watch right before the first blast.

Tariq breathed in deeply and exhaled. "I think it's safe to tell you now. When Badr stopped letting me see Theresa I became alarmed. I called Langley, Virginia to reach CIA headquarters."

In her shock, his mother invoked the name of God in Arabic. "*Wa'Allah!* The CIA? How? Have you been working for the Americans all this time?"

"When I was taken prisoner after the Gulf War, I was questioned. They felt they could turn me because of my experience in America, so they gave me a number. I had memorized it, though I never thought I would use it. Until a few weeks ago."

Ghassan spoke up. "But cell phones, satellite phones are illegal."

Tariq nodded. "Except for high-ranking members of the party, including the Mukhabarat. I borrowed the colonel's SAT phone one day when he stepped out of the office. I made a quick call. My information on Theresa and her father convinced the men at Langley I was serious."

Ghassan pressed. "How did they know they could trust you?"

"They didn't, at first. But I made another call the day of Theresa's interrogation. I had learned from Badr that Qusai Hussein would be there for the questioning. After I told Langley, they had another source verify it. I wasn't ready to fully betray the government until I saw what they were prepared to do to her. I worried about the danger to all of you. But Grandfather convinced me to go ahead."

Theresa raised her head. "You talked to your grandfather about me?"

Tariq glanced in the rear view mirror but wouldn't maintain eye contact. "Yes. I had to get you out of there. He agreed. So last night, I killed the two agents watching our house, and took their SAT phone."

He held up a pocketsize gray device. Theresa recognized it as the one he used after their escape. She had assumed it was a cell phone.

"I made another call, telling them Qusai was likely still with Badr at Headquarters. He had been gone the day before but I saw him return last night. I reminded them that I wanted to get you out. They told me to wait for their call…that they might be planning something that would help."

"The bombing?" Ghassan asked.

Tariq nodded. "In the middle of the night, a Baghdad agent called. He said they were going to target the Headquarters, as well as a few other places, and I should get Theresa out immediately. He didn't tell me exactly what time the missile strike would begin, only that I had half an hour to take her to safety. I was to call him back to verify she was safe."

Theresa remembered his brief call in Arabic during the drive to his house.

Tariq's mother shook her head again. "You are working with the CIA? How do you know you can trust them? Who is this Baghdad agent?"

He paused. "I don't know. But I have his phone number in case anything goes wrong."

"But are we not safe now? What could go wrong?"

Tariq spoke bluntly. "We will not be safe until we are out of the country. But for now, you should try and get some sleep. All of you. You've been up half the night."

Ghassan countered. "So have you. Why don't you pull over and let me drive?"

He glanced sideways. "I will, in time. Close your eyes, Ghassan. I'll wake you when I'm tired."

Theresa tried to sleep, but couldn't. Images of her father's gaunt face in prison kept flashing before her eyes, interspersed with the scarred cheek of Tariq's grandfather. She looked to her right at the flat desert speeding past, spotted in dawn's light with scrub here and there. She felt as empty as this land.

A SCOUTING MISSION

(Near Halabja—March 20, 2003)

Barham laid on the horn. A long blast followed by four punctuated honks. The blaring sent the Kurdish shepherd and his sons running and cursing to drive the sheep off the road near Halabja so the PUK command vehicle could proceed. Peter took a few pictures before rolling up his passenger side window to drown out the bleating animals shoved to one side or the other.

"It looks a bit like Moses parting the Red Sea, doesn't it?" Peter knew Muslims accepted Moses as a prophet. He wasn't sure, however, if Barham knew all the biblical stories about him.

"Moses raised a stick. Allah parted the Red Sea." Barham looked to make certain his friend understood the difference.

"I know what you're saying, but God told him to do it. And that's basically what happened here. You gave the

command by honking on the horn and Moses here…"
Peter pointed at the scurrying shepherd. "He raised his
stick to get things going. The sheep are parting."

His friend regarded him suspiciously. "Did you just
compare me to Allah?"

"Well, no. I was just making a…never mind."

"How many cups of coffee did you have this morning?" Barham waved his thanks to the shepherds after
passing through the last of the flock.

"More than enough."

Barham gave him a sidelong glance. "I thought so.
Too much coffee makes you say things you shouldn't."

Peter rolled his eyes. "Well, you woke me at five to
tell me about Baghdad. Did you think I wanted to sleep-
walk through this mission? It takes a lot of coffee to get
going. The earlier I wake, the more I drink."

"Try tea. One cup of *chai* and I can do anything."

Peter raised an eyebrow. "Maybe you are God." The
Kurd gasped and Peter hastened to apologize. "Sorry.
That was the coffee talking."

Barham grunted. "Keep your mouth closed until it
wears off, okay?"

"Okay."

Peter turned to look behind. Their SUV was the
first in a small convoy of cars filled with members of
Barham's brigade. The Kurd had outlined their mission
simply: his group was to scout out the roads leading to
known Ansar camps and determine any weaknesses in
the Ansari defense. The main attack would launch any

day now. Barham and his commanders wanted to be ready.

Peter knew his friend itched for the battle to begin. Barham had told him about a battle last December in which some Ansar fighters had successfully attacked a PUK post near this area manned by the Kurd and some of his men. Barham had survived the initial attack, but barely escaped capture. Many of the PUK fighters captured that day had been executed.

"The next time I face those Ansari dogs, I will kill three for every one of my men they murdered." Barham spat on the ground after making the vow, as if to seal his promise.

Peter had learned a good deal more about the Sunni Islamic fundamentalist group since his first encounter last August. Their full name, *Ansar al-Islam fi Kurdistan*, meant "Supporters of Islam in Kurdistan."

From their bases, northeast of Halabja and in and around several villages and two valleys, these militants advocated and enforced what they called "the propagation of virtue and the prevention of vice."

Among other things, this meant men must grow beards, women must cover their heads, and Kurds could no longer listen to music or use satellite dishes. Since their establishment two years ago, hundreds of villagers in the area had fled.

What a shame, Peter thought. Looking out at the green rolling hills gradually leading up to the snow-topped Zagros Mountains of Iran, he snatched glimpses of yellow and violet wildflowers growing along the road. He had noticed again the lovely lake south of Halabja and thought how pleasant life might be here, were it not for all the war.

Barham interrupted Peter's daydreaming. "There is a petrol station up ahead a few kilometers."

"Are we low on gas?"

"No. But I want information. The owner deals with the Ansar every day and may know which routes are least protected."

"Good. I'm ready to take a…uh, I have to relieve myself after all that coffee. I was about to ask you to pull over." Peter stretched his arms out to the sides. Since his torture in Abu Ghraib, he could no longer raise them over his head without pain.

Barham glanced his way. "It might be a good spot for lunch, too. His wife will prepare something if we pay. Are you hungry?"

"Always." Peter grinned at his friend.

Barham grinned back. "I know what you mean. I ate two hours ago and already my stomach is complaining."

"But you've got about twenty men. Can she feed all of us?"

"She will not have to. You and I are the only ones who will eat. There are three or four routes branching off this road. While we eat, the others can scout out most of the routes and report back. You and I will check the remaining one."

"Sounds good."

They approached the small, pockmarked concrete station cautiously. Most of the paint had faded or been blown away by errant gunshots. Peter wondered how often the station had been caught in the crossfire of warring parties. Once Barham saw no other vehicles around, he flipped on his right turn signal. The cars behind followed his lead as he pulled into the station, kicking up choking clouds of dust.

A middle-aged Kurd in brown baggy pants came out to see how much gas he could sell. Barham rolled his window down and spoke to him in Kurdish. The man looked disappointed at first. But a smile and a nod soon followed with a glance in Peter's direction.

Peter looked at Barham. "What did he say? Can I use the toilet?"

"Yes, and he will feed us. I told him you were paying."

"Thanks. You're very generous with my money."

"No problem."

"Are you sure there are no Ansar around?" asked Peter.

"No, but he said he has not seen any yet today. I do not want to stay out here too long, though. Our car is too easy a target parked here in the open. You go on inside. I will give the men their orders."

Peter got out. He groaned as he walked toward the door of the station. His body stiffened too easily these days. Prison had aged him a decade or two. He entered the station office, looked in the back and found the toilet. Once finished, he came out to find Barham listening as the station owner waved his arms this way and that to emphasize the words he spoke in Kurdish.

Barham replied briefly. The owner tipped his head politely and walked away.

"Where's he going?" asked Peter.

"To his house up the road to get his wife started on lunch. Go sit. I will pull the car around the back so it cannot be seen by any passing Ansar."

"What if some stop by while we're in here eating?"

Barham reassured him. "Not to worry. He has a room in back where we can rest and eat in privacy. There is even a television."

Lunch proved simple, but filling: flat mountain bread, yogurt, cucumbers and tomatoes, and a kind of lamb stew. Barham scooped the last of the yogurt on his plate with a rolled piece of bread. One of his men entered to report back.

Peter waited until they finished talking. "What's the news?"

"The road they checked was clear. So I will have to mark it on the map. It is definitely one we could use. I told him to get the information from the others as they come in. Once they have all reported, they can return to Sulaimaniya."

"Without us?"

Barham finished chewing and swallowed. "Certainly. I know the way. We will check the last road before heading back."

Peter nervously rubbed his ring as he pushed back from the table.

The Kurd laughed and shook his head. "Still the ring. Money kept us alive in prison." He held up his AK-47. "This will keep us alive out here."

"A little luck can't hurt." Peter stood and dug in his pocket for a wad of bills. "Will he take dollars?"

"This close to the war he will insist on dollars. Be generous. He risked his life and his family by feeding us."

Peter counted out fifty dollars and handed the money to Barham. His friend approached the station manager and presented the payment, thanking him again in Kurdish. The man's eyes bulged at the sight of so many dollars and he bowed several times as the two walked out his door.

They walked around the back, got into the SUV, and buckled up. Looking out the window and up into the hills, Peter could make out small ebony pinpoints revealing the different Ansar positions. His skin buzzed.

Barham put the key in the ignition. "Ready?"

"Sure." Peter touched his ring again as the car engine started.

They drove several kilometers until they came to an unmarked road leading off to the right toward the hills. Barham stopped, pulled some binoculars from the glove compartment, and handed them to Peter.

"What are these for?"

"Scouting. You look through them."

"I knew that. I meant what am I looking for?"

"Movement. Signs of guns or roadblocks. If you see anything suspicious, tell me."

Peter hung the strap over his neck and trained the lenses on the dots in the nearby hills.

Barham nudged him. "Don't look at the hills. Look at the road ahead. Any danger will come from there."

The Kurd pressed down on the accelerator and turned onto the dirt road. Peter peered through the glasses. Bumps in the road made focusing difficult and caused the binoculars to gouge against the bone under his eyebrows.

After a while, Peter lowered the glasses. He glanced at his friend. Barham steered with his left hand, keeping his right down next to his gun. He had unlocked the safety. Peter raised the binoculars for another look.

The road ahead seemed clear but it curved around a hill. Barham murmured something in Kurdish under his breath and slowed to a stop.

Peter lowered the glasses. "What's the matter?"

"You stay. I am going to climb up this hill here on foot and look around where the road turns."

"You're leaving me here with binoculars?"

Barham smiled, pulled a pistol from his waistband, and handed it to him. "Here. I will be back soon."

Peter watched as his friend started up the hill, his AK-47 slung across his back. As he neared the top he crouched lower. Right before the crest, Barham hugged the ground and inched forward until he could peek over. He scanned the area slowly. Peter took another long look through his binoculars. Nothing. Why were hairs prickling on the back of his neck?

The door opened on the driver's side and Peter whirled, pointing the pistol.

Barham held up his hands as he got back in the car. "Don't shoot. You don't know the way back."

"Don't scare me like that. What did you see?"

"There is a small grove of trees up ahead on the right. I watched it. There was no movement. I think we are safe now. But they could definitely use it for a defensive position. When we get back to town I will mark it on the map."

Peter was ready to leave. "Let's go back now."

"I want to go on about two more kilometers. The road curves again there and I could not tell what was ahead of it."

Barham started up the engine and eased the car ahead around the turn. Peter held the glasses up to his eyes, focusing on the trees his friend had mentioned. No movement. He scanned ahead to locate the next bend in the road. Barham also concentrated on the distant curve. Both missed the turbaned heads peering out from behind the big oaks.

One bearded man signaled. Immediately the SUV was raked with machine gun fire. Peter had time to drop the binoculars and turn before shots hit him in the arm and neck.

"I'm hit! Barham, they're…" A third shot struck him above his left eye, and killed him instantly.

Barham stopped the car, trying to throw the gear into reverse. A bullet ripped into his right hand as he reached for the shift. Another tore into his shoulder a second later. He ducked down and played dead.

Crouched over his gun next to his dead friend, Barham peeked up and saw five bearded Ansar fighters quietly stealing forward. The Kurd pulled down Peter's limp body to clear his field of vision. He waited until the first of the militants reached the road before lurching up, aiming his gun out the window and blasting away, left-handed.

Two Ansari fell dead and one collapsed, wounded in the stomach. The fourth fighter opened up on the SUV again. A bullet caught Barham in the midsection. Another grazed his cheek. He dove down for cover. He was bleeding all over now.

Weak, Barham could do nothing when the fourth man opened the passenger door and dragged Peter's body out. The Ansari looked at the Kurd, judged him dead, and turned to empty the Canadian's pockets. He stuffed Peter's passport and credentials in his baggy pants. He almost missed the ring. Grinning, he pulled it off and held it up to shine in the sunlight.

The militant started to shove it onto his own finger when Barham made one last move. He sat up, raised his gun and fired. He missed. Automatic gunfire caught him from behind the car. The fifth Ansar fighter had made his way around, unnoticed. Several shots hit the Kurd in the back of the head, propelling him forward.

Barham laid on the horn—dead.

THE PETROL STATION

(Near Halabja—March 20, 2003)

Tariq snored in the front passenger seat. He had driven for three hours before switching with Ghassan to catch some overdue rest. They changed again after lunch, and now the older man was pulling his second shift. Tariq's mother dozed peacefully in the warmth of the late afternoon sun. They had left the desert far behind now, taking less-traveled roads leading up into the hills of Northern Iraq.

Theresa longed to sleep, but feared the dreams that might come. So she gazed, heavy-lidded, out the window. She saw a beautiful lake and wondered if this was the lake near Halabja—the same one where she and Peter had first been captured. It looked familiar. Ghassan glanced over. He must have shared her thought.

The servant nudged the young man awake and pointed. "Tariq. Is that the lake? Are we approaching Halabja?"

Tariq sat up, rubbed his eyes and looked. "Yes. How long have I been sleeping?"

"Three or four hours."

He looked at his watch, then glanced back at Theresa and his mother, who had wakened at the sound of voices.

The older woman sat up and adjusted her abaya. "Where are we?"

"A little south of Halabja," Tariq answered. "There's a petrol station several kilometers ahead. How are we doing? How is the fuel?"

Ghassan checked the gauge. "The tank is about a quarter full. It depends on how much farther we have to go."

Tariq ran some quick calculations in his head. "Sulaimaniya should be about seventy-five kilometers away… maybe eighty. Let's stop at the station and re-fuel to be safe. I can phone my contact from there. Now that I can give him an approximate arrival time, he'll make arrangements for someone to meet us outside the city."

Theresa spoke up. "Can we eat soon, or should we wait?"

Tariq replied without looking at her. "I'll see if I can arrange some food for us at the station. The manager lives nearby and he has often accommodated us in the past…for the right price."

"You know the area?"

"Yes. I was stationed in this region for several years."

She continued the conversation, hoping he would shift to look at her. "I was captured near here, wasn't I?"

He nodded without turning. "The Ansar camp alerted us to your presence the day before. They wanted to take you themselves, but we convinced them to hold off until we could make the arrest."

"You mean you thought you convinced them." She recalled the look of hate in their leader's eyes as he had pointed his gun at Peter.

"Fortunately I got there before they could do something stupid."

Theresa felt uneasy. "What if we run into some of them again? They could contact Badr."

Tariq shook his head. "They know me well. They wouldn't have any reason to call Badr. Besides, I'm certain the colonel died in the missile strike."

Ghassan saw the station ahead on the right. He turned off the road and pulled up to the pump.

As he got out of the Land Rover, a Kurd in brown baggy pants came to help. Tariq stepped out to meet him. Seeing the young captain in uniform, the station manager beamed and the two spoke at length while Ghassan filled the tank. Tariq's face stiffened and he turned back to the car, signaling Theresa to roll down her window.

She did, but he looked past her to his mother when he spoke. "You should probably go in and use the facilities. There's a toilet in the back, but try and be quick. He says there's an Ansar patrol nearby. I would prefer avoiding them. There was some trouble earlier today involving a foreign journalist."

Theresa tried to keep her voice steady. "What happened?"

"He says their car was ambushed. The reporter and a PUK fighter were killed. As you know, they aren't friendly to Westerners...particularly now."

"What nationality was the journalist?"

Tariq shook his head. "He doesn't know. But let's not take chances." He opened her car door to help her out. "I'll make my call while you're inside. Can you wait until Sulaimaniya to eat?"

Theresa held onto his hand a moment longer than necessary. "I can wait."

He froze, caught her smile, and pulled his hand away to help his mother out. Theresa felt confused and slightly hurt, but gathered her abaya close around her and followed his mother through the door of the station. They located the toilet and each held the other's robe while they took turns.

When they came back out, Tariq was talking on the satellite phone. Ghassan finished cleaning off the windshield while the manager topped off the fuel tank. The women settled into the back seat again while Tariq concluded his conversation.

Putting the phone in his pocket, he motioned Ghassan over. "Everything is set. A U.S. Special Forces officer will meet us outside the mosque south of the city. They will take me in for debriefing."

The servant raised his eyebrows.

"Ghassan, this is their regular procedure."

"Are they arresting you? What will happen to us?"

Tariq tried to reassure him. "No. I've been acting as an agent for the past month. I have to give my report. I'm sure they have many questions for me, but they're certainly not going to question you."

Ghassan still seemed unsure. "At least, let me meet the officer before you approach him. I do not want you walking into a trap. Let me talk to him first. What is his name?"

Smiling, Tariq gave in. "All right. We're supposed to meet a Lieutenant Grange. Now, let's get going. I'll drive."

Ghassan handed him the keys. "Grange. Can I use the toilet first?"

"Yes, but hurry." Tariq turned to pay the station manager as Ghassan scurried inside.

As he was putting the last of a huge wad of dinars into the Kurd's hands, a battered looking car pulled in behind the Land Rover. Tariq turned to see two armed Ansar fighters emerge. One walked up to the men while the other checked out the robed occupants in the back seat. Theresa pulled the abaya around to block the second man's view of her face and hair.

The station manager called the first fighter by name.

"Ahmed." Indicating Tariq, he spoke excitedly in Arabic.

A smile spread across the Ansari's bearded face when he recognized Tariq. Theresa gathered from snatches of their conversation in Arabic that it had been more than two years since Tariq had dealt with this leader face to face. Before he entered the Mukhabarat. Ahmed hailed his old friend, embracing and kissing him on both cheeks. Theresa decided she should continue to pretend not to understand. They weren't over the border yet, and out of danger. If they were caught, only Tariq knew she could speak the language, and she wanted to keep it that way.

She looked at Mrs. Awali, turning away from the inquisitive eyes of the second Ansar fighter. "What are they saying?"

His mother whispered. "Apparently they knew each other before, when Tariq served in this area with the Republican Guard. He is asking why Tariq is here when the bombing of Baghdad has begun." She listened a moment more. "Tariq told him Badr gave him permission to get his family out of Baghdad, away from the bombing."

"These guys know Badr?"

His mother nodded. "They are speaking as if they do." Another pause to listen. "But Ahmed doesn't understand why he has brought us this way to the north where the Kurds are. Now he is asking more about Badr." Her eyes strayed to the left. "Oh, no."

Theresa turned to see what his mother had seen. Ghassan had come to the door of the station. The Ansar fighters hadn't seen him yet. Tariq flashed a warning with his eyes, urging him back out of sight, before turning to continue his conversation.

The other fighter had gotten a better look at Theresa when she turned, and now approached Ahmed, whispering in his ear. Ahmed looked her way immediately and walked over to the car. Before Tariq could stop him, he had opened the car door.

His English was poor, but sufficient. "You. Out."

Terror held her back against the seat. Tariq started to explain in Arabic, but Ahmed ignored him. The militant reached in and pulled Theresa out of the car. She tried to keep the abaya wrapped over her face, but he grabbed at it and pulled it down.

His surprise at seeing a Westerner soon turned to suspicion and anger. All aimed at Tariq. He barked an order to the other fighter and Tariq's mother was dragged out of the other side of the Land Rover. The fact that she was, indeed, Iraqi did little to appease his anger. He turned on his old friend with a flurry of questions and accusations.

Tariq saw Ghassan move forward from the station to intervene. He stopped him again with a look over Ahmed's shoulder. In the next minute, they were being herded toward the battered car. Tariq held up the keys to the Land Rover, pointing at the vehicle and saying something in Arabic. Ahmed grabbed the keys, tossed them to the frightened station manager, and instructed the Kurd to move the car back out of sight.

All three—Theresa, Tariq, and his mother—were forced into the back of the Ansar car. Ahmed got behind the wheel while his comrade took the front passenger seat, shifting to hold a gun on the captives.

The windows had been rolled down and, as the car sped away, Theresa saw Ghassan run out of the station office yelling.

He shouted something in Arabic and called their names: "Tariq! Tahira!"

The Ansar fighters had not seen or heard him, but Theresa had. Stunned, she turned to look past Tariq at his mother. "Is your name Tahira?"

His mother swallowed before answering in a whisper. "Yes."

The man pointing the gun yelled at them in Arabic. He added English for Theresa's benefit. "No talk!"

Even if Theresa could have spoken, she wouldn't have known what to say.

TAHIRA

(Sargat Camp—March 20, 2003)

Theresa sat on the filthy dirt floor, her head in her hands. She peeked through her fingers to see the hem of Mrs. Awali's abaya trailing the ground as the older woman paced back and forth across the room. Every so often the robe stopped while its wearer listened at the door. Eventually, it moved again.

She and Tariq's mother had been locked in this holding room for half an hour. They had not spoken one word to each other. The drive from the petrol station to this Ansar camp in the hills had been silent, as well, partly due to the fighter's armed threat. Theresa knew that, even had they been allowed to speak, no words would have crossed their lips. It was if they had silently agreed to ignore each other.

The drive to this camp had taken twenty minutes. All that time Theresa wrestled with the implication of

Mrs. Awali's first name. Was it a coincidence? If so, why had she seemed ashamed to admit it? Tariq had not appeared upset at Theresa's question. Why had his mother?

Theresa had also reviewed her vision during the drive. She was certain her father had called the woman in bed "Tahira." Could this be her?

She waited until the older woman had passed and turned again. Theresa looked up through the web of her loosely clasped fingers to snatch a glimpse of Mrs. Awali's face. Even in her upper fifties, the woman was attractive. Yes, she decided, this could be the pretty Iraqi she had remembered from the Alwiya Club.

But was the vision about her parents' bedroom real? It had pulled such heaving sobs from her breast that there had to be substance to it. Theresa had studied enough psychology in college to know that dreams and visions could range from nonsense to symbolism, from symbolism to real, long-stored memories. Where on that continuum did this one fall? All the others, so far, had been real memories, packed up and stored away in the recesses of her brain until pulled out in vision form by her episodes. Was this vision any different?

The abaya stopped in front of her. "Theresa?" The voice was tentative, almost plaintive.

Theresa remained silent and kept her head down. She feared the answers to her questions. Perhaps if she said nothing the pacing would resume.

The black robe gathered in folds on the floor as Tariq's mother knelt to make eye contact. "Theresa? Do you remember me?"

Tears flooded her eyes, wetting her fingers. It was true. This was the same one she had met, the young Iraqi woman her father had known. She had seen them together. At the pool, and…that other place. She felt her hands being pulled away from her face. When her swimming eyes opened to meet his mother's gaze, she saw Tahira's jaw clench. The older woman's eyes filled. For a moment the two shared unspoken pain.

Theresa tried to turn away, but Tahira cupped her averted face with a hand, gently guiding it back. "You do. You remember. Do you remember everything?"

Theresa's face crumpled. All the feelings of a nine-year-old, whose love and trust were betrayed, flooded her heart, breaking it all over again. Her body shuddered and gave way to long sobs as Tariq's mother grasped her, drew her close. At first, she resisted, even tried to push away, but Tariq's mother held her in until she went limp.

Tahira whispered over and over again as she rocked the younger woman. "I am sorry. I am so sorry for everything, for all of your loss. I think you can never forgive me."

Several seconds passed this way until Theresa's shuddering ceased and her sobbing dissolved to silence. Embarrassed and unsure, Theresa stiffened again. Tahira drew back.

Using the hem of her own robe to dry her hands and face, Theresa asked without looking, "What does Tariq know of all this?"

The door opened before his mother could reply. Tariq walked in, nudged by a gun. The door slammed shut after him and they heard a locking bolt slide noisily into place.

His mother rose to grab his arms. "Where were you? What did they do to you?"

"They didn't touch me. We just have to be patient a while longer." He looked from her to Theresa. "Are you both all right?"

Theresa nodded without looking up. She knew her face still bore signs of crying. Unsure as to how much Tariq knew, she tried to act as if nothing else was wrong.

His mother pressed him. "I thought these were your friends. Why are they treating us this way? What is going to happen to us?"

"Probably nothing. Ahmed was angry and suspicious because of Theresa. I told him Badr allowed me to use her as a shield to ensure your safety. That we weren't sure about the positions of American troops in the North."

"Was he satisfied?"

Tariq shook his head. "He thought it strange that I would bring you this way. I told him I had friends in the area. I was going to leave you with them for safekeeping, and return with Theresa to Baghdad."

Theresa looked up in alarm. "We're going back?"

"No. That's just a story I gave him. But he's holding us here until he can check it out. He took my phone. He's trying to call Badr."

Tahira exchanged looks with Theresa. Neither wanted to voice her fear.

Tariq seemed to know what they were thinking. "Don't worry. Badr died in the explosion. Besides, communications are bad right now. Everything is in chaos. Ahmed was having a difficult time reaching anyone in charge."

Theresa stood, her legs wobbly. "But how long will they hold us here?"

"I'm not sure. But I think if he hasn't reached the colonel by tomorrow he'll let us go. At least some of us."

Theresa drew in a sharp breath. She pointed to herself with a questioning look.

Tariq continued. "He wants to keep you as a shield for him and his camp. But we will escape before that. We left Ghassan back there. He knows our contact in Sulaimaniya. He won't leave us stranded here."

They heard voices approaching.

Tariq spoke more urgently. "Theresa, I think they're going to put you in a separate place."

"Why? I don't want to be alone."

"It's not proper for you to sleep in the same room with a man who is not your relative."

She argued. "But your mother's here to watch. Nothing's going to happen."

Tariq shook his head. "They're very stringent, fundamentalist. They want you separated. Theresa, it's only one night."

The voices were louder. The bolt slid back and the door swung open. Ahmed strode in with two other Ansar militants. They grabbed Theresa by the arms and dragged her out.

She looked back over her shoulder. Tahira was holding on to her son.

BEDSIDE INTERROGATION

(Mansour—March 20, 2003)

Ibrahim al-Awali heard the car long before the pounding began at the door. Amina had fed him his supper in bed and cleared it away so he could enjoy a bit of reading before turning in for the night.

Flipping through T.E. Lawrence's *Seven Pillars of Wisdom*, an old favorite, he had stopped at chapter eighty describing Lawrence's treatment while detained by the Turks in Deraa. Despite the harrowing account, Awali's eyelids were beginning their final bows when he heard the car approach and sweep into the driveway.

Car doors opened and slammed shut. Awali marked his place with a prescription note and closed the book. Weak from the cancer, he shook slightly as he set the thick old volume on his nightstand. Footsteps rushed to the door and the pounding began. He took a sip of water to help clear his throat, and prepared for his visitors.

He heard Amina turn off the running water, and open the door. The orders shouted in Arabic and her whimpering replies told the old man enough: the Mukhabarat had arrived.

Awali heard footsteps in the hallway. An armed man in plain clothes kicked open his bedroom door and aimed a gun. He called over his shoulder, "Sir. In here."

A man in his early fifties appeared at the door dressed in a colonel's uniform. His face bore contusions and scratches, his left hand was bandaged, and he leaned on a wooden cane. This would be Badr, thought the old man. The officer scanned the room and entered, limping.

Awali made the first move. "Good evening, Colonel Badr." He knew by the surprised look on the man's face that he had guessed correctly.

Badr dipped his head and smiled malevolently. "Ibrahim al-Awali, your grandson was not entirely truthful. He led me to believe you were at death's door. And here I find you surprisingly alert."

"Tariq never sees me at my best, I'm afraid."

Badr nodded. "Apparently not. Where is your grandson? He did not report for work today."

Awali feigned surprise. "Was he supposed to? I assumed...we all assumed that with the explosions last night..."

The colonel cut in. "That I would be gone? Dead?"

"Not at all. Why? Is that how you got those wounds? Were you there?"

"Where?"

"Intelligence Headquarters, of course. The word spread quickly in the neighborhood. Amina told us early this morning."

"So Tariq and your daughter were still here this morning?"

"Of course."

Another security agent entered and whispered in Badr's ear. The colonel nodded and dismissed him.

"You still have not answered my question, Awali. Where is Tariq now? You said 'Amina told us.' Well, where is everyone else? My men have searched thoroughly and no one is here but you and your maid."

The old man reached for his glass and took another sip of water. "She is as much my nurse as my maid. And they have gone. The explosions last night convinced my daughter it would not be safe to remain in Baghdad. I asked our servant, Ghassan, to take her beyond the city limits this morning. Tariq went with them to make certain they would have no trouble at the checkpoints."

Badr pulled up a chair and sat down, laying his cane on the floor. "And why didn't you leave? With your... nurse?"

Awali sat up straighter. "I am a loyal Ba'athist. I will not flee for safety's sake. I was born in Baghdad. I will die here."

"Indeed."

The old man caught the threat in Badr's reply, but said nothing.

The colonel fished a cigarette out of his pack and, using a gold lighter, lit it with some difficulty. "Is not your grandson a loyal Ba'athist, as well?"

"Of course. Tariq will return once his mother is safely situated."

Badr dragged deeply on the cigarette. He blew the smoke out through his nostrils. "And where did he take his mother? North? East? West to Amman?"

Awali knew he had to be careful now. The longer this questioning took, the greater his grandson's chances for success. "My son—Tariq's uncle—has a small date farm northwest of the city. I assume that is where they were going."

"Assume? You didn't ask?"

"No. I trust Tariq to make a wise choice. When all of this is over, they will come back."

Badr leaned forward eagerly. "I thought you said Tariq would come back as soon as he had safely situated his mother."

"I did. And he will. When I said 'they,' I meant my daughter and Ghassan."

A new look came into Badr's eyes. Awali could tell the man didn't appreciate being made to look the fool. The colonel leaned toward the nightstand and picked up the book by Lawrence. He glanced at the title and looked at Tariq's grandfather. "You have a particular appreciation for the colonialists?"

"Not at all. I have an appreciation for Arab nationalism. As did Lawrence."

The colonel opened the book and scanned the pages Awali had been reading. He looked up. "The Turks were good at torture. But I think you will find we have improved upon their methods."

Awali said nothing.

Badr smiled, put the book back on the nightstand, and told the man at the door to wait outside in the hall. He pulled his chair closer to Awali's bedside and began to examine the various bottles of pills next to the book as he spoke.

"Before we return to the subject of your grandson, I would like to clear up the mystery of Professor Nathan Fuller. Are you familiar with the name?"

Awali made up his mind to drag this out as much as possible. "Fuller? Fuller?…Nathan Fuller?" He gently squeezed his lower lip between his thumb and forefinger, as if contemplating. "The name is familiar. But I can't quite place it. You say he is a professor?"

Badr gave a brusque wave with his hand. "Do not toy with me, Awali. You know he was a professor. You are the one who had him arrested."

Tariq's grandfather opened his mouth and looked up at the ceiling as if he had just remembered. "Ah, yes. You mean the Political Science professor from America.

Yes, he was suspected of being an agent for the CIA, as I recall."

"And do you recall what happened to him?"

The old man looked directly at Badr. "I believe he was murdered by a gang of thugs in prison."

Badr's eyes glared and his mouth tightened. "Don't you mean to say executed? Not murdered, but executed?"

Awali thought for a moment. "No. He was definitely murdered."

The muscles in Badr's jaws flexed. "It is not murder when it is ordered by decree of the Ba'ath leadership."

"Ah, but you see the Ba'ath leadership did not order him killed."

"Is not Saddam Hussein our highest leader?"

Awali knew his answer would put a noose around his neck, but he spoke without faltering. "Yes, but he wasn't in 1965. And so it was murder."

Badr raised his voice. "Are you calling our president a murderer? Do you realize, at the very least, I could have your tongue cut out here and now for such an offense?"

The old man shrugged.

Badr's eyes squeezed to slits. "You would like that, would you not? You could not talk without a tongue, and the shock of it would probably kill you."

Awali smiled to goad him. "Well, Saddam didn't commit that particular murder himself. He did not do the actual deed…"

Badr opened his mouth, closed it, and gritted his teeth as he spoke. "No. He did not. My uncle and another man carried out the execution. Both died for it because of you."

"They deserved to die. They murdered an innocent man."

"Innocent?" Badr spat. "He was an agent for the CIA!"

"He was not." The more agitated Badr became, the calmer Tariq's grandfather grew.

"But you took sworn statements that he was!"

"They were either lies or misunderstandings."

"Did Theresa Fuller lie about her father?"

"Theresa?" Awali feigned confusion by pressing his brows together.

"The nine-year-old daughter. The one whose name you circled."

The old man waved his hand in the air. "Well, you can get a nine-year-old to say anything. I am sure you know that, even without the crude methods I imagine you use today."

Colonel Badr clenched and then unclenched his right fist. "It is easy to get a child to talk, yes. Almost as easy as convincing an old man. We can get an old man to say anything and everything."

Awali reached for his glass of water. Badr grabbed it and placed it on the floor, out of reach. Picking up his cane, he pulled himself up so that he stood over the old man.

The colonel's tone became almost compassionate. "We can do this here, or back at headquarters. Which would you prefer?"

Tariq's grandfather leaned forward, coughed and locked eyes with him. "I have always wanted to die in my bed."

FORGIVING

(Sargat Camp—March 21, 2003)

The thin abaya served poorly as a blanket. Rather than freeze in the cold night air, Theresa walked in a circle until dawn, wearing an oval path into the dirt floor of her windowless hut. She had been too bothered about her past to sleep anyway.

She tried to make sense of everything. First, she was told she helped to put her father in prison. Then she had recalled her father's infidelity. Might there be a connection between the two? After all, her father had slept with the daughter of a Ba'ath official. That same official subsequently pressed for her father's arrest as a spy.

In her heart, Theresa knew the charge was false. Her mother had never wavered on that point. Ruth Fuller had always referred to the whole incident as a "terrible mistake." Up until now, Theresa had assumed her mother meant the Iraqi government had mistaken her father for a spy. Now she wasn't so sure.

She circled the bare room without pausing for rest, all the while thinking. In the hours before dawn Theresa reached a new conclusion: her father had not been arrested for spying, but for having an affair. The "terrible mistake" was not the false charge of spying, but the sin her father had committed.

At the rising of the sun and the call of the muezzin, she stopped, physically exhausted. She knelt to say a new prayer.

This supplication, voiced in her mind, was different from any other she had ever attempted. Back in Baghdad, she had pleaded for herself, pitied herself. But after spending most of the night reviewing her life, apologizing for her choices, and regretting her mistakes, Theresa had come to a new understanding of the part she had and had not played in her father's imprisonment. If she had not testified against him, he still might have been sent to prison. This time, her prayer went beyond herself. For once, Theresa considered the others affected by her father's "terrible mistake."

She thought first of her father. How he must have suffered for his weakness. Not only the physical suffering of prison and death, but the emotional pain he must have felt when he looked into the eyes of his forgiving wife and unforgiving daughter. And what of the spiritual agony? Here stood a man, supposedly saved by

Jesus, who had chosen to turn his back on God, however briefly, for momentary pleasure with a woman. Theresa thought of him, imprisoned and racked with guilt, and wept.

She considered her mother, held at arm's length for decades now. Her mother, who had done nothing to deserve such pain and grief. Rather than console and comfort her, Theresa had blamed her in the irrational way a child faults a parent for not preventing bad things from happening. She thought again of the wasps, and shook her head and cried.

Along with her mother, she had neglected her brothers and sisters. With their father gone, they relied on each other even more, yet hadn't she made herself the family outcast? With each attempt by the others to draw her in, she strayed farther. When they did get together, she listened to the stories, but never offered any of her own. Even as they tried to fortify the family bridge, she weakened the connections with her cynicism and sarcasm. Now she wished and wept for a chance to reach out and rebuild.

Theresa's tears fell even for Tahira. She didn't know the woman well enough to understand her motivations, but she knew now what it was like to be in love. Could she have held her feelings in check had Tariq been happily married? She remembered the suffering in his mother's voice as she had begged forgiveness hours ago. How many years had his mother lived with the guilt, knowing she had broken a home, a family?

And the old man, Tariq's grandfather. Hadn't he felt what any father would toward the man who took his daughter's virtue? It was impossible to forgive his use of a child in the process of vengeance but, having seen his dying and cancer-ridden old body, she could feel little but pity for him now.

She shed tears for all of them. This time, in her prayer, Theresa asked nothing for herself. She pleaded for them—that they would find peace, understanding, and forgiveness.

And a strange thing happened. The very things she sought for them...came to her. A peace settled over her, not unlike the soothing calm she had known as a child newly baptized. In the cold mountain air, her body warmed from within. Tears traced a path from her closed eyelids down her cheeks, pausing at the line of her jaw before dropping. Head still bowed, she raised a hand to wipe both eyes and chin, and dried it on the abaya.

In that moment, something even more amazing happened. She felt the press of someone's hand on her shoulder. Theresa opened her eyes. She had heard no one enter the room. Who could be standing behind her? She wanted to turn and look, but hesitated. And in that pause the hand lifted. It was gone. Turning, she saw no one. Had she imagined it?

Only the peace remained. Her mind filled with a new acceptance of herself, her father, and her family. And Tariq's family. As Theresa forgave them, she felt forgiven. Spent, but happy, she rose from the floor, longing to embrace Tahira again. She yearned to see Tariq, tell him of her prayer, and feel his gentle touch.

When a breakfast of bread and tea was brought by one of the militant's wives, Theresa asked to see the others. The guard at the door refused. Either he was under orders to keep them apart, or he didn't understand her request and knew how to say only, "No."

Theresa ate the bread; she left the tea untouched, and lay down to catch up on the sleep she had missed. She no longer feared her dreams. Wrapping the cloak around her, she closed her eyes and thought longingly of a hot Baghdad summer.

She must have slept for hours. Hands shook her roughly, startling her awake. Confused at seeing the daylight gone, Theresa first thought the scene was some extension of a dream. But Ahmed appeared at the door. He barked an order in Kurdish. The same rough hands that woke her now grabbed her arms, pulled her up, handcuffed her and thrust her outside.

Theresa awkwardly drew the abaya close around her in the frigid night air. As they walked toward the main cinderblock building, which was slightly larger than the others, she tipped her head back to see thousands of stars. The night was clear. She could make out the snow-tipped peaks in the distance.

She had been transported so many times from cell to cell, interrogation room to interrogation room, and prison to prison. Theresa no longer cared where she was being taken. She was still alive. That mattered. She breathed in the fresh mountain air while she could. These Ansari seemed to smoke as much as most Arabs, and there was no telling how clear the air would be wherever they were taking her now.

They came to the door of the main building and Ahmed knocked. That struck her as strange. Theresa had thought him the leader of this base. She heard muffled voices inside. The door opened and she immediately recoiled. At the door stood the Baghdad prison guard, the one with body odor. And she heard a voice beyond him that chilled her far more than any night air.

"Come in, Miss Fuller. The air is cooler up here in the mountains. We would not want you to catch your death of cold."

Ahmed pushed her in without following and the smelly Mukhabarat guard closed the door behind her. He stood there to bar escape. Theresa blinked twice at the sight of Badr, scraped, bruised, and injured...but very much alive. A satisfied smile slowly spread across the colonel's face. He shifted his eyes over to the wall at her left. She followed his look and sucked in a breath. Tariq and his mother, shackled, hung by their arms from ropes tied to hooks in the ceiling. Their bare feet were bound, as well, and reached part way down into tubs of water. Both had been gagged. At least they were alive.

Pointing his cane, Badr spoke drolly. "Take off that ridiculous abaya. It doesn't suit you, Miss Fuller."

"I would rather keep it on, if you don't mind."

"But I do mind." He stepped forward and snatched it off.

She held her cuffed hands up in front of her chest and shifted her feet nervously.

The colonel sneered. "Have no concern. I am not going to remove the rest of your clothes. At least not yet. Go ahead, have a seat."

He indicated a chair behind her. When she didn't move, he signaled the guard, who reached forward and pulled her into the chair. She glanced again at Tariq and his mother, searching for any marks of torture.

Badr cleared his throat. "We have been waiting for you to join us. Now that you are here, we can begin."

"Begin what?" She threw it out almost as a challenge.

"A trial of sorts. But first, I must say it was not easy to find the three of you. After the building exploded—missing me for the most part, as you can tell—it took much of the day to ascertain the fact that you were gone, Miss Fuller."

She parried. "I would imagine that after such an explosion several people would be unaccounted for. Even blown up in the blast."

He smiled slightly. "True. But not in your section of the building. I found that interesting. It was almost as if they were trying to miss you. But how could that be? How could they know where you were?" His eyes strayed to Tariq.

Theresa drew his attention back. "If my area wasn't hit, what took you so long?"

"We had to dig through a few floors to get to your section. When we did, and found you were gone, I immediately thought of our young friend here." His eyes traveled again to Tariq. "And lo and behold, when I arrived at his house, he was gone too. As were his mother and servant."

He addressed the captain. "By the way, where is Ghassan? I believe that is what your grandfather called him."

Unable to speak, Tariq threw an earnest look at Theresa. She returned the barest of nods.

Theresa lied for all of them. "He deserted us back in that town after Baku…Bakubah? The town that started with an 'M.' Miqa…"

"Miqdadiyyah?" Badr prompted.

"That's right. We filled up on gas there. While we went in to use the restrooms, he left. He even stole some of our supplies. He probably would have taken the car if Tariq hadn't held on to the keys."

Badr clicked his tongue in mock disapproval. "It is so difficult to find an honest servant, is it not?"

She wasn't sure he believed her story but nodded her head all the same.

"Well, thanks to Tariq's grandfather, I found out you were going north. And thanks to my old friend Ahmed— who suspected something was up and reached me on the satellite phone Tariq so thoughtfully provided—here we are all together at last."

He pointed with his cane to another chair in the corner and the guard quickly pulled it over and set it in front of him.

Theresa spoke up. "Colonel, Tariq's mother has nothing to do with any of this. You may as well let her go."

"You are always asking me to let people go, Miss Fuller. First it was the Kurd and his son. Next it was your maid."

"They were innocent, just as Mrs. Awali is innocent."

He cocked his head. "Is she now?"

"Yes, she knew nothing of my escape."

He chuckled. "Is that what you think this is all about? You think I came all the way up here for you?"

She didn't know what to say. That was precisely why she thought Badr had tracked them down.

The colonel eased himself down so that he now sat four feet away from Theresa. He propped his bandaged left hand on top of the right holding the cane in front of him, and looked from her to Tariq to his mother and back to Theresa.

"You know there are very few innocent people in this world. Most of us are guilty of something in our past, are we not?" He pointed to her. "Take you, for example, Miss Fuller. You turned your own father in as a spy."

She clenched her teeth. "I didn't turn him in. I was questioned. My answers were manipulated. I'm at peace now with what happened long ago."

"Are you? I am happy for you. But do you know everything that happened that summer in 1965?"

"I believe so."

"Then you know that Tariq's mother here is not wholly innocent."

Her eyes wandered to Tahira and Theresa gave her a reassuring smile. "I'm at peace with that too."

Badr raised an eyebrow. "My, we are forgiving." He glanced over at Tariq and his mother and sneered. "What a loving trio you make. And I emphasize the word 'loving.' But I wonder, Miss Fuller, if you know every detail of the story. Has Tariq told you everything?"

Her smile wavered. What was he getting at?

"Has he told you about his father, for example? His real father?"

She glanced at Tariq. Panic filled his eyes. Badr apparently knew something she didn't, something upsetting. Theresa said nothing and steeled herself.

"I had a lovely chat with Tariq's grandfather before he died."

Tahira's eyes squeezed shut, and she began to keen. Theresa heard her muffled wail of agony. Tariq's eyes blazed hatred and he kicked out with his feet, sending water splashing onto the floor. Badr laughed.

Theresa cut in. "How did he die?"

The colonel considered a moment. "He died in bed. Painfully. But in bed."

"You tortured him? The man was on his deathbed! He was dying from cancer."

Badr fiddled with his bandage as he spoke, to allow his thumb and fingers more mobility. "I merely made certain it was his deathbed. I was only honoring his wish."

"What about his nurse? Did you kill her too?"

"Amina? She was useful in loosening the old man's tongue. Alas, she did not survive the strain. But the important thing is that Awali told me a rather interesting tale before he died. One that I think bears repeating at this time."

Theresa's voice was cold. "I already know about my father and Tariq's mother."

Badr fixed her with his eyes. "You cannot be aware of all the details. Otherwise, I do not believe you would have behaved the way you did with Tariq in your cell."

She drew back. Tahira craned her neck to look at her son. He hung there looking mortified.

"Oh, do not pretend to be shocked. I am sure you suspected your cell had a hidden camera. Tariq certainly knew it did. When his maneuvers in your cell became obvious, I had a second one installed, unbeknownst to him. Videotape is a very useful tool in the regime. Why else do you think I allowed you so much unsupervised time together?"

Theresa shot a glance at Tariq. She was glad to see he looked as exposed as she felt. He avoided her eyes, as she did Badr's.

The colonel continued. "The audio was malfunctioning the day of his last taped visit, no doubt thanks to Tariq. Otherwise, we might have caught on to the plan you were hatching. Of course, you made your feelings for each other all too apparent, even without audio."

His leering made her defiant. "So we love each other. So what?"

He smirked. "You say you know about your father and Tariq's mother. Let us see if what you know matches what I learned."

Badr stood and hobbled over to the suspended woman. He slowly circled her as he spoke. "Tahira fell in love with her dashingly handsome American professor. A married man with five children. But no matter, love is blind. Is it not, Miss Fuller?"

She said nothing.

"And so they carried on an affair, right under the noses of their families. This might be all right in American society, but we must note that Tahira was the daughter of an important, leading Ba'athist in a Muslim society. A society that forbids such extramarital relations. Indeed, a woman found in such circumstances would be killed, generally by a member of her own family, for it is unforgivable to bring such dishonor to the family name."

Badr now faced Tariq's mother. "But Ibrahim loved his daughter. Once he found out she was pregnant by this professor…"

Theresa gasped at the same moment Tariq groaned. They looked at each other. Her shock met his anguish.

Noticing, Badr smiled and continued. "Ibrahim sent her off to Beirut to marry a cousin, have the baby, and finish her studies. Of course, the cousin did not stay around. Why should he? Tariq wasn't his child."

Theresa felt as if she had been thrown overboard in a storm. Slowly she was drowning, with wave after wave washing over her head. She strained to breathe.

The colonel turned now to face his American prisoner. "All might have ended there without your family being affected any further, except for the matter of honor. You see, Ibrahim wanted your father to pay for his 'indiscretion.' So he had him arrested as a spy and thrown in prison. All this to cover up the sin of his daughter."

Badr lifted Tahira's chin roughly with the end of his cane and challenged Theresa. "Are you still at peace with all of this? Do you really forgive this woman? Wouldn't you like to hurt her in some way? After all, she came between your father and mother. Their adultery led to his imprisonment. An imprisonment that led to his death. Here, I will hurt her for you."

The colonel motioned the guard to hand him a cigarette. He lit it, crooked his cane around Tahira's waist to prevent her squirming away, and held the burning end against the tender skin of her left underarm for a long three seconds. Tahira's scream, however muffled, lasted even longer. He moved to repeat the procedure on her right underarm.

"Stop it!" Theresa yelled. "I don't want you to hurt her. I've forgiven her. And my father."

"And him?" The colonel flicked the cigarette at Tariq's face. It glanced off and dropped, sizzling out in the tub of water. "Do you forgive him, too, for holding and kissing you that way? You think he did not know?"

Theresa hung her head and closed her eyes. "I don't know. I can't believe…he can't be my half-brother."

Badr walked over and pulled her head up by the hair. "Believe it. Look in his eyes. See how he is torn? He hates himself for lusting after his father's daughter."

Theresa looked in those black-brown eyes. Eyes that had given her comfort, humor, reassurance, love. Now all she saw was a mix of confusion, pain and longing. Tariq vehemently shook his head but she looked away.

Badr released her hair and Theresa dropped her quivering chin to her breast. She tried to stem the tears flooding her eyes.

The colonel couldn't resist one last jab. "He has ruined you, just as she ruined your father. It is rather ironic, is it not?"

Theresa shuddered. Had Tahira ruined her father? No, he had entered the affair with eyes open. Though apparently weaker than she had thought, her father was not a stupid man. And what of Tariq? When had he learned the true nature of their relationship? Since the night of their kisses he had behaved coolly toward her. She had noticed the change. He must have found out about his mother's affair only recently. No, Theresa could not blame him. He had showered her with kindness, given her a reason to endure.

Badr tipped her chin up. "So why not carry out your own poetic justice? Exact your vengeance. Tell me about Tariq. Is he working for the CIA?"

She looked into his evil eyes and lied easily. "No."

"How is it he helped get you out minutes before the building was attacked?"

"We got lucky."

Badr sneered. "So you still want to protect your lover? Or should I say your brother?"

Theresa shrugged.

"You condone incest, then?"

She bit hard on the inside of her lip and tasted blood. "There has been no incest."

He circled her, taunting. "Oh, yes, there has. If not in fact, then in your hearts. I saw the way you clung to each other, kissed each other…"

Theresa groaned. "Stop it. What do you want from me?"

"I want the name of his CIA contact."

"He's not CIA and, even if he were, what makes you think he would tell me his contact?"

He stopped in front of her. "Let us find out, once and for all." Badr spoke Arabic to the guard at the door. The man stepped forward, pulled out a small black instrument and handed it to the colonel.

Badr turned it over in his hands and pushed something. Immediately, Theresa saw a jagged blue electrical arc pass between the two ends of the instrument. A taser. Would he use it on her? She recalled the machine back in the prison and her heart began to pump harder.

He approached Tariq and his mother, and turned to face Theresa. "You did not care for my treatment of your maid, did you? Let us see how you respond when you see your lover tortured."

He barked out an order. The guard stepped forward, ripped Tariq's shirt open, unzipped his pants and pulled them down around his knees. Water sloshed on the floor as Tariq struggled to resist.

When Theresa looked away, Badr instructed the guard to move behind her and hold her head, forcing her to watch. As the colonel pulled Tariq's shirt to expose the left side of his chest, Theresa closed her eyes. Six seconds of snapping and crackling joined with Tariq's muffled screams to complete an awful picture in her mind. When she opened her eyes, she saw him hanging limply, his head drooped on his chest.

Badr yelled again in Arabic. The guard holding her let go and went to untie the gag from Tariq's lolling head.

The colonel addressed her again. "Miss Fuller, I do not think you fully appreciate the pain your lover is experiencing. So I have decided to let him speak for himself. Are you still unwilling to tell me about his CIA connections?" At this, Tariq lifted his head.

Theresa searched Tariq's eyes for permission. Even in his weakened state, he shook his head. She looked at Badr, shook hers as well, and closed her eyes again.

"No? Very well." He turned the taser on and jabbed it into Tariq's side. Ungagged, his anguished cries pried her eyes open and she watched him arch back, twisting and writhing, unable to remove his feet from the water.

She pleaded. "Colonel, I don't know anything. This is pointless."

"Is it? This is a man who plotted against President Hussein. Because of him and others like him, our leader and his sons almost died the other night. I don't think this is pointless at all."

He placed the taser on the front of Tariq's underpants, well below his navel, and flipped the switch again. The captain's screams brought a sickening smile to Badr's face and a look of horror to Theresa's.

Her mind raced. If she couldn't stop this torture, could she, at least, redirect it?

She cried out. "Stop it. You're going to kill him and you'll never get the information you want."

Badr turned to her, triumphant. "So you admit there is information to be had."

"I admit nothing. I don't know anything. He is the only one who might know, but you're going to kill him this way."

She saw Tariq shaking his head, pleading with his eyes, but Theresa went on. "He won't ever talk. He'll die first. What do you hope to gain by any of this? Do you think your government can hold out against an American invasion?"

Badr's tone turned cold. "Yes, I do. But even if it does not, I have a personal interest in this."

"What do you mean?"

"You would not understand. But Tariq does." The colonel turned back to face the captain. "Because of your mother and your grandfather, my uncle died. Because of them, I had to return to this country. Leave my dreams behind me. You understand only too well what I gave up. I trusted you, treated you as a son, and you betrayed me."

Tariq's reply was barely a whisper. "And I once respected you as a commander."

"What are you talking about?" Theresa asked the colonel. "What does your uncle have…"

"Never mind. Suffice it to say, for reasons of my own, both must die."

"Then why haven't you killed them? Why are you torturing them?"

Badr whirled around to face her. "Because, unlike you, I do not think the outcome of this war is a foregone conclusion. And if the captain here has any useful information that might thwart the enemy, I will get it before he dies. Our president will be most grateful."

Theresa bobbed her head at the taser in his hands. "You won't get anything from him with that."

Badr looked down at it, and shifted his gaze to Tahira. "Maybe not directly. Perhaps I am hurting the wrong person."

She guessed his intention. "She doesn't know anything either."

"No, but an only son would not want to see his mother hurt."

Desperate, Theresa made another suggestion. "Hurt me. You said he loves me. Use it on me."

Badr smiled indulgently. "How noble of you. To risk your own life for the woman who ruined your father. No, I have seen what electrical shock does to you. You would be of questionable use under any kind of extended stress. I think I will have you returned to your cell for now. Things here might become a bit too...stressful."

"I would rather stay."

"As you wish." Badr motioned to the guard, nodded at Tahira and whispered something in Arabic. The guard walked over and cut the ropes tying the older woman's hands and feet. Tariq's mother instantly collapsed to the floor, tipping the tub of water over. She lay on the wet ground for a minute, nursing her sore wrists and shoulders. But when the guard pulled her up and started ripping open her jacket and blouse, panic filled her eyes.

Alarm spread through Theresa. "What are you going to do?"

Badr spoke calmly. "I thought you wanted to stay. Have you ever seen a woman raped?"

Theresa's mouth fell open.

"I thought not. You had better go. I would not want you to interrupt with another seizure. As soon as I am done here, you and I will be returning to Baghdad."

He gave orders in Arabic and the guard left Tahira's side to summon an Ansar fighter waiting outside. Badr spoke to the fighter briefly, indicating Theresa. As the Ansari picked up Theresa's abaya and pulled her from the room, she looked back to see Tahira's gag pulled down. Rage and terror filled Tariq's eyes.

Theresa stumbled back toward the other building and her holding room as the mother's first screams melded with those of her son in the night air.

A GOLD RING

(Sargat Camp—March 22, 2003)

She heard the screams in the distance, joined by yelling and cursing in Arabic. Even from her room with the door closed, each shriek tore at Theresa's heart. How long would this go on? Still handcuffed, she clumsily pulled on her abaya and wrapped it close, trying to cocoon herself.

Theresa did her best to think clearly. The continued screams must mean Tariq hadn't broken. How could he stand it? She tried to keep the horrible images out of her mind, but even with her ears covered, they crept in. Was Badr taking part? Theresa saw Tariq closing his eyes to the scene. How could they force him to watch?

Her back was to the door when it opened. She whirled to see the leering face of her Ansar guard in the moonlight. He closed the door behind him and took a few steps toward her.

"What do you want? Why are you here?" Theresa's voice pitched higher than usual.

He didn't attempt to speak. Setting his gun down without taking his eyes off her, the shabbily dressed man with the dirty beard eased forward. The gleam in his eyes and the curve of his lips gave him away.

Theresa opened her mouth to scream, but he was instantly on her, clamping one dirt-streaked hand over the bottom of her face to stifle any sound. With the other, he grabbed her cuffed hands and wrestled her to the ground. She tried to bite his fingers, but only tasted dirt mixed with garlic as he squeezed her jaws shut. He lay on top to immobilize her. His one free hand tore at the robe, ripping it, and groped at her shirt underneath.

She could barely breathe for the hammering of her heart. His beard scratched and his greasy hair smelled of goats and sheep. Theresa felt both terrified and nauseated.

At first, he only lay there, panting and feeling her. She hoped it would end there. Perhaps he couldn't go through with it. After all, these were supposed to be zealous Muslims. But when his weight shifted and she felt him groping lower, searching for her zipper, her heart sank.

Theresa stopped struggling. What was the point? Tahira had been raped. Why shouldn't she suffer too? They were all going to die. With this realization came the tingling up through her throat. As he unzipped her pants, she fixed her eyes on the shadow of a stain on the ceiling, ready to give up to the episode and the violation.

The Ansar fighter, sensing her surrender, slowly loosened his hand. When she didn't scream, but lay there staring into nothing, he smiled and stood to remove his pants.

Something flashed in the moonlight and Theresa pulled her gaze off the ceiling to track it. A gold ring graced the fourth finger of the fighter's right hand. She fought the waves in her head to focus on the ring. She made out the Canadian maple leaf etched into its burnished surface. It was the ring she had given Peter. How did this man get it? Then she remembered the ambush of the journalist they had heard about. Had Peter returned to Iraq, looking for her, only to be killed by this man?

A sudden anger built past the episode and adrenaline pumped through her body. She watched the man drop his pants. She would only have one chance.

When he stooped to lie down on her again, she kicked out hard and fast. She struck him with full force in the groin, and scrambled to her feet as soon as he keeled over to the side in surprised anguish. Grabbing his gun with both hands, she brought its barrel crashing down against his skull.

The waves still lapped in her head, but she had no time to lose. Ignoring them, she rifled through his pants pockets and found the handcuff key. After several attempts, Theresa freed herself. She zipped her pants and, gun in hand, headed for the door. Halfway there she remembered Peter's ring. She hurried back, pried it off the man's finger, and shoved it in her pocket. The Ansar fighter began to stir, so Theresa clubbed him twice more with the gun, before rushing back to the door.

With the fighter unconscious, Theresa peeked out to make certain no other guards stood watch. Seeing no one, she stepped outside. She had no plan and wanted nothing more than to stand still, let the episode have its way. But the yelling and screaming from the main building propelled her forward. She tried to keep close to the buildings and stay away from the open, stooping under windowsills when necessary.

By the time she approached the third house, the clamor from the main building had intensified. She clearly made out Tariq's voice, yelling and pleading in English.

"Don't! Wait. Don't do it."

Frantic, she broke into a run. Out of nowhere a hand clasped over her mouth. Another grabbed her gun, and she felt herself pulled back behind the third building. Strong arms held her. When she swiveled to look, she made out a man. Theresa struggled to focus in the dark. A soldier. He brought his finger to his lips, signaling her to be quiet. A second heavily armed soldier held her AK-47 in one hand while pointing his own machine gun at her chest. Sucking in breath, Theresa noticed the night-vision scope extending eerily in front of his eyes. The black face paint. When she saw the green triangle patch with a yellow triangular lightning bolt superimposed over a white dagger, her heart soared.

She nodded and the man removed his hand. It was difficult to form words, but she forced herself to fight the waves. "Special Forces?" she whispered.

The man nodded. "Lieutenant Colonel Haines. Are you Theresa Fuller?"

"Yes. How did…?" Her breathing was ragged.

"Your friend, Ghassan. He's waiting in the chopper. He contacted Lieutenant Grange and briefed us on your situation. Where's Tariq al-Awali?"

She pointed to the main building. Theresa could hear Tariq pleading and crying. "Hurry. Badr has him and his mother." She started forward.

He held her back. "Badr and how many others?"

"One other. Tariq's tied up…hanging from the ceiling."

"Which side of the room?"

Theresa tried to ignore the colors in her head. "The left. His mother's on the left, too, but they took her down…to rape her."

The Delta Force commander looked grimly at his comrade and whispered into a microphone in his helmet. "Haines here. Target 1 found. Set demos at building one for five minutes. Position to provide cover. Outer buildings, ten minutes. Moving to apprehend targets two and three now. Rendezvous with chopper at LZ in ten. Out."

Haines handed the AK-47 back to Theresa. "Are you okay?"

She nodded.

"Stay here while we get them." He started to move forward, shadowed by the other soldier.

Theresa followed. "I'm coming."

"You're safer back there."

"No. Not by myself."

Haines gave in. "All right. Just stay behind Gonzalez here. And don't enter the room till the firing's over."

They snaked across to the main building and hugged the wall inching toward the door. Two other Special Ops poked their heads around the building's sides and signaled ready. Haines motioned Gonzalez to the other side of the door, leaving Theresa behind the commander. The sensations within her battled for attention, but a greater fear kept her from surrendering to their pull. She saw Haines count to three with his fingers.

At three, Haines kicked the door in, crouched low and spit his gun several times to the right, while Gonzalez stood and aimed left. Theresa saw the Baghdad prison guard struck by several of Haines's bullets. He fell. At the same moment, Tariq screamed. Theresa turned. Badr was bending over Tahira, semi-conscious on the floor, injecting her with a syringe. To avoid hitting the woman, Gonzalez aimed for the colonel's back. Badr jerked forward and fell over the bruised and battered body of the older woman.

Theresa ran in behind Haines, and rushed to Tahira's side. Gonzalez kicked Badr off the woman and knelt to remove the syringe. Seeing Tahira only partially clothed, Theresa grabbed the older woman's abaya from the corner of the room. When she turned around to cover her up, her blood froze. Badr was rising up behind Gonzalez with pistol drawn.

"Look out!" she yelled, dropping the robe.

Gonzalez whirled in the same moment Theresa aimed and squeezed the trigger of the AK47. The bullets caught Badr against the back wall, pinning him in a frenzied dance. Seconds later, she stopped. The colonel slid down the blood-smeared wall, a sick smile pasted on his pale face. Gonzalez put his muzzle to Badr's head and made the kill certain with one last shot.

Theresa looked down at the AK47 in her hands and let it clatter to the floor. A sour taste filled her mouth and she felt like gagging. She fell to her knees beside Tahira, instead, and pulled out the syringe still sticking in her arm. The woman thanked her with a weak smile.

Haines had freed Tariq. He stumbled, weeping, to crouch by his mother as Theresa finished covering her with the robe. The older woman raised her fingers to caress his cheek. She took his hand and put it over Theresa's.

Theresa looked at Tariq. "What was in the syringe?"

He choked on the words. "A poison." As he answered, his mother grimaced, let out a slight breath, and rolled her head to the side. Vacant eyes signaled her death. Tariq wailed, burying his head under hers.

Haines crouched down next to the captain and shook him to get his attention. "This building's gonna blow in a minute and a half. Gonzalez here can carry her. Let's go." He nodded to Gonzalez and the other soldier bent down.

Tariq put his hand out to restrain Gonzalez. "I will carry her." He secured the black robe carefully around her, hoisted her up in his arms, and followed Haines and Theresa out. Gonzalez brought up the rear. Weakened from the torture and burdened with the dead weight of his mother, Tariq stumbled at the doorway. Gonzalez took Tahira from him and urged him on.

They ran flat out as other Special Ops laid down covering fire. Snipers took out several Ansar fighters who dared to emerge, then caught up with the group right before the main building blew. The explosion rocked the ground and Theresa was blown forward. Getting up again, she ran on, approaching the last of the outer buildings.

Theresa could see the chopper, an MH-47E Chinook, in the near distance. The last of several Special Ops units were unloading and running to take up positions in the surrounding hills. It was then that she realized their rescue was only part of a major offensive. The three blades on each of the Chinook's two hubs rotated furiously in preparation for takeoff. Eight other Delta soldiers converged on the huge chopper as explosions continued to rock various parts of the camp.

Theresa rounded the corner of the last building when it blew. She felt herself lifted off the ground in the blast, a huge deafening sound reverberating in her ears. Everything went black.

THE UNSEEN HAND

(In the Chinook—March 22, 2003)

She stood in the prison courtyard. In the blinding sun, her father bent low to hug and kiss her goodbye. He had meant to kiss her lips but she turned at the last minute so his whiskers scratched her cheek instead. He straightened up and she took a step back to look up at his sad face.

His lips moved but, again, the glaring sun blinded her. A roaring in her ears drowned out the sounds coming from his blistered lips. Rather than turn away, she kept looking. A cloud passed over, blocking the sun and erasing the glare. Her vision cleared and everything grew silent.

Her father spoke and this time she heard.

"I love you, Theresa. And I forgive you. Don't ever blame yourself for this. It was my fault. Maybe some day when you're older, you'll understand and forgive me too."

She rushed into her father's arms, holding him close one last time and feeling the pulse of his heartbeat.

The pulsing stopped, replaced by a roaring, and her eyes fluttered open. She looked up to see Tariq above her wrapped in a blanket and gazing intently ahead. Her head lay in his lap and he held her hand to his heart. She heard the sounds of weeping nearby.

Theresa glanced around in confusion. "Where am I?"

Her words seemed to shock him out of a trance. "Theresa. You're awake." He drew her close to his breast. "I thought I had lost you too. Praise Allah. You're alive."

Before he realized what he was doing, Tariq bent and kissed her on the lips. Drawn in for the first seconds, Theresa stiffened when she remembered. He noticed, flushed, and pulled back.

Tariq swallowed before speaking. "I'm sorry. I…I was just so relieved. I don't know what came over me. I'm sorry. We're safe and on our way to the nearest U.S. air base."

She sat up slowly and looked around. They were in the back of the chopper. Haines and his men had gathered at the front to give them some privacy. She heard sobbing again and turned to see who was crying. Ghassan sat several feet away cradling Tahira's body in his arms, rocking back and forth and mumbling in Arabic.

Tariq responded to Theresa's questioning look. "He's been with the family a long time. He probably feels he let us all down. But he's not to blame. I am."

Tariq's watery eyes held a world of desolation and loneliness. Theresa reached out to touch the scar above his eye. Cradling his face between her hands, she silently drew him into her embrace.

Ghassan's weeping subsided as he looked up to see the couple embracing. A minute later, when Tariq pulled back from Theresa in obvious confusion, the older man gently laid Tahira's head down on the floor of the chopper and made his way toward the pair.

He crouched down and took hold of both their hands. "You love each other. Don't turn away from that love." Then he joined their hands together.

Tariq pulled his hand back. "Ghassan, she is my half-sister."

"She is not."

"Grandfather told me."

Ghassan joined their hands again. "Her father was not your father. Your mother was young and afraid. She knew her father would kill any Iraqi who made her pregnant. When she found she was with child she panicked. She did not want to tell anyone. Instead, she made advances to the professor and he responded. She used him as a cover."

Theresa drew her hand up to her mouth.

Ghassan looked at her and shrugged apologetically. "She believed an American would not be punished. I am so sorry for the pain we brought to your family. I hope you can forgive us both."

Tariq opened his mouth dumbstruck. "You? You are my father?"

Ghassan looked down, barely nodding for fear that in this moment of revelation he would be despised and rejected.

Instead, Tariq reached out, kissed him on both cheeks and pulled him close. Tears of joy and relief streamed down the cheeks of both men.

As father and son held each other close, Theresa thought of her own father. Almost in answer, a hand pressed lightly once again on her right shoulder. Rather than turning to look, she placed her left hand there and whispered a prayer of love and thanks.

Tariq pulled away from his father and looked at Theresa through wet eyes. He took her left hand, kissed it lightly and pulled her to him. As she tilted her head up and his lips closed on hers, the unseen hand lifted, replaced by Tariq's.

49655457R00229

Made in the USA
Middletown, DE
22 June 2019